W9-BQT-015

Carriers of Genius:

Conversations with the Mothers of Twelve Famous Men

Walt Disney
Albert Einstein
Benjamin Franklin
George Gershwin
Howard Hughes
Norman Rockwell
Roy Rogers
Teddy Roosevelt
Walt Whitman
Frank Lloyd Wright
Fred Astaire
George Washington Carver

JAN HELEN MCGEE

WISE Ink
CREATIVE ★ PUBLISHING

ISBN: 978-1-63489-909-3
eISBN: 978-1-63489-908-6

Library of Congress Catalog Number: 2016936480
Printed in the United States of America
First Printing: 2016
20   19   18   17   16   5   4   3   2   1

Cover design by Jess Morphew

WISE Ink
CREATIVE ★ PUBLISHING

Wise Ink Creative Publishing
837 Glenwood Ave.
Minneapolis, MN 55405
www.wiseinkpub.com

To order, visit www.SeattleBookCompany.com or call
(734) 426-6248. Wholesaler and reseller discounts available.

For my mother, Lorna, who pushed and
pulled out my best self, and for my children,
Layla and Gavin. I am so lucky
to be your mama.

Contents

AUTHOR INTRODUCTION   7

1   WALT DISNEY'S MOTHER   10

2   ALBERT EINSTEIN'S MOTHER   40

3   BENJAMIN FRANKLIN'S MOTHER   61

4   GEORGE GERSHWIN'S MOTHER   95

5   HOWARD HUGHES'S MOTHER   126

6   NORMAN ROCKWELL'S MOTHER   141

7   ROY ROGERS'S MOTHER   165

8   TEDDY ROOSEVELT'S MOTHER   185

9   WALT WHITMAN'S MOTHER   211

10   FRANK LLOYD WRIGHT'S MOTHER   240

11   FRED ASTAIRE'S MOTHER   261

12   GEORGE WASHINGTON CARVER'S MOTHERS   283

Author Introduction

In elementary school, we had to report on a historical figure. I wanted to pick a woman but could only think of three: Martha Washington, Betsy Ross, and Joan of Arc. I didn't feel a kinship with any of them, so I picked a man instead. Today, I still feel irritated. As my dad used to say, "It stuck in my craw."

When I turned fifty, I thought about my legacy and what I had contributed. Motherhood topped the list. I decided to research mothers and give them a voice. I picked twelve famous men that I admired from various genres to see the impact their mothers had on their lives. Libraries offered much information, but for every twenty facts about the fathers of these men, only one appeared about their mothers. Information came obliquely, with one reference to a maternal grandfather but no mention of a mother. I often read an entire book about the son to extract one fact about his mother. I realized that with so few distinct facts in the history of women, I could only do them justice if I opened my heart. I gleaned their feelings as I gathered facts about their ancestors, home life, and tragedies. I thought about how mothers I know react to both pain and joy.

As I moved through ten years of research, I realized I wanted to meet these women. Facts were just not enough for me.

I needed to hear their voices and know their feelings. I began to open my paranormal senses to these women. You see, for as long as I can remember I have been highly intuitive—what many people call psychic—but I kept my abilities a secret for forty years. After my son's birth, my abilities increased and I quietly worked pro bono on murder cases. It was difficult since I absorbed the victims' pain, so at age fifty-five, I cut back dramatically. Today, I do a few cases a year.

I opened up about my skills in 2005 when a police detective and the production company from the Investigative Discovery channel approached me about a murder case I worked on in 1993. I agreed to be part of a television show called *Psychic Witness* on the episode "Circle of Enemies." In that case, I told local police where to find a murderer who killed his best friend. In the television reenactment, I played myself.

In the same way I worked on murder cases, I connected with the mothers of these men. I gathered my strength, concentrated, and accessed a special part of my brain. The best way to explain it is that I go down a pathway similar to a memory for you. Let's say in a grocery store you see a woman you think you recognize. As you try to remember, you focus with all your brainpower. Slowly information unfolds. Suddenly you know her name, the red dress she favored, and her favorite restaurant.

I call it time travel. I took the facts, transported my brain and body backwards to the past, and—in their present time—talked with these women. I smelled them and sensed them. I felt their pleasure and pain. With my eyes, I saw them as hazy or wavy, but my other senses stayed keen. At home throughout my day, I listened for their voices. When I heard them, I pulled out the notebook I carry and wrote fast. Other times I sat, intuitively waited for them to speak to me, and then wove their voices with my research.

I interviewed and spoke with them near the end of their lives, a time when most people no longer edit their past. Their openness to speak with me came from my unspoken intuitive abilities, my empathy, and their desire to set the record straight about their sons.

Some of the mothers offered more difficulty than others. Roy Roger's mother communicated easily since we had music in common. Walt Whitman's mother took a long time to understand since her life was full of troubles. Albert Einstein's mother seemed cold and distant until I realized her strong feelings for her two daughter-in-laws.

In many of these talented men, three common denominators stood out—they played music or were exposed to it, they relied on their intuition to explore creativity, and they approached schooling in unusual ways. Many of them disliked the rigidity of school, and some could not see the benefit of it at all.

These stories are about the men from the perspective of their mothers. I present them as fiction since I don't want to argue whether or not I can really time travel. Some say I don't have those skills, but I see it as my truth. The facts in these interviews are well researched, but—like love—my intuitive abilities can't be proven. I have waited a long time to come forward.

Forgive any mistakes I've made in my interpretations. Remember, mothers don't always know best.

1

Interview with Flora Call Disney

MOTHER OF WALT DISNEY,
BUSINESSMAN, BORN DECEMBER 5, 1901

I love Mickey Mouse more than any woman I've known.
—Walt Disney

JAN HELEN MCGEE

I've read a lot about Walt and his work. Can you tell me about him?

FLORA DISNEY

A lot's been written, and not all of it good. When a man finds success, people distort the truth. Like other families, we went through hard times and we made mistakes. My daddy had a saying that supports that fact:

"Looking back on life is easier than living it," he said.

So here you are, asking me to go back in my mind and tell

you about Walt. In cowboy talk, that's a tall order. Maybe my daddy's words will ring true, that looking back is easy. He turned out to be right about a lot of things, but young children think they know best and can't see that. Maybe this talk won't be so hard. In life, it's the changes and beginnings that give us trouble.

JAN HELEN MCGEE

I need to tell you right away, I loved *Snow White and the Seven Dwarfs*, and Walt won an Oscar! Do you visit the studio and watch him work?

FLORA DISNEY

No, I don't go there, and it troubles him that I don't like his new animation. But I do spend a lot of time pretending, and Walt doesn't mind that a bit.

Did you like his old animation better?

I never cared much for cartoons.

The voices of some of the characters hurt my ears.

That I understand. Now, I think I'll tell Walt's story in order, like a history lesson, since I used to teach.

I'm a teacher too. Maybe you can start with your ancestors?

My family, the Calls, left England in the 1600's and moved to upstate New York. Back in those old days, they had problems with hostile Indians and bitter cold. Two hundred years later, my father Charles and his parents and sisters moved to Ohio.

What work did they find?

Grandpa farmed, but he wanted more for his children. My aunts became teachers, and my father graduated with high honors from Oberlin College in 1847. After that, my father's wanderlust led him on an unsuccessful gold hunt in California. When that didn't pan out—oh, excuse me, I like my little jokes—he traveled some and then returned to Ohio. There he met my mother, Henrietta Gross, a German immigrant.

Mama and Daddy had a little wedding and then moved into Grandpa's house. My father settled down a bit and became a teacher, and Mama had ten children. I'm the seventh, born April 22, 1868, and my full name is Flora Call Disney.

What a pretty name. I almost named my daughter Marigold. Do you like your name?

It suits me. I'm hardy like a plant.

Did you meet your husband in Ohio?

No, we didn't stay there. One day Daddy opened his eyes and realized that all eight of us girls had crushes on the neighbor's eight sons. Some men would've seen that as a boon, but my daddy said they drank too much. We moved to a rough Kansas frontier town.

I have to switch to my husband Elias's family so I can tell how we met. Elias's Disney ancestors were French peasants from the cheese-making town of Isigny. You hear it? It sounds just like Disney.

Yes, I do hear it. I find it fascinating how names begin and change.

At some point, Elias's grandfather, Arundel, moved to America. Next, he moved to Canada, where he worked in the sawmills and then started his own. He married Mary and they had eight boys and eight girls. Kepple, his firstborn, married Maria, and they had ten children. My husband Elias was their firstborn.

Kepple had the same wanderlust that his son—my husband—possessed, so he joined an oil drilling team, rented out his farm, and then sent Maria and the children to live with her sister for two years. Kepple never did strike oil. Another year, he took off to drill salt wells, but that didn't work, so he started farming again. Then he heard about the California gold strike.

My husband Elias and his brother Robert were grown enough to go along, but when they hit Kansas they all decided to stay there and bought a three hundred acre farm. Kepple telegraphed Maria and told her to sell their property in Canada and join them in the States, so that's what she did. The men cleared stumps and rocks and got it ready for cattle and wheat. Guess who lived two miles away from them?

You and your family?

That's right! With that distance, our families had contact like a neighbor in town. The timing was off, though, since I was a child when I first laid eyes on Elias. I liked him, but grown men don't notice little girls. I paid attention, though, whenever a conversation involved the Disneys. I found out he lived a sin-free life and quoted whole passages from the Bible, and due to his daddy's strict rules, he snuck into the woods to practice his violin. Even back then, Elias had his own ways. A new place called and he was itchin' to go.

"Ants in his pants," my daddy called it.

Staying in one place didn't suit Elias, so he got a day job putting down railroad tracks across Kansas and Colorado. At night he formed a musical group with two other men. He played his fiddle out in front of saloons and collected tips in an upturned hat. Sometimes they played for square dances. When Elias finally came back home from laying track, he saw me in a different light.

How old were you by then?

About grown, fourteen.

What were you like?

I had a good sense of humor, and everyone raved about my pies, apple butter, cakes, and bread. I acted dreamy, but I had a good head on my shoulders. Elias and I lived close so we saw each other a lot. I mooned over his blue eyes and copper hair, and my heart bumped and thumped as he sang tenor at the end of the day. Don't let on and tell him if he comes walking in here, but I liked his singing voice much more than those folk tunes he played on the fiddle. I don't think he'll show up while we're talking, but now that we live here in California, he wanders all over the place.

Besides those things I mentioned, Elias liked that I play organ. In time he got a crush and courted me. I was also close with his sister, because we roomed together when we trained to be teachers. After that finished, I taught at a grammar school. Then my daddy got sick of bad winters, and after a three-day blizzard, he blurted it out.

"I have had my fill. We are moving south," he said.

You had to leave Elias?

I was upset. We moved near some relatives all the way down in Lake County, Florida.

How did you and Elias reconnect?

Elias and his father, Kepple, came down to Florida to experience it firsthand. Kepple moved away, but Elias lived with us for a short time. Then he moved close by and delivered mail with his horse and buckboard.

At some point Elias figured out that he loved me, but it

took a while for him to propose. I kept hoping he would, because all the time he was complimenting my soft temperament and curvy hips. See, I'd been so skinny when we first met. We both liked fresh air and new places. He especially liked to wander. Maybe some opposite attraction came into play. I have a silly sense of fun and Elias is serious.

Finally he asked my daddy's permission, and I accepted. By then I was nineteen to his thirty. We had a small wedding at my parents' home on New Year's Day in 1888 and then took our honeymoon in Daytona Beach by the ocean. After we had our fun, Elias got a job there managing the Halifax Hotel. When summer came, all the guests went back up north and we had to move out. I returned to teaching, and then I realized I was going to have a child. That news proved useful when my so-called "delicate situation" helped convince the postmaster at Kissimmee to give Elias a rural mail route. I guess the man was a father himself and wanted to help us out.

That must have been a relief. Then you had your child.

Herbert came in 1888. Motherhood settled me, but Elias couldn't change out of his restless pants. He was tired of mail delivery and got it up in his head to buy an orange grove. He wanted my savings, but that wasn't enough, so I asked my parents for more. What a mistake. I thought the orange grove would satisfy Elias, but it didn't. All of a sudden, he enlisted to fight in the Spanish–American War, which left me to run the orange grove and care for the baby on my own. What a time.

After seven days of boot camp training outside of Tampa, Elias realized the reality of military work didn't coincide with his dreams. He craved adventure but hated rules. Every day he was gone, I wrote him letters and said the work was too hard for me, especially with the baby and all. I couldn't do it by myself. One day he just walked out of camp.

Weren't you worried they'd put him in jail?

I was scared to death. When the military police showed up to get him for desertion, Elias kept on spraying the trees. I was certain they'd cart him off. I don't know what Elias said to convince them he had a bum knee, but they gave him a medical discharge. He could talk anybody into almost anything.

After that stint, he worked hard in the orange grove from morning till dark. I did all I could, but little Herbert took up much of my day. Life seemed fine, but in no time at all, Elias decided we had one big problem—my parents. He complained something fierce and said things that hurt, made comments about their nosy and overbearing attitudes. I tried to understand his feelings, but I loved my momma and daddy. I saw it differently, more like an expression of concern when they gave advice. Elias talked about making some changes, but before we could do anything we had a string of bad luck.

Nothing worse than bad luck. What was it?

That terrible frost of 1889 destroyed our whole orange harvest. I felt crushed, almost at life's end. I couldn't stop worrying, but Elias proclaimed the good Lord would provide. In the midst of that worry, my poor daddy had an accident while clearing some pines. He didn't have the strength to recover, and he died. I mourned him something fierce, but the Lord gave us a new life: another baby on the way.

I'm sorry about your father's death, but a baby is a joy. What did you do after the loss of your orange crop?

Elias heard about the Chicago business boom, and I agreed to go. For a dollar a day, he did carpentry work on the World's Fair buildings, and we saved what we could. On the side, Elias got orders and commissions for the furniture he made. We bought a plot of land, and then I drew up some house plans and Elias followed them. Single-handedly, he built our house. After our neighbors admired it over and over, Elias bought the land next door. I drew up the plans, and we built two more houses. I hammered and sawed planks right along with the men.

You were the architect *and* helped build! Now that's unusual for a woman. Did you think you'd stay in Chicago?

I felt settled, but I don't know what I could've been thinking. I pretended for a time that we'd have a permanent home. I just spent too much time pretending.

But that's enough about work and profit. Let me talk about my babies. At the end of 1890, Raymond Arnold came into the world, and in '93, Roy Oliver. I had such a fright with Roy. As a baby, he got real sick and I thought he might not make it. Luckily, we got a special milk formula for him and he improved. Elias said my praying and our religious beliefs helped.

At the time, we were active Christian members at St. Paul's Congregational Church, where we got friendly with the minister Walter Parr and his wife. Elias became a trustee, and when the minister was absent, Elias took the pulpit. He was a pretty good preacher, as you would expect, since he did a lot of preaching at home. You see, another of my little jokes.

You still like them?

I do.

I didn't want you to miss them with all those notes you're taking. You have an interesting job, I must tell you.

I learn a lot when I hear about the lives of others.

I want you to write that my life was not all hammers and wood. In the church, I was the organist. At the weekend church hoedowns, Elias played the fiddle for square dancing. It was a sweet time.

After a space of about nine years, I found out we had another baby coming. The minister's wife was in the same way, so our men decided that if we had boys, they'd name them after each other. That's how Walt got his name, in honor of Reverend Walter Parr, even though we thought about that name for Ray. Walt's full name is Walter Elias Disney Jr., and he was born in my bedroom on December 5, 1901. What a pretty baby he was, those fine features and that golden hair from my side. When the Reverend's baby arrived, the church people called our two boys the "consecration babies." Right before Christmas we had a joint christening ceremony. Two years later I had my baby girl, my angel, Ruth Flora.

That makes five children.

What a handful. One is one, two is ten, three is a hundred, four is a thousand and five makes ten thousand. Day-to-day living consumed me. Meanwhile Elias kept getting more and more upset by all the sin around us: the saloons, whiskey, poker, and loose women. He wanted to raise our daughter in an upstanding manner, so he decided to move us away from Chicago. It's embarrassing to say, but so much time has passed that I can tell you. Part of our reason for moving concerned debts Elias owed to members of the congregation. I stood by my husband and put on a cheerful face.

Elias went off to Missouri where his brother Robert lived, and he found a forty-five-acre mixed fruit and stock farm he could run. Our two oldest sons, Herbert and Raymond, helped Elias pack up our belongings, and the three of them went on a boxcar with the horses. My three youngest and I took the train. What a good little adventure. In Fort Manson we visited with my sister, and her husband gave the children presents. Roy just adored his air gun. We were all sorry to leave. Our time away from Elias meant a more relaxed way of life. He meant well, but he could be stern and disapproving.

I had a father like that.

I don't know what possesses men to be that way. Elias would fly off at nothing, and his mean words smacked harder than any paddle.

And you stayed with him.

I loved him, and that counts for a lot.

I agree. Love binds. My mother never left my father. How was your new home in Missouri?

The children and I loved it, all the color in the sky and trees, with enchantment in the countryside and open fruit blossoms. The farmhouse had no electricity or running water, but we had more space than in our old house. In those first days, we felt like pioneers. The children discovered hidden spots for hide-and-seek and played stickball. I read them to sleep—fairy tales by candlelight—and soothed them when they heard their first hooting owl. Nights meant magic and days burst with painted surprises. In his free time, Walt began to draw in earnest on that farm.

So that's where Walt got his start. Did anyone influence him?

Walt loved Elias's brother Edmund, who visited every few months. I called him Ed but Walt called him Uncle Elf because he had a small, hunched body and a lined, tanned face. Ed's mind was simple, but his charm bubbled. Since Elias disapproved of treats, Ed snuck hard candy and chewing gum to the children. Walt and Ed took off on daily expeditions and caught frogs, grasshoppers, and field mice to study. Ed taught Walt so much, how to fish and how to mimic bird sounds.

Every few months Ed moved on to another relative's house. After he left, Walt called him "the boy who never grew up." What happened later is so sad. Ed was with another relative when he took bad and had to be sent to a home for the retarded. None of us ever forgot him. I think Walt used Uncle Elf's looks for some of his drawings, and he learned to make the sounds for his cartoons from his imitations.

Another influence on Walt was Mother Maria, Elias's mother. Before Walt got old enough to start school, she visited and spent a lot of time with him. I never understood how a woman who loved games and mischief could be the mother of Elias. What opposites. I remember one trick she pulled: she gave Walt these little candies that turned out to be sugarcoated laxatives. Do you remember those Cascarettes?

I read the cascara tree was overharvested because Cascarettes were so popular.

Were they? I put my foot down on that stunt she pulled. She heard it from me.

Did any other relatives or friends come to visit?

Elias made the acquaintance of men who liked to talk socialism, and they came home with him. All kinds of men—some tramps—but good folk nonetheless. If the tramps hadn't bathed, I tried to be polite and asked them to take their meals out on the back steps.

"There's more fresh air out there," I said. Elias would've put them right at the table along with the family.

What was it like when Walt started school?

Ruth and Walt started at the same time. It bothered Walt that he was two years older, but in time that worked itself out. I remember the time Walt played Peter Pan in a school production and the day he and Ruth went to their first motion picture show, a movie about Christ. But every single day, Elias and the boys worked hard on the farm. After one particularly good harvest of apples, Elias had money to buy more land, so he offered Herbert and Raymond a part of the profits if they worked the farm. They weren't too sure about the idea, but they said alright.

For two years in a row, the crops failed and we took heavy losses. Elias got even more short-tempered. He would hit and yell when he caught the boys reading frivolous books instead of the Bible. By then, Herbert was nineteen and Raymond seventeen, which was too big to put up with that. They got tired of his temper and said they were finished. After a bitter quarrel they left a note and ran away from home.

"We are tired of Dad treating us like wicked children," they said.

I felt so sad, but grown men have to make their own lives.

The day always comes when our children leave home, but that doesn't make it any easier. What did they do?

Herbert got a job with Sears and Roebuck, and Raymond got work in a bank. They wrote me letters, and to get back at their daddy, they pulled practical jokes. In the outgrown clothes they sent home to Walt and Roy, they filled the pockets with cigarette butts and pictures of loose women. That put Elias in a stew. For a time, he refused to speak Herbert and Raymond's names, and at one point he insisted they never set foot in our house again. I think he felt more hurt by their leaving than any pranks they pulled. He thought they'd stay on the farm with him forever.

How old was Walt then?

He was about eight, and that meant Roy was sixteen. They formed a bond like the two older boys. That's what brothers do. Maybe their fear of their father drew them together. Elias didn't believe in allowances or toys, and he didn't approve of most of their behavior. He found fault with so many things and gave them whippings every day.

I felt the opposite from Elias. I believe every boy needs time to relax and play. The children turned out alright, but sometimes I look back. I wanted to do the right thing and stop the whippings, but it was just too hard to go against my husband.

How did you cope?

I pretended it wasn't going on. Maybe I could have paid attention and done something early in our relationship. I don't know what; maybe I could have tried harder to kid Elias out of his black moods or simply recognized how bad it was. Other women might've done it differently if their husband acted like that. I just tried to get along and adjusted the best I could. When my husband wailed on them, I went out into the fields so I couldn't hear.

I'm sorry. Did the boys ever fault you?

No, they put all the blame on their daddy with his short temper and hard ways. Elias ran away from problems and all the time changed things around to suit his beliefs. I'm glad they weren't mad that I didn't put a stop to it. I kept my mouth shut and loved Elias for his good things. Walt had it the worst since he was so like his daddy, with two warring sides inside each of them. As a result, and I don't think it's intentional, they hurt those they loved and they hurt themselves with their tempers. But we were a family, so we stuck together.

Roy adjusted better since he was all business from a young age. That business sense turned out to be good for Walt, and it helped him get successful. Roy was older, and he felt sorry for Ruth and Walt, so he did odd jobs to buy them toys. In one of Roy's jobs, he washed the town hearse and then pretended to hire Walt as his assistant. Even though Walt stayed in the hearse and played dead, Roy paid him. We kept the extra money and toys a secret from Elias. He had such strong beliefs, even at Christmas, when he insisted we get the children practical things like underwear and shoes.

Roy sounds like a wonderful older brother.

Roy took good care of Walt. He bought paper and sketch pencils for Walt's drawings. I did what I could to encourage Walt since he had a sensitivity that many boys don't show. Every night I read Walt fairy tales to ease his pain from his father, and when he grew up, those fairy tales played a part in his cartoons. Walt loved that farm and everything about it, especially the animals. Jackrabbits hopped and Roy shot them, but softhearted Walt sketched them. One time, on the side of our white house, Walt and Ruth used bits of tar to draw pictures. Their daddy punished them for that.

Did Walt have a favorite farm animal?

He had a pig he liked a lot named Porker. He'd climb on that pig's back, and off they'd go across the farmyard. Then Porker waded into the slimiest part of the pond, dumped Walt off in the mud, nudged him in the rear and went off squealing. They had the time of their lives. Walt acted pure crazy for animals. He gave them names and said each one had a distinct personality all its own. He talked with them every day and made up stories about their lives.

For his animal and bird drawings, Walt barely had any proper tools, and his lack of paper frustrated both of us. He made drawings on toilet paper with charcoal, but we had to use it later and couldn't save it. One time my sister Maggie gave Walt some paper and a box of pencils, and I managed to buy a book for his drawings, and as I said, Roy helped some.

Life on a farm changes through the seasons. Do you remember any bad winters?

I remember one. Elias took sick with a terrible case of typhoid. As he lay up in the hospital, I worried. I couldn't let myself think he wouldn't make it. Thank the Lord, they released him to come home, but he had to rest and couldn't work. Doc Sherwood spent a lot of time over at our place caring for Elias, so he saw Walt's art. He especially liked the drawings of the pig and the hen. One day, Doc took Walt over to his own barn and gave him crayons and cardboard and told him to make a picture of his horse. He paid Walt a nickel and kept the picture. Walt showed me that nickel with pride.

His first salaried art start!

Walt loved to draw, and like Mother Maria, he loved to clown and pull pranks. We definitely needed something to offset the darkness surrounding Elias. After he got sick, I spent a lot of time nursing him. I cooked and sewed and cleaned, but Roy had it worse. He ran the farm, which meant little time for schoolwork. Those were difficult days.

Elias decided to sell the farm. The auction made the boys sad, but we got a good price. Best of all, the sale freed up time for Roy to do his lessons. He was so good at arithmetic. Maybe he even had an inkling back then that he'd go in business with Walt. Their partnership thrived and they both worked hard, even though the boys were different, with Roy serious as Walt entertained. At school, the other children loved Walt's stories and cartoons. Before we left, Roy and Walt finished out the school year.

We moved to Kansas City, Missouri and I enrolled the children in good schools. They adjusted, but Elias had a hard time since his illness sapped his strength. He had enough energy to attend church and speak at his Christian meetings in favor of socialism, but he had little energy left over to make a living. For a time, right after he bought a newspaper delivery route, he felt well enough to handle it, but then he lost his stamina. So every day before and after school and on weekends, Roy and Walt delivered the newspapers. Those industrious boys got up at 3:15 a.m., and many days I pulled the wagon while Walt delivered newspapers. I was still strong.

Roy was practical and older. Did he resent what he had to do?

Roy's schooling was complete and he was grown, so he did get fed up with his daddy. He didn't like the way Elias made them work while he kept the money. I accepted Elias as he was, but Roy couldn't understand him at all. Behind his back he called him a capitalist exploiter. Walt wasn't as outspoken, so he just went about his business. By then, he was ten and needed pocket money, so without telling us, he got a job at the candy store during his lunch recess from school. Walt kept his feelings hidden, but Roy got more and more upset. I did what I could, made butter and sold it, along with eggs from my chickens. Elias tried another business where he imported butter and eggs from a dairy in Marceline and sold them to the paper route customers. One morning, Roy went missing. It gave me a terrible fright, and I wanted to report it to the police, but Elias forbade it. A week later I got a letter from Elias's brother Will, who said Roy was there helping him harvest. When I told Elias, he had an outburst.

"I told you I never want to hear his name again. He's turned his back on us and on God," he hollered, just like when Herbert and Raymond first left.

How did you cope with that situation?

In time, Elias's anger dissolved, but Roy never came back home. He got drafted in the Army, but he enlisted in the Navy instead and fought in the war.

How did you deal with that?

I found solace in Ruth and Walt. They were good students. Ruth liked most of her subjects, and Walt enjoyed Charles Dickens, Mark Twain, and adventure stories with Jimmy Dale, junior secret agent. To buy art supplies, he got a better part-time job at the pharmacy. Outside the family, Walt did more things on his own and made a friend, also named Walter. At Walter's house, they had drama productions with Walter's sister, and on the weekend, Walter's father took them to the movies. Walt was crazy for motion picture magic, and he talked nonstop about the characters, especially Charlie Chaplin as the Tramp. In between movies, Walt kept drawing.

My son got into so much trouble in eighth grade. What about Walt?

I remember one incident at school. Walt had trouble with a teacher who didn't like the political cartoons that Walt copied out of Elias's socialist magazines. We got a letter home about that, but it was only the tip of the trouble. As Walt made it clear that he wanted to draw, Elias protested.

"If you are foolish enough to want to be an artist, then you should learn the violin instead. That way you can be in a band and earn some money," Elias told him.

Elias saw music as better than art, instead of realizing the two represented the same thing. After Elias tore up some of Walt's drawings, he forced him to practice the fiddle, which Walt hated. Anyone could see that Walt didn't have a natural talent for music like Elias did.

When Walt came to me to talk about Elias, I told him I hated that Elias destroyed his artwork, but I just couldn't speak up. I was too scared, so I did what I did best. I cooked, cleaned, mended, and tried to be cheerful. I distracted Elias enough that Walt got his drawings done, and I encouraged Walt to find his own way. Instead of manual arts with the boys, he took domestic science and homemaking with the girls. He thought he'd learn more about art in those classes.

Now here's a surprise: in 1917 Elias had another itch to move. Oh, my little joke, acting like it's a surprise that Elias wanted a change.

You said at the start he was restless. Where did you head next?

This time he wanted to go back to Chicago to work for a friend in his jelly factory. When I wanted Walt and Ruth to finish out the school year, we argued back and forth. I finally gave in, and Ruth and I left with Elias.

Herbert; his wife, Louise; and their daughter, Dorothy, moved into the house where we'd been living, so Walt could finish that grade. That summer, Walt sold newspapers, cigarettes, and soda pop for the railroad and saved most of his money. The job didn't last long, but he adored everything about the trains, the adventures, and all of the people waving goodbye.

When fall came, Walt joined us in Chicago and attended McKinley High, where he developed a crush on Su Pitowskia, a fellow student who wrote for the school paper. She had a brother in the war and was especially patriotic. At first she didn't notice Walt, but her dedication influenced him. He thought she was pretty, and soon she started to watch him draw. Walt was named junior art editor, and in the evenings he attended the Chicago Academy of Fine Arts. Some of the teachers there drew cartoons for Chicago newspapers. When Su started at the academy, the two of them went to patriotic meetings together and got close enough to exchange class rings.

At the school, Walt used live birds and animals as his models, and a man from the *Chicago Herald* taught him cartooning. One day Walt visited the *Chicago Tribune* and decided to be a newspaper cartoonist. To find ideas for his cartoons, or that's what he said, he attended a few burlesque shows, which upset Elias.

Some nights, when Elias went to his political meetings, Walt and I talked about Roy and the war. Elias was still mad, so he burned Roy's letters in the stove, but I remembered enough to tell Walt the latest information. Those letters influenced Walt's decision to join up.

What was your reaction to that?

I opposed that idea. First off, Walt was underage and underweight, but mostly, I couldn't stand the thought of three of my boys fighting. Walt tried to convince me and then begged Elias to sign the enlistment papers. Elias refused, so I finally signed both our names. Walt changed his age to read seventeen and joined the Red Cross Ambulance Corps. After training, he sailed on a converted cattle boat for France.

Weren't you scared for your sons?

I tried not to be. I wrote lots of letters. Twice a week Su wrote to him. Walt kept her picture under his pillow to look at when he felt homesick. He wrote to both of us that he used his drawing ability to make signs for the new people coming into the camp. One funny sign had some hairy legs with pants around the ankles. He put it right outside the water closet.

"And DON'T steal the toilet paper!" it said.

Walt even painted cartoons on the canvas flaps at the sides of the Red Cross Jeeps, and for extra money he drew pictures of the soldiers in his unit and sold the caricatures. Another moneymaking scheme involved making souvenirs for the boys coming back from the front. With his buddy, a boy he called Georgia Cracker, he got surplus German helmets and shot bullet holes in them and then used dirt and paint and decorated them to look like real sniper helmets. Walt wired half his money home for me to bank, along with letters and some drawings, which I loved. My favorite showed his German shepherd puppy Carey, with his little head leaning out of Walt's musette bag. In those pictures, I could tell Walt longed for home. He told me that even drawing didn't help him feel better, so he applied to leave the Red Cross.

When we picked him up at the train station, he looked so tall and filled out. What a thrill to see him safe, but my heart hurt for him because his homecoming didn't turn out the way he expected. He arrived with gifts for Su, but she had engaged herself to another fella. At first Walt wanted to throw the French perfume and new clothes away, but I convinced him to pass them on to my friends instead. For a long time after that, he couldn't trust any female but me.

"I'm through with women," he said.

War can wreak havoc on romance.

Poor thing, more bad news waited for him. When his friend got discharged first, he took Walt's little dog Carey home with him. Poor Carey died of distemper or worms or something during the crossing. Walt was so distraught. He wanted me to give back that sweet picture he'd drawn of Carey, but it was my present and I cherished it. I don't know why it was so important to me, but I knew he'd remember that dog in his mind.

Right away, Walt looked for a job. The *Tribune* had no openings for cartoonists, so Elias offered Walt a job at the jelly factory, but he refused, and that caused a row. They yelled and cursed at each other and used words I can't repeat, and Walt decided to leave home. I pleaded with him, but he had only one answer.

"Come with me," he said.

Did you consider going?

No, my place was with my husband. I gave Walt a big hug and promised to take care of the money he'd saved.

Where did he go?

He moved to Kansas City where Roy worked in a bank, and the two of them lived with Herbert and his family. Roy offered to pay Walt's share of the board to Herbert, and Walt slept in the parlor. He called long-distance to tell us he got a job as an apprentice in an advertising agency. That made me happy, but Elias couldn't say a kind word. He didn't even try.

"You'll soon be out of a job again," he told Walt.

Walt saw five movies a week in his free time. A few months later, he decided to go into the animation business with another fellow. He wired me to send the five hundred dollars from when he was overseas. Elias forbade it and said we needed to know more details about why Walt wanted it. So there wouldn't be trouble with me in the middle, Walt told me to send half. That calmed Elias down.

Walt used the money to make animated, short cartoons he called Laugh-O-Grams. It tickled me to realize my night-time fairy tales influenced his stories. With those cartoons, Walt had a clear path.

It's impossible to know how we'll influence our children. Wait, you haven't moved in a while.

Here it comes again, you'll see. The jelly factory failed.

Elias couldn't find a carpentry job, so we moved back to Kansas City. I liked all of us together, but it didn't last long. Poor Roy got sick with tuberculosis and had to go to California to recover. Herbert transferred to Oregon, so we joined him. Walt moved to California and lived with Elias's brother, Robert, near the hospital where Roy convalesced. Each day Roy's health improved.

Where did Walt work in California?

Someone in the industry had seen and liked his animated feature *Alice's Wonderland*, so Walt decided to direct films. He needed a stable man to help him, so he convinced Roy to do the finances. Their first cartoon was *Alice's Day at Sea*. As time passed, Walt began to want to work with ideas, so he hired an animator to draw his plans instead of doing it himself.

Roy kept busy with the books. In his free time, he dated Edna Francis, with a promise to marry her if he recovered from the tuberculosis. In the spring of '25, he upheld that promise. The wedding was held at Robert's house, with Walt in his old brown cardigan as best man. The maid of honor, Lillian Bounds, was chosen by Roy since Edna didn't know anyone in Los Angeles. Lilly worked as an inker at Disney Productions and Walt liked her.

It had been a long time since Su broke his heart, but in all that time, Walt had little interest in a steady girlfriend. In Kansas he dated two girls, but he wanted to be friends, nothing romantic. For a charity ball, he took both of them.

"I need financial security and some maturity in age before I get married," Walt claimed.

When people pushed him about girls, he told them all the

same thing.

"I prefer animals to people," he said.

So he felt differently about Lilly?

She adored him and accommodated his personality. Walt has a tendency to be exacting, so I was glad he found her. When I met Lilly, she was twenty-four to Walt's twenty-eight. Born and raised in Idaho, she was built solid like me and she had fine-looking hair. All her family had musical talent, and all the girls sang beautiful harmonies.

How did Walt and Lilly's relationship develop?

Most days after work, Walt gave her a ride home and then stayed for dinner at her sister Hazel's. That's where Lilly lived. Walt said Hazel sure did know how to cook. Soon after Roy's wedding, Walt made Lilly his secretary instead of an inker. The problem was she made a lot of mistakes during dictation.

"She was so bad I had to marry her," he told everyone.

Walt's proposal sums up his personality. One night, while driving his old car, he came out with it.

"Which would you rather have me buy? A new car or an engagement ring?" he asked Lilly.

"An engagement ring," Lilly answered.

He bought her a three-quarter-carat diamond ring with blue sapphires. They married in July of '25, just three months after Roy's wedding. Lilly's brother had the wedding at his house in Idaho. We weren't able to make it, but Lilly's widowed mother lived close by, so she attended. Roy wasn't invited because he and Walt had a fuss over something—maybe about all the time Roy spent with Edna. Those boys had their spats over the years, but Walt always said Roy was one of the kindest fellows he'd ever known. After Walt stirred up trouble, he'd make it up to Roy. There was a peace pipe on Roy's office wall that Walt gave him one time.

Anything else you heard about Walt and Lilly's wedding?

Lilly wore a lavender gown and giggled the entire ceremony. Her wedding ring was white gold with six tiny diamonds, which looked pretty on her hand. Their first night as man and wife was spent on the train going west, and Walt developed a terrible toothache. On their way to Mount Rainier, Lilly said he looked a sight, with his swollen face and a scarf around his head. After a dentist visit, they took a steamer out of Seattle and then stopped in Portland to see Elias and me. Later, Lilly wrote me that she felt happy and Walt was sweet. I knew she'd be a good wife, because she worshiped Walt and let him have his way. She was quiet and didn't like crowds or parties.

So after the wedding, Walt and Roy got past their problems?

With a little bit of work they patched up their differences and then bought plots of land next to each other and had houses built. At work, Walt made cartoons featuring a mouse. First it was Mortimer Mouse. Then he changed it to Mickey. He added sound to his next project, *Steamboat Willie.* To pay for that, he sold his open Moon four-seater car. I guess it paid off, because that first-ever animated sound cartoon turned out to be a good idea.

Did anything change for Walt on a personal level?

I worried about him. Because he loved what he was doing, he worked all day, and after supper he went back in. To keep him company, Lilly went along to the office, and when he worked late into the night she slept there on the davenport. I wrote letters as often as I could and kept track of him from the letters Roy wrote me. He told me Walt developed some tics and twitches in his face and a bad cough from too much worrying about the studio. Roy thought Walt could be on the verge of a nervous breakdown.

You must have been so concerned.

His insomnia and constant handwashing worried me most, but I tried to concentrate on the true satisfaction he got from his work. I put my worry into action when I wrote Walt and suggested a vacation. Poor Lilly especially needed one. Both her sisters had children, and Roy and Edna had Roy Jr., but Lilly had problems. Her little dog comforted her, but a dog can't take the place of a child. They took my advice and went on a two-month sightseeing trip to Washington, DC; Key West; and Cuba. That helped.

After they returned, Walt made *Three Little Pigs*. I liked that song, "Who's Afraid of the Big Bad Wolf?" With that success came good news. In '33, Lilly carried a baby to term: Diane Marie. Walt and Lilly moved into a new house with a swimming pool built into the rocks, which was impressive enough, but then all my neighbors started talking about Walt's splash in the newspapers. He announced that all orphans would be admitted free to the opening of any Disney movie. Walt had good business ideas.

It sounds like Walt's health improved.

It did, and then he started to exercise. He played polo every morning, but then a ball hit him and knocked him off his horse, and he hurt his back. So he replaced polo with badminton, golf, swimming, and horseback riding in Griffith

Park. Lilly rode there with him.

After Diane turned three, Lilly adopted Sharon Mae. Lilly pretended she'd birthed her, but she hadn't. Later, she set that right, but in the beginning she thought it wasn't anyone's business but her own. Soon after Sharon joined the family, Roy became awfully concerned again about Walt's nerves, so he convinced Walt to take their wives on a working vacation to Europe. Roy wrote me from over there and told me that all the attention and admiration overseas brought Walt's health back.

What about Herbert and Raymond?

After Walt and Roy's business grew, Herbert transferred his post office job to Los Angeles. He moved there with his family in hopes that his daughter could get a job at the Disney Company. Then Raymond moved to California to set up a life insurance business for Walt's one thousand employees. I missed my boys when they left, but Roy visited pretty often. He had something to say about Herbert and Raymond's move.

"Bees to the honeypot," is what he called it.

Whenever he visited, Roy wanted Elias and me to join them in Los Angeles. Elias was too weak and old to work long hours, so he did odd jobs as a carpenter. Then Roy put his foot down.

"You're getting on in years. We want you close," Roy said. We just couldn't decide.

I understand that quandary. As we get older, it gets more difficult. What was Walt working on at that time?

That's when *Snow White and the Seven Dwarfs* debuted, but the extra work presented problems in Walt's marriage, with him gone so much. I guess it was worth it when he won an Academy Awards Oscar for that movie. About that same time, Roy visited and talked us into coming to Los Angeles for our fiftieth wedding anniversary party. All four of my boys attended our celebration in Hollywood, but Ruth couldn't make it. After the party, we did move to California, even though it meant leaving Ruth back in Oregon with her husband.

That takes me to the present. Roy and Walt bought us this brand new cottage and that chair where you sit. The only problem is the furnace is acting up. I told Alma—she's our housekeeper, but she's off today, that's why you didn't meet her, wonderful woman—that we better get it fixed or we'll wake up and find ourselves dead.

I hope not! How do you like it here?

This cottage is pretty, but I miss the farm. There was so much more to do. I wouldn't mention it to my boys, but I don't especially like it here. I feel sad sometimes, like nothing matters. I miss the familiar. Roy lives here in Toluca Lake, right around the corner, so I look forward to a visit from my grandson Roy Jr. every day after school.

How sweet that he stops by. I would love to have a grandchild. How does Elias feel about the move?

He feels different than I do. He likes California and helps out a little with carpentry at the studio. He still wants to lecture about socialism, and he wants everyone to have a pious attitude.

Elias is eighty and I'm sixty-nine now. Nobody told me sixty-nine would feel this tired. I think I lost some of my humor. The children worry about me, but I don't like talking about my pain. I admit I'm a little frail and my legs are weak.

You said you don't like animation. What exactly do you dislike?

What grates on me is that voice he used for Mickey Mouse.

"I don't like it. It sounds girlish," I told him straight out.

"That's my voice," he said.

It's an unnatural sound, and it reminds me too much of some confusion when he was a boy.

Confusion?

It was a long time ago, but he would dress up in my clothes to scare his brother and little sister, or come to the front door in my dress and hat with make-up and a wig he'd borrowed. He loved dressing in costumes, so I guess he was creating characters, but it never sat right with me. Maybe his confusion had something to do with how hard Elias was on Walt growing up. Elias followed a strict interpretation of the Bible, and I believe his good heart got tangled. I forgive his cruelty, but it took a long time for the boys to forgive, especially Walt. He felt things stronger, so he suffered more. His troubles in the past helped him invent all those other worlds.

That's it. I've told the worst and best of it. I hope I've cleared up some things. Too much of what's printed isn't correct, and true facts get misunderstood. I'm proud of Walt's accomplishments. He made his dreams come true.

In what ways are you and Walt alike?

We both have a good sense of humor, but we feel set off from other people, lost in our own world. Some days we don't quite know what's real. Walt draws his thoughts, while I keep mine in my head. I guess we spent too much time on those fairy tales. And we have the same eyes.

Now please excuse me. Ever since I had a small stroke, the doctor suggested ninety minutes of rest to lower my blood pressure. I like a nap, but first I have to go find Elias. He needs to rest his eyes and take it easy, same as I do. If you want, you can take a look at this book I made filled with Walt's accomplishments. It gives you a sense of how hard he worked. When he had problems with the real world, he escaped into fantasy. Makes sense to me. That's how I cope.

―――――――― ⟨⟩ ――――――――

INTERVIEW WITH WALT DISNEY
ON THE DEATH OF HIS MOTHER

I don't want to talk about it, but I'll briefly explain. The report says the carbon monoxide fumes from the gas furnace were the cause of my mother's death. Alma and the neighbor weren't able to bring my mother back, but they did revive my father. Without Mama, he's a lost person. I take some comfort in the fact that Mama is now in heaven. I will always think of her as a ray of light.

2

Interview with Pauline Koch Einstein

MOTHER OF ALBERT EINSTEIN, PHYSICIST, BORN MARCH 4, 1879

———— ❧ ————

I believe, on the whole, that love is a better teacher than sense of duty—with me, at least, it certainly was.
—Albert Einstein

JAN HELEN MCGEE

Hello, Pauline. I think with our interpreter and my meager German, we can make it through this interview. What a privilege to be the mother of Albert Einstein. How were you able to foster Albert's abilities?

PAULINE EINSTEIN

First I want to ask you a question. Do you play an instrument?

JAN HELEN MCGEE

I play piano and some violin.

PAULINE EINSTEIN

I love the piano's combination of wood, strings, and keys, and I adore the resonance of the violin. Music has such value. Who is your favorite piano composer?

Tchaikovsky. Who is your favorite?

I have two: Beethoven and Mozart. That's enough; you passed the test. Now I'll tell you about Albert's abilities and how they came to him. It could have been my husband Hermann and his interest in mathematics, or my interest in literature, or a combination of both. Close instruction worked best for Albert, so I tutored him until he was seven and I made sure he had violin lessons. Until he was thirteen, he fought against them.

What changed?

After he mastered the skill, he began to feel the music. His movements relaxed and his emotions evolved. By then, he understood the mathematical structure of music, and that acted as an extension of his thinking process. He said research and music were born of the same source and complemented each other through the satisfaction they gave.

Now you live here in Lucerne with your daughter?

Yes, with Maja and her husband, Paul.

She's pretty.

And smart.

Albert and Maja are similar in that way?

Yes, although they're so different. Maja fit in socially, while Albert had his own agenda before he could talk. We adapted to his determination, which I found more difficult than Hermann since I have less optimism and a strong will. My background might explain more of my personality.

Tell me.

I come from southwestern Germany, and my family is Jewish. My father, Julius Derzbacher, who adopted the name of Koch, was a royal court purveyor who ran a successful grain business with his brother. During my childhood, my family and my uncle's family lived together in the same house. My mother, Jette, and my aunt alternated cooking and domestic chores each week, and my father and his brother shared business responsibilities.

That's an unusual arrangement.

To you, but it felt normal to me.

How did you meet your husband?

We met when Hermann worked as a partner in his cousin's featherbed company. I was a teenager then.

What did you like about him?

His optimism and his gentle nature. He adapted well to life.

Where did his family come from?

He was born in Buchau and attended high school in Stuttgart. At that time most universities didn't admit Jews, but it wouldn't have mattered since his parents didn't have the financial means. Unlike our son, Albert, Hermann's mathematical inclination remained untapped. At work, he studied a situation from every angle before he committed himself and he had difficulty saying no, which created some business trouble. He had a smart, clear mind, but in business he was too friendly.

What did he look like?

Hermann was a large man with a pair of rimmed pince-nez and a thick mustache that tickled my face. His looks pleased me, yet we had different interests. I adore German literature and piano, and I consider myself sophisticated. I love to laugh. My downfall is my teasing wit, which can strike a fatal blow. Hermann used to say I found it difficult to understand the difference between a tease and fun. My humor might be hard to imagine since I doubt I'll express it with you. My stomach has been hurting me.

I'm sorry. Can you continue?

I feel better than most days, and today I have an important job to do.

Your eyes are such an unusual shade of gray, and I love your hair.

My broad forehead lends itself to the style I wear today, piled high on my head. Its thickness remains, although it used to be darker. Hermann liked my hair and that I was tall and slim. I always told him I have a face neither beautiful nor plain.

How old were you when you married Hermann?

I was eighteen and he was twenty-nine. We lived in Buchau for a year and then moved to Ulm, an old city on the Danube in the foothills of the Swabian Alps. With narrow winding streets and a great cathedral, it boasted the tallest spire in Europe and the country's biggest organ. The river Blau flowed in a cutting beside our street and ended in the Danube. I enjoyed the rural feel and the smell of the near-by forest. My father made everything easier when he helped Hermann set up a small electrical and engineering work-shop. We lived a few hundred yards away in an apartment in a four-story building.

When was Albert born?

Albert came on a sunny Friday, March 14 of 1879. We chose

the letter A from Hermann's father, Abraham. His birth, I took in stride. Albert's size is what surprised us.

"Much too fat! Much too fat!" my mother said. She had a way of telling truths with few words.

Hermann and I worried about Albert's weight, but our main concern was his large and angular head. The doctor assured us that in time he would be fine, and Albert did turn into a beautiful child, with my hair and eyes and Hermann's chin. His arrival brought us happiness, which we needed at the time, since Hermann's business had some trouble.

Did his business trouble bring changes?

When Albert was only six weeks old, we had to move to Munich, where Hermann joined his brother Jakob in his electrochemical company. My family provided loans for Hermann and Jakob to convert the buildings close by into a small factory. Jakob used his technical knowledge as an engineer to run the works and Hermann attended to business and sales.

We lived next to Jakob's family in a house with big trees that was set off from the main road. I tended our garden and cooked and cared for Albert. I was positive about his intellect, but I worried about his reluctance to talk. The doctor reassured us there was no need for alarm, and after my parents visited, Mama wrote and consoled me.

"Albert was so good and dear, and we talk again and again of his droll ideas," she said.

My own mother saw Albert's speech improve slowly, but I was too impatient. In her letter, she chose not to mention that he repeated his words two or three times over.

How did you learn to accept his unusual ways?

I made a firm decision to encourage his abilities and force a sense of calm. Albert had a temper if things didn't go his way or when he wasn't being paid enough attention. It might have started with the birth of Maja, since a sibling can cause the first child to feel left out. Now Maja and Albert love each other dearly.

Tell me about her. Were they always close?

Maja, my lovely daughter. She came into the world on November 18, 1881. Such symmetry to that date. Her given name is Maria, and she has eyes like mine and Albert's. Our children's temperaments differed, though. Maja played with other children in the garden, but those same children called Albert "father bore" or the "dopey one" because of his lack of interest in them. He preferred complicated, indoor games that required perseverance and patience, and he wanted to be alone or with an adult. He didn't fit in with children, and he thought in pictures instead of words. We nurtured his curious nature and accepted him.

What are some fond memories you have of his childhood?

My favorite memory is what I called our Sunday excursions. I chose a destination, we discussed which way to go, and Hermann selected a route. Germany is beautiful, with romantic lakes and stunning mountains, so we absorbed the sights as the children played. When we tired, Hermann loved to stop at Bavarian taverns for sausages, radishes, and good beer. He adored our family time since he worked hard during the week. Jakob's and his business had over two hundred employees, and it provided the first electrical lights for Munich's Oktoberfest.

When Hermann came home in the evening, his positive nature remained solid. With the children he was kind, and he talked to them as real people. After dinner he read Shakespeare and Goethe aloud. Hermann and I loved the sound of each other's voices, mine soft-spoken and his more robust. We carved out time alone and time just for the children. We believed in good instruction combined with freedom.

What kind of freedom?

We encouraged Albert at age four to cross the street on his own and explore. Unlike other mothers, I had no fear he'd make a mistake. I wanted his mind and intellect open to experience, not closed. During the time I tutored Albert, I encouraged creative thinking. Sometimes I look back and wonder if our early isolation made him unsocial, but on the other hand, he's always been Albert.

When the time came for him to attend school, the closest one practiced the Catholic faith, like most of our neighbors. Hermann and I were raised Jewish, but we didn't attend synagogue, we ate pork and shellfish, and we ate dairy and meat together. Hermann thought organized religion was ancient superstition, and he believed a guardian angel guided him. We decided the Catholic school was acceptable, but Albert felt like an outsider.

Did Albert show genius as a child?

Let me think. Remembering those early years takes energy.

Should I come back another time?

No, I'm fine. Albert and Maja both had strong intellects. Albert's abilities developed at a later age. When he was young, I thought he had a reading problem. At nine, his speaking voice had little fluency and he hesitated, reflected, and repeated before he answered questions. He withdrew from life and had little interest in communication. When things didn't matter to him, he acted absent-minded. He forgot to put on his socks and never combed his hair. When he sat in a corner to do his work or ponder, we left him alone with his thoughts. Our devotion knew no bounds. Albert claims his slower development helped him wonder more, and he believes it made him delve deeper into problems of space and time.

Outside of school, I continued with his instruction. I play piano quite well, but at first the piano held little interest for Albert. When he was six, we bought a violin and I hired a violin teacher. Albert hated her rote lessons. Once, in the middle of a temper tantrum, Albert threw a chair and chased her away. I simply hired a replacement. With my coaxing and insistence, Albert continued his lessons. With your knowledge of violin, you know how difficult bowing can be, the relaxation combined with the steady pull of the bow across the strings. Albert knew what he had to do, but putting it into practice was another thing entirely. We played duets over and over until he got it right.

I have to concentrate so that I don't saw the strings instead of pulling the bow. I had that problem my entire childhood. I think it's due to my piano background, the pounding of the keys.

Albert's high level of concentration made it possible for him to plod along towards an accomplished sound. I pushed him since music is a place to lose one's soul. In time, his strong interest in music might have been called an addiction.

He played violin so much that it seemed like a third arm extended from his neck. Every evening we played Mozart and Beethoven sonata duets. I enjoyed his playing, though his performance was not professionally gifted. What mattered was how music made him feel, and the waves and flow of music gave us a connection beyond mere mother and son.

He stayed with violin instead of piano?

Eventually Albert did learn to play piano, and he became so good that he found new harmonies and invented transitions in songs. Music acted as a release for him. Whenever he felt anxious or restless, he went for long walks or played his instruments, and he used music as an aid to solve math and science problems. Albert's study of the structure of music enhanced all his abilities.

Maja just peeked into the room.

She's become protective of me. I'm glad she cares, even though I didn't give her the time I gave Albert. She was solid and Albert so unusual. We did all we could for him. Once when Albert was ill, Hermann gave him a compass to keep him occupied. The invisible force that forever pointed north intrigued him. Another favorite toy was a building block set that he used to construct models. Both Albert and Maja loved to make houses of cards and one of Albert's rose fourteen stories.

My brother Casar had a strong influence on Albert, who considered Casar his best-loved uncle, especially when he brought him a model steam engine when Albert was nine. And Hermann's brother Jakob helped Albert learn algebra.

So your entire family promoted his intellect?

We all saw Albert's potential, but too often the schools

didn't see it. Only a few teachers approved of him, despite his talent for Latin and mathematics during his two years in elementary school. At ten, after he transferred to the Luitpold Gymnasium, some teachers believed in him and some didn't. At that school, Albert took Latin and Greek, geography and history, and simple mathematics. His introspective nature meant he kept to himself and he never complained, but the school's discipline and rigid army structure made him suspicious of authority. Despite the problems, he ranked at the top of his class, usually first.

What did he do outside of school?

Albert enjoyed the company of Max Talmud, a Russian Jew and medical student who came to our home for dinner each Thursday. Both Hermann and I found it important to host students with limited means. Max and Albert talked about physical science, and Max gave Albert a mathematics book. After he read it, they discussed the problems inside. In addition to Max's support, we bought textbooks every summer for the grade ahead so Albert could study in advance.

At twelve, Albert discovered geometry, which he called a "holy endeavor." He found Euclid to be a great delight, and he loved to read science books. Math and science are what counted with Albert. He thought about his childhood fantasy of riding on a beam of light and noted his observations. As he sat quietly, he allowed his subconscious to solve tricky problems.

How would you describe your involvement in Albert's future?

I was ruthless in my determination, although I had little control over some aspects of his learning. For example, at the gymnasium, everyone had to be taught religion because the state required each child to be instructed in a faith. A distant relative and a teacher at the school gave that instruction to Albert, who then walked to and from school and sang songs that he'd composed in praise of God. During that time, Albert observed the Jewish faith and disliked our lax religious observances, but that changed as he grew older. Later Albert doubted a personal God but felt religious in his ability to wonder at the universe, his commitment to social justice, and his belief in a cosmic intelligence.

Many things seem important now, that might not have seemed so then. Let's move to 1894, when our lived changed. It had to do with business once again, when Hermann and his brother had financial setbacks, after which my parents stepped in and offered Hermann a business venture. Since they lived in Genoa, Italy and made the investment, they wanted a say in the business, so Hermann and Maja and I moved there.

What about Albert?

He was fifteen and needed to finish high school. I hated to leave him alone in Munich in a boardinghouse with a distant relative, but we had no choice. Albert taught himself calculus, but with the three of us gone, he grieved. He missed my cooking and his friend Max, who had moved to New York for a medical career. I wrote as often as I could and Albert wrote back, but at the time he gave no hint of his dejected state. I only knew he dreaded school, ignored what bored him, and hated Greek. He told us later he felt like a high-strung outsider with no interest in sporting activities and trouble with friendships. He decided to join us in Italy.

Albert approached the principal of his school with a letter from our doctor, Max Talmud's older brother. The letter explained his nervous ailment and included a note from his math teacher that referenced his stunning abilities. Instead of a release, the man expelled Albert for his skepticism about the need for most of his subjects. If I had been there, I would have stormed the man's office.

Were you overjoyed when he joined you in Italy?

At first we were disappointed that he left school, but as he opened his heart, we realized the depth of his loneliness. In fact, the timing was excellent, since Albert would have been forced to join the German army at seventeen. He hated the military. I remember as a child he shuddered and cried when he saw soldiers on the march at military parades.

After his move to Italy, his feelings against Germany became so strong that he decided to renounce his citizenship and change it to Swiss. He constantly badgered us until he convinced Hermann to make the application. For four years, Albert waited and saved money for the citizenship fee. In 1901 he became a citizen, and the Swiss excused him from military service for varicosities and flat and sweaty feet.

Was anything else different for Albert in Italy?

The first spring and summer there, he worked at our electrical apparatus family business and learned about electricity, coils, and magnets. He hiked the Alps and visited my brother Julius. After one visit, Maja and I saw his mood had changed. Instead of nervous and withdrawn, he was jaunty and amiable. That meant the three of us get along better, but he had a problem with his father that stemmed from Hermann's disappointment over Albert's career choice. Albert wanted to be a philosophy teacher. They argued over it constantly.

"Philosophical nonsense," Hermann said.

He insisted Albert learn a sensible trade at a technical school for electrical engineering. Albert followed that advice, under pressure, of course, and applied to the best school, Zurich Polytechnic, even though he was two years younger than the others. In the subjects he loved, math and science, he passed the entrance exams, but he didn't pass French, literature, or politics. At the school, a physics professor noticed Albert's high scores and recommended that he audit classes. The director suggested that Albert take a year to prepare at a cantonal school.

Did he take his advice?

He did, and what a perfect move. That progressive school was the complete opposite of the gymnasium. It encouraged individual thinking and a visualization of images, and its teachers recognized Albert's distinct talent. My family agreed to pay his school fees after I convinced them it was an investment in the future.

The next year, at Poly, Albert lodged with his history and Greek teacher, Jost Winteler, and Jost's wife, Pauline. His friendship with them flourished, and he fell in love with their beautiful daughter Marie. Evenings found Marie on piano and Albert on violin, and on weekends he joined the Wintelers on bird-watching expeditions. All of us became so close that Maja later married Marie's brother, Paul.

How wonderfully convenient! Did he continue with his music at the school?

He played in the orchestra.

Did he come home to visit?

He visited often. We lived in Pavia then, since Hermann had a precarious year financially. Albert hated the dingy streets and rundown buildings, but he played violin for the local young women. I heard fire in his playing, and his abilities were good, but not remarkable. No matter.

And the Winteler's daughter Marie?

She left to teach first graders, and she and Albert wrote letters. Even before I met her, Albert let me read two of her charming letters. I enjoyed their relationship and the Winteler's proper background.

My heart fell when he came home for spring break and told me he no longer wrote to her. He gave no explanation to either of us. When Marie wrote me to ask about his situation, I tried to be lighthearted. I explained his lack of letters could have been due to the family weakness: laziness. I couldn't answer with any clarity since I didn't know his feelings. I convinced him to write to Marie's mother and explain that the relationship was over. I put aside my disappointment during the little time we had together.

How did you pass the time as a family?

Albert, Maja, and I treasured wordplay for fun, and in the evening they played wonderful duets. They shared little secrets and laughter as they sat with their heads together, and they made fun of me as young people are prone to do. They teased me to the point where I had to flee the room to get away from their torment. I acted displeased, but I cherished their closeness.

The two of them banded together to work on Hermann, and he finally agreed that Albert could leave engineering and study for a teacher's degree. Once again I convinced my family to pay for his schooling. Albert repaid them later by paying for Maja's schooling. I loved that my parents understood the importance of education. Their generosity extended to giving us summer vacations at the charming Paradise Hotel in Switzerland.

It must have been delightful. Tell me more about those vacations.

Maja and I would arrive at the hotel early in the summer, and Albert would join us later. What a sight, my unusual son in his frayed clothing, his arms filled with a haphazard load of books and papers. It surprised me every summer that he joined us. At that time, Albert said my thoughts and ideas bordered on the narrow and conventional. I disagreed, of course.

Albert was far different from me, and some days he confused me. Sometimes he'd act cheerful and positive like Hermann, and other times his cynical and reserved behavior offended me. I know he hated the boring chatter of my friends.

I used to wonder why he joined us on those summer vacations, but now I see three things attracted him: his sister Maja's presence, a chance to indulge his passion for sailing, and extended time for violin. His music delighted hotel guests, even those offended by his rumpled appearance and lack of socks. Those summer days with my children brought me such pleasure. Then, too soon, displeasure.

What kind of displeasure?

A new woman in Albert's life. After her arrival, we lost the ability to laugh. I can barely speak her name. Mileva Maric. I never understood his attraction. I know why she loved him, with his intellect and casual air, not to mention his black hair and big eyes. Though his research came first, many women loved him, and he liked to be around them.

That one, she studied physics. Albert admired her thought process. I never approved of any part of her. I didn't like her Serbian and Greek Orthodox background—she was from Hungary—and I didn't approve that she was four years his senior.

How did they meet?

At Zurich Poly. I thought it peculiar that she was the only woman in his school who studied physics. She had no sense of humor, and she walked crooked from a congenital hip problem. At first, I underestimated their relationship and thought it casual.

As Albert became enamored with her, I worried and lectured him that if he got too close to her and allowed things to happen, it could set back his career. I was terrified she'd trap him, and trap him she did. She bewitched him with her intellect and lovely singing voice. Hermann fought that relationship as hard as I did, and when Albert wanted to get married, he stood firm against it. We secretly called it the Dollie Affair, after Albert's nickname for that creature. Their relationship put a blight on our family's last days together.

Are you feeling badly? Can I help in any way?

Let me walk to the window, slowly, due to my stomach trouble. Even the dull color of a winter garden levels my mood.

I enjoy the browns and grays of winter. Take your time.

In the fall of 1902, at age fifty-five, my dear Hermann had a heart attack. Albert was working as a clerk in the Swiss Patent Office in Bern, but he came immediately to Milan to see his dying father. Together for the last time, Hermann gave Albert his consent to a marriage. I disagreed but could do nothing. Albert had a respectable salary at the Patent Office, and that job brought creative thoughts. He loved to speak Italian, German, and French there.

Those last moments of Hermann's life, such a horrid time. He insisted we leave the room so he could die alone. This I understood, but Albert felt guilty. He worried that he hadn't worked hard enough to forge a close bond with his father. I told him that the path he chose met with Hermann's approval.

So there it is, loss and regret. Let me sit down again and hope my stomach settles. Death isn't something anyone handles well.

What did you do?

I did my best to be strong, and I told Albert to go back to work. I moved in with my sister Fanny and her husband and took time to recover. My heart was broken in pieces, but I needed to be practical, so I began housekeeping for a widower. I missed my husband, but the work of caring for another suited me. My children and I wrote letters when we couldn't see each other. Albert's contained too much news of that woman, and a bitter bile formed in my throat when I read them. The two of them hadn't married, and I hoped it wouldn't come to pass.

When I saw Albert, I cried and cried. I told him she'd destroy his future, and I warned him of the mess that would occur if she got with child, and I was sure she would. Nothing worked. He continued on with her, a woman unfeminine, old, and unhealthy. A woman who found it impossible to be pleasant or intimate. A stern and blunt companion, small and sad, a jealous witch. He needed a wife, not another book like himself. My warnings and sulking did nothing to change his mind.

In January of 1903, they married. Their wedding breakfast reception was small, and they delayed their honeymoon. I wept and resigned myself to a lost battle. Albert wrote and claimed the woman was a good cook. He told me she knew science and had a curiosity towards it, and he said they were freethinkers who shared progressive ideas.

What brought you comfort?

It helped a little when my grandson Hans Albert was born, and then Eduard two years after. We call Eduard Tete. Hans is called Albert, and he loves to question, and he has a scientific mind like his father. In other ways, they aren't the same. The boy loves school while Albert hated it. Poor Tete is shy and sickly and spent time in a sanatorium. He inherited something that came from that woman's younger sister, Zorka, who was born with mental problems and limitations.

Albert loves both his sons, and even though that woman did what she could to ruin it, Albert is a good father. In between his projects and his job as a full professor, he taught the boys something each day. He taught Hans Albert violin.

Did Albert keep up with his own music?

He played in a quartet with musicians from Prague. He also paid for Maja's studies in Paris until she decided to take a post as a governess. His life would have been perfect except for that wicked woman.

Did anything change with her, or in your relationship with her?

She kept being demanding, and they separated right before the war. Albert stayed at his professor job in Berlin. She took the boys and moved to Zurich. The loss of his boys wrenched Albert's heart to the point that he said he was no good as a father. I don't know what the boys thought, since that woman turned them against him and kept them apart. Her goals were isolation and alienation.

When Albert asked for a divorce, she had a breakdown and had to be admitted to the hospital. She left the boys with the maid. I think she invented her illness to get Albert back into her life. He didn't go back, but he cried over his sons' wellbeing. I pointed out that he had more time for his studies and clever ideas. Albert feels truth should come ahead of all other desires.

Albert worried so much over Tete's frailty. During their little time together, Albert loved to hear Tete play the piano, since music calmed his emotional and rebellious nature. With Hans Albert, he had no worries. Together, they spoke of science, mathematics, and music, and they hiked and took boat rides. Poor Tete couldn't join them when he had fevers and inflamed lungs, but Hans Albert had excellent health and common sense.

How is Albert's health?

Better than most. One time he had a physical setback, and he lost fifty-six pounds during a bout of stomach trouble, nervous exhaustion, and severe depression. The doctor thought wartime food shortages caused his stomach problems and put him on a special diet. For his exhaustion and depression, he needed a woman to care for him. The timing was perfect for Elsa to step into his life, and she became a lifesaver to Albert. Her mother is my sister Fanny, and her father is Hermann's cousin, Rudolf Einstein. As children, they played together. Elsa nursed Albert back to good health, and their love grew into something more. Elsa lived with her daughters, Ilsa and Margot, and was divorced from her merchant husband.

Unlike the nasty one, Elsa is warm, motherly, and undemanding, with beautiful blue eyes—nearsighted, though. She provides everything Albert needs and organizes his details so he can work. She knows he's the educated one, and she's awed by his fame. He succeeded in getting rid of that other one with a promise of the Nobel Prize money that he'd won. After the divorce, Albert married Elsa.

He married his double cousin?

Why not? You think close cousins shouldn't marry? I firmly disagree. They don't have children together. Elsa ensures Albert has solitude and study. When the publicity gets so bad that Albert can't breathe or work, Elsa takes food to his study and makes sure no visitors interrupt him. She encourages his violin playing to lighten his negative thinking. He plays the piano alone, but he plays violin in the kitchen for Elsa since that room has the best acoustics.

Albert tells me everything in letters, and he provides financial help for me. I moved out of Fanny's house, then kept house for a wealthy banker, and then moved in with my brother Jakob when he lost his wife.

Soon Maja will interrupt us again, so I should explain her worry. I'm ill with abdominal cancer and just recently left the sanatorium.

I'm sorry to hear about your illness.

I have decided to spend the end of my days with Albert, so Maja will take me to Berlin to live with him and Elsa. I'll stay in his study and I'll be fine.

I wish you well. You'll enjoy your time with Albert and Elsa.

I do love both of them. To get back to your first question, I think the way I raised Albert had something to do with his abilities. I taught him and encouraged him, but more than that, I recognized who he was and I let him be.

INTERVIEW WITH ALBERT EINSTEIN
ON THE DEATH OF HIS MOTHER

When my mother discovered she had stomach cancer, she chose to spend her last days with Elsa and me. Maja brought her here, and we made a bedroom in my study. Even with the help of morphine, she suffered. Mutti died at the end of February. I wept.

3

Interview with
Abiah Folger Franklin

MOTHER OF BENJAMIN FRANKLIN
PRINTER, PHILOSOPHER, AND INVENTOR,
BORN JANUARY 17, 1706 (N.S.)

———— ✸ ————

Every morning hath gold in its mouth.
—Ben Franklin

ABIAH FRANKLIN

For months now I have declined this meeting. Pray excuse me, I do not wish to be uncooperative. My life is quiet by choice, with my faith and home of most importance.

JAN HELEN McGEE

Thank you for meeting with me.

ABIAH FRANKLIN

I proceed with caution due to my private nature.

JAN HELEN McGEE

Is your son Benjamin the same?

He keeps many private thoughts hidden. His anecdotes

are available to all; thus, you could think the opposite. Please understand, when we finish here that will be the end of it. I will return to my everyday life and endeavor to put aside the fervor surrounding my eighth child.

You have your cider. May I get you anything else?

No, I am comfortable. I will try to do you justice.

I am weak and some days short of breath, yet I will be as open as the Lord allows.

I am sorry for your weakness. I hope this won't tax you. Can you begin with Benjamin and, of course, all of your children?

Pray speak up. I am grown so deaf.

Please tell me of Benjamin.

Benjamin is the youngest of our ten boys, named for my husband Josiah's closest-in-age brother, Benjamin the Elder. After our Benjamin was born, we leased a small house here in Boston on Milk Street across from the church. It had a clapboard structure, so we improved its sorry appearance with bright-colored paint.

How small was the house you leased?

Two rooms on each of two floors, one chimney in the middle, and the cellar with space for my vegetables. The garret became the children's domain. In the hall, Josiah boiled his soap and made his candles. He kept his books there.

Outside the door of our house, he hung a twelve-inch blue ball from an arm of iron. That blue ball proclaimed his trade, like the cobbler with a shoe and the blacksmith a horseshoe. I see many differences from that time; when streets had open gutters in the middle, the pigs collected garbage and vermin ran everywhere. I am pleased by today's progress.

Benjamin arrived on January 6, 1705. I remember the day clearly, a Sunday. I see that as a blessing, though some of my neighbors feel that to have a child born on Sunday bodes bad luck. God's kind providence does not allow for such foolishness, and superstition does not align with my faith. Benjamin's birth on Sunday meant services at the church, so the very day Benjamin was born, Josiah wrapped him in thick blankets to protect him from the cold wind and carried him across the street to be baptized. In my mind it seemed too soon, but in my heart it felt right. The Lord's blessing is important for a child's start.

How is Benjamin similar to your other children?

All have loving natures, with individual characters and varied paths. Few of them have Benjamin's sense of independence. I give credit to my husband Josiah, who fostered freedom of thought and openness to choice. He is more of the world with its change, while I tend to keep my days constant. When my children were young I nurtured them, instilled good in their hearts, and gave them strength for proper deeds.

Are they similar to you?

Within all of my children I see a small part of myself. With Benjamin it is curiosity. While my curiosity enlightened my children, Benjamin's took him down different paths. His choice to live far away from us means I seldom see him, though I think of him with a fond heart and wish he could be with us. With God's blessing, he stays safe from harm.

Do you have any physical similarities with Benjamin? From whom did he inherit his ways?

We have high, domed foreheads and narrow lips. His personality reminds me of my father. He was a dissenter who did not conform to any wrong.

I have heard that Benjamin is not the first man in your family with a fondness for sayings.

Here is one of Josiah's favorites: "Honest work brings due reward."

I follow this creed. My reward is my faith and my children. My firstborn is John, and then Peter, Mary, James, Sara, Ebenezer, and Thomas. After Thomas is my youngest son, Benjamin. Then Lydia and Jane. God blessed me with no troubled births. I am uncomfortable talking about myself, and my mind jumps from here to there. I will try to stay with you.

Please tell of your father.

Benjamin and my father, Peter, both had wit and ambition. Father shared my Quaker belief. When he was eighteen, he left England for Massachusetts with his father John, his mother, Meribah, and his sister. They were like Puritans on a pilgrimage for religious freedom. On the ship, Father fell in love with my mother, Mary Morrill, who sold her labor for passage to the New World. After they arrived in Boston, my mother left for Salem as a servant indentured to a Puritan minister.

Father settled near Boston, worked as a miller, weaver, and shoemaker, and saved his earnings. It took him nine years to accrue twenty pounds to settle my mother's debt and buy her freedom. In 1644, they married.

What similarities existed between your parents?

They had practical and rebellious natures, with a keen interest in life. I inherited my curious nature from them. I remember childhood conversation at meals, exploration of the countryside, and even the familiarity of chores. In the evenings, Father wrote verse and shared it with us.

As in every family, we had failings. Bless him, Father could be impatient. The positive side of that energy meant a strong spirit, which he used to further the good of others. That is one of the traits Benjamin has inherited. They both believe in liberty, and their conscience dictates their lives. Benjamin has more freedom than Father, who had as his primary concern a quest to find religious tolerance.

Was he able to find it?

He was.

Where did they live?

Martha's Vineyard and then Nantucket.

What were your father's interests?

Father had a variety of skills in addition to milling and weaving. He acted as surveyor, clerk of the court, and schoolmaster to the local English children and the Algonquian children. Not one English man but himself could speak a word of Indian. With his teachings, he converted many Indians to Christianity. In time, he became a Baptist, and that is the faith he taught them.

If he was the only man to speak the language, he must have been helpful in many ways.

Through his work as an interpreter, Father secured compensation for the natives in the sale of their land. Though other men believed Father should fear them, he disagreed. They caused him no heartache, and he understood their plight. It was the authorities, not the Natives, who caused him grief.

After the Indian war began, Bibles were burnt and lives were lost. My father wanted peace. When he refused to hand over a deed book in a land dispute, authorities charged him with disobeying the magistrate and fined him twenty pounds. His estate did not amount to half that, and they arrested and imprisoned him.

Imprisoned? How dreadful.

In the midst of bitter cold and snow, with no proper prison, they locked him in a pen where the neighbor's hogs rested the night before. He slept on a board with no hay to soften his night. For a man of peace in a time of war, he felt it a sane place to live. In his solitude he wrote a poem of protest called *Looking-Glass for the Times.*

Were you able to see him?

I was ten years of age then, and one day each week I visited him in the hog shed and watched him write. He made it clear to me there was a time for silence and a time to speak.

How long until they released him?

After a year and a half, the authorities suspended his case. Father kept on with his work on the street and sold pamphlets that criticized the local officials and their actions against the natives. When I speak of his writings, it brings my thoughts to Benjamin, who admires Father's poem of outspoken views. In my mind I hear Benjamin's voice.

"He wrote with manly freedom," Benjamin said time and again.

My father did not deserve the trouble in his life and this is not merely my belief. When others spoke of him, honorable mention was made.

And your mother, the same?

Mother functioned as his supportive helpmate and more. Her two boys and seven girls saw her as a good and worthy mother. I was her youngest, born on Nantucket on August 16th, 1667. My family presented a path of right and good, and I thought I would never leave. All that changed at age twenty-one when I was on a boat to visit my married sister, Dorcas. I met Josiah.

Will you share Josiah's early days with me?

He was born northwest of London, England, on the day before Christmas in 1657. His ancestors were blacksmiths and had interests in both writing and reading. His great-grandfather was Thomas. His grandfather, Henry, wrote poetry. His son, Thomas, is Josiah's father.

What were Josiah's father's qualities?

Thomas was a reasonable man with a strong temper, which he kept in check. He was dark in complexion and had a thin build. He ran a day school, practiced the trade of blacksmith and functioned as clerk to both the county courts and the archdeacon. He had skills in chemistry, astronomy, and surgery, and he was a gunsmith. He tinkered and built a clock and erected chimes in the church steeple. Gifted in music, he constructed his own organ and played for his own amusement.

And Josiah's mother?

Jane was a good and kind woman. Both of Josiah's parents were devout people who wrote their favorite Bible verses on the walls of their house.

On their walls?

They did.

Their children?

Thomas, John, Benjamin, and Josiah.

Please tell me more about Josiah's mother, Jane.

She loved to sing the Fourth Psalm. Music might have brought her and Thomas together when she sang and he played the organ. She was intelligent, and she took pleasure in discussing the prophets from the Bible. She loved to recite from the book of Malachi and speak of a just God. She put together and organized the women's Thursday church meetings to sing Psalms, pray, and discuss the previous Sunday's service.

When Josiah was still an infant, Jane became ill with fevers, weakness, and coughing. It continued until Josiah was a mere five years old, when she entered heaven. Somehow those children made it through. They worked hard and divided household tasks.

Death and life. What trade did Josiah choose?

When he entered his teens, he was put to apprentice as a maker of ink and a dyer of woolens and silk with his brother, John, an agreeable man. Josiah came of age to marry, and at nineteen he chose Ann, three years his senior. He needed to support the two of them and the children to come. Since the shop did not provide enough money for both families, Josiah had decisions to make. He thought he might start a new trade, but the law in England meant he needed to apprentice again with no income. This put his mind to thoughts of New England and its religious freedom. At that time, no one in England had a choice. To become a member of the Church of England had been the rule.

And that rule became his incentive to leave England.

Yes. With fortitude for a new life and heavy heart for the

old, Josiah, Ann, and their first three children—Elizabeth, Samuel, and Hannah—embarked on the eight-week ocean voyage. They settled in Boston, and Ann bore two more children, Josiah Jr. and Ann, and then two baby Josephs. In Boston, the demand for dyed cloth was low and Josiah had to adapt. The entire city had only one tallow chandler in attendance, and he chose that trade.

His first step to make soap and candles meant a purchase of fat from slaughterhouses. All but the poor used candles, and except for slovenly people, everyone needed soap. I remember the joy of people who bought soap and could avoid the making of it.

It deposits an acrid odor on everything.

As a child, I disliked soap-making more than any other household chore. The smell overwhelms, and it takes all day to make lye from ashes and simmer it with fat. Josiah is a strong man who never minded the heat and smell. He worked hard, and when Benjamin turned three, he received a contract to make candles for the night watchmen of the town.

Can you tell me more about his faith?

Josiah attended Old South Meetinghouse and became a member in full communion. His character encouraged the townspeople to seek him out to arbitrate church and town affairs, and his prudent conduct enabled him to settle difficulties without confrontation. To relax in the evenings, Josiah drew pretty and exercised the musical talent he learned from his parents. He played violin and had a sonorous voice. When our church leader was unable to attend services due to illness, Josiah set the tune for the psalms and gave the closing prayer. At home, he had prayer meetings.

Can you share what happened to Josiah's first wife, Ann?

Ann lost Joseph, their sixth baby, after five days. How sad for any woman whose baby cannot live to see old age. I am told that one in four babies does not live past their first year, which makes me feel that the Lord has truly blessed me with my own children. With God's help and benevolence, I try to accept my own losses.

Your losses?

With time, my losses will unfold. The Lord giveth and taketh away.

You mentioned another Joseph?

When Ann gave birth to her seventh child, also named Joseph, the Lord took her into his fold. A mere thirty-four years old. To add to Josiah's sorrow, within a fortnight, baby Joseph followed his mother to heaven. So much sadness for Josiah and his children.

You met Josiah on a boat?

He was leaving a sheep farm in Cape Cod with mutton fat to make tallow for his candles. Josiah was a widower of thirty-two. I was twenty-one. I admired his knowledge and his talk of freedom, and he appreciated my steady ways. With five children and no one to mother them, Josiah had need of a woman with my excellent constitution. Through our shared faith, we started to care for each other.

We married in November. I had just turned twenty-two. I brought a root of mint from Mother's garden to plant in the yard of my new home and then took to task my lot. Five children to mother: Elizabeth, Hannah, Josiah Jr., Samuel, and Anne. People worried over my young age, yet I knew those children needed me. As for Josiah, since he lost his own mother so young, he did not want to provide a hollow life for his children. Many times over, he told me the thoughts in his heart.

"I am ever grateful that you mothered my children after they lost their own," he said.

And then you had children of your own.

John, Peter, Mary, James, Sarah, and my poor Ebenezer . . . I cannot say his name without being overcome with tears. I shall take another deep breath, quiet my thoughts, and take my mind to a more constant place. Over and over, I tell myself to accept God's will. I know you have questions, and I am sorry I cannot speak of it now. I do not know if ever I can speak of it. Let us talk of kitchen concerns. Do you bake? Pies?

Yes, I enjoy apple pie, even though it takes time to peel and cut. Baking means physical work mixed with the enjoyment of something sweet.

Baking a pie takes me away from everything unpleasant in my mind, and the smell of hot fruit reminds me of Mother. Where did I leave off in my story? Oh yes, my children. I next bore sweet Thomas, Benjamin, Lydia, and at forty-five, my youngest, Jane. She is the closest to Benjamin. They call each other Jenny and Benny.

With constant industry and God's blessing, Josiah and I set forth to raise our children to be pious. Josiah worked hard with great responsibility and was given the post of constable. At home he proved handy with tradesmen tools, and at work he enjoyed continued success. That meant our everyday life had an ease that others did not have, and for that I am thankful. I took time to bake, yet I gave little notice to my victuals, which were plain.

What did you eat on a regular basis?

Breakfast was bread and milk or cornmeal mush with milk. For evening I served stew, soup, vegetables, and pudding. All my children were taught to eat what was in front of them; thus, Benjamin has never been attentive to his food. At our evening meal, Josiah insisted the children converse on ingenious topics to improve their minds. To help them, Josiah did not limit topics to his own ideas. Instead, he invited well-educated acquaintances to share supper. Evening meals could be lively, with my demeanor in contrast with others. I listen more quietly than my outspoken husband and children.

Did you have music?

After our evening meal Josiah sang for us, which endeared my heart to him. We encouraged music in our home, although conversation was primary, and our children learned to develop their own ideas. Proof of that is with our headstrong son, Josiah Jr. Our sons John and Peter had more of an ability to conform, so they trained under Josiah in candle making and soap. Josiah had a saying concerning a man's toil.

"Seest thou a man diligent in his calling, he shall stand before kings, he shall not stand before mean men," he said.

Josiah Jr. developed a strong dislike for Josiah's trade and he chose another path. Two years before Benjamin was born, he shipped out to sea as a merchantman bound for the Indies. After a long silence and no letters to console us, our concern deepened. Nine years after he left, he arrived back home smelling of tar and pitch and then soon left again for the sea.

Is it difficult when our children grow. What did your chores include?

My chores were the same as any other mother. I cared for the younger children with the help of the older. I spun wool, wove cloth, baked and roasted, cleaned, tended the garden, sewed, and knit. I fed the children and made them comfortable with a constant fire and warm clothing. I kept my husband's accounting books. I sang psalms with the children and taught them their prayers, proper manners, what colors to wear, and activities permissible on Sunday. We spent four hours in church, where, by age three, Benjamin could recite the Lord's Prayer.

How did Benjamin get on with the other children?

An incident with Thomas comes to mind. The two boys bickered endlessly. As the elder, Thomas teased Benjamin relentlessly until the day Benjamin knocked Thomas onto his bottom. Angered by that behavior, Josiah insisted that Benjamin memorize long passages of the Bible.

When did you leave Milk Street?

When Benjamin turned six, we bought a house on Union and Hanover Streets in the business district, where we had three times the area. I thanked God for the comfort of more space, and for forty years we resided there. We lived in the back of the house with the workroom in front. Nearby, the Long Wharf built and serviced ships and provided excitement and exploration for Benjamin. Like other adventurous boys, he enjoyed robust activities and boxing. He was full of energy and sometimes acted willful and unpredictable. At home, he did obey.

What were Benjamin's strengths?

He was an affectionate child with love that was not measured. He possessed high intelligence and taught himself to read, and at five years of age he read the Bible. Soon he consumed the two hundred fifty sermons in Reverend Willard's *Complete Body of Divinity*. Benjamin devoured the written word and any money that came into his hands he spent on books. One of his favorites was *The Pilgrim's Progress*. John Bunyan, a simple thinker who became a preacher, wrote it in prison. Benjamin told me Mr. Bunyan was the first English writer to use dialogue in telling a story. Benjamin loved words and writing came naturally to him. He studied incessantly.

At seven, he changed. As all boys of that age, he wore pants. No long, loose gowns and hanging sleeves, no full and flouncy attire. He began to write verses and asked his father to send them to London to Benjamin Elder, the writer in our family, who wrote back full of praise.

"Go on with your pen," he said. His encouragement put Benjamin on that path.

How did Josiah help?

Josiah fostered Benjamin's mechanical curiosity and his inventive nature.

How was he inventive at such a young age?

He taught himself to swim by tossing an egg ahead of him. When it sank, he swam to retrieve it and tossed it again. With a boy, speed is everything, so his need to swim faster pushed him to develop an invention. He gathered two oval pallets similar to painter's pallets and put them in the palm of his hands with a hole for the thumb. They presented a good idea, but their weight oppressed him. For his feet, he made webbed sandals. He used the pallets and sandals and swam with a kite so the wind pulled him across the lake.

You mentioned Benjamin liked to explore.

He fished for minnows in the salt marsh and at the harbor he watched tall sailing ships load and unload. Benjamin and his friends played on the Common, the grassy meadow nearby, and put sticks on their shoulders to imitate the red-coated soldiers of the British army who marched around Fort Hill. One time, and it makes me feel shame for him, Benjamin and his friends took stones that were meant for a nearby house and built a wharf. He was not a wicked child. He merely had a mind full of mischief and a body full of energy. He loved to tinker with ideas.

"Ideas do not feed a man and his family," I told him many times.

Josiah insisted Benjamin look forward to his future, and yet the boy had his own mind, like Josiah Jr. Instead of concentrating on morning and evening prayers, which lasted one hour, Benjamin opened his eyes and studied geography from the four large maps in the hall.

A friend of Josiah's saw that Benjamin would make a fine scholar and Josiah took heed. Benjamin's formal education began. He was Josiah's tenth son, and Josiah believed in tithing ten percent, so he decided to devote Benjamin to the service of the church in the hope he would preach as an adult.

That seems to be an unusual view. Where did Benjamin attend school?

At eight years of age, he started at South Grammar, a

school with free tuition supported by public funds. The school had one hundred students, and it trained pupils in Latin and Greek so they could pass into Harvard College. At that time, only most men, not women, could read and write. Benjamin had such a gift for reading that, by the middle of the first year, he moved to the top of his class. It was suggested he skip a grade, yet arithmetic held him back. Soon Josiah gave concern that Benjamin did not have the unquestioning devotion needed for ministry.

Benjamin has his sayings, so it seems he does preach.

That could be a way to view him.

Did he stay at Boston Grammar?

No, Josiah took Benjamin from the Latin school and continued his education with George Brownell, who held school in his home two blocks from ours. That school was open to both boys and girls, which was unusual. At that time, not even half of the grown women could read and write. I dearly wish I had been blessed with more learning in that area. With God's grace, I get by.

I appreciate my own background in learning.

You are young, and today's education has a forward direction and more subjects are taught. At George Brownell's school, the main stress fell not on composition but on writing with a good, clear hand. It suited Benjamin, but once again he did poorly with arithmetic. He had such trouble and I am not sure why. In life he was quick, yet formal teaching and testing proved difficult for him. I wanted to help although I did not have the skill. I wanted his teachers to make the subject matter clear to him, yet that did not happen. After two years, Benjamin's formal schooling ended.

Did you ever hear news of Josiah Jr.?

Word arrived that his vessel had been lost at sea during a storm. Distress overcame the children, who missed him sorely. The loss affected Josiah most of all, whose grief manifested in quiet. We consoled ourselves knowing he chose his own path. I grieve to think of it.

I am so sorry.

I can say this, for all our lives thereafter we gave thanks that Josiah Jr. was our only son who chose the sea. Eventually, all our children had a trade or worked on a farm.

The sea can take away a life and leave no hope in its place.

After that tragedy, Josiah forbade a career at sea for his sons. He could not bear to lose another child.

That is understandable. When did some joy come back into his life?

After that news, Josiah experienced a pleasant reunion with his brother, Benjamin, who arrived from London. In time his joy became less so. Benjamin Elder lost his wife and nine of his ten children, and Samuel, the only one to survive, worked in America as a cutler. Josiah understood Benjamin Elder's heavy heart and invited him to live with us. When he arrived, he was sickly and forty-five years of age. For four years, until he moved to be with Samuel, Josiah's brother shared our home.

Were the brothers similar in views?

Josiah worked hard and spent his evenings constructively, while hour after hour Benjamin Elder composed rhymes. Not pious enough to be a minister, he wrote sermons and family stories for amusement. When Benjamin Elder lived in London, the brothers wrote affectionate letters, but together they had disputes. Josiah thought Benjamin Elder should work as hard as he did, which did not come to pass. Benjamin Elder claimed his age prevented him from a switch from silk dyeing to a new craft.

I kept my counsel. I noticed the Elder's encouragement of Benjamin's love of books and his praise of Benjamin's own verse and ballads, while Josiah felt an irritation at the time spent foolishly. Some days, Josiah's criticism of young Benjamin rained down harshly upon his head.

"Verse-makers are generally beggars. Your writing is weak," Josiah said.

That might sound insensitive to you, if you choose to make judgments.

It would be wrong of me to judge your life since I have not led it.

Writing and reading held interest for Benjamin, and Josiah kept that in mind. It came time for a decision, though Benjamin was too young for an apprenticeship. Josiah held hope he would join him in his work, as our firstborn son, John, had done before he moved to Rhode Island to set up his own business. Benjamin helped Josiah with easy tasks, like sweeping floors and making deliveries. What bothered Benjamin most were the flies.

What do you mean?

Benjamin described the slaughterhouse as a cloud of flies. There, they got chunks of sheep and beef fat, piled it high in a wheelbarrow, and hauled it home. After they boiled water in a large tub, the fat melted, the waste sank to the bottom, and the tallow floated. For candles, Benjamin cut twisted cotton threads for wicks and poured the tallow to fill the metal molds. Benjamin disliked the smell of rancid animal fat, and boiling lye for soap disagreed with him even more. Only the customers appealed to him. He shined around people, and they in turn enjoyed his company.

Was Josiah able to understand Benjamin's feelings?

Josiah accepted his dislike of the trade. After he refused Benjamin's strong inclination for the sea, they walked and observed joiners, turners, braziers, and bricklayers and then poured over choices and discussed trades. Josiah wanted to apprentice him to Benjamin Sr.'s son, Samuel, a blacksmith turned cutler, though when Samuel asked for money for Benjamin's keep, Josiah stormed away.

You boarded Benjamin Sr. for four years. I can understand Josiah's anger with Samuel. What did he decide upon?

Since Benjamin took to books as troubled men take to drink, it seemed fitting to apprentice and learn the printing trade from his older brother James. Josiah had sent James to London to study and then to buy a printing press and type. When he returned, he set up his own shop three blocks from us. We paid James ten pounds, and at twelve years of age, Benjamin signed the apprentice papers to indenture himself to James until he turned twenty-one. It included an agreement that he would not marry, play cards, drink alcohol, or attend the theatre.

Benjamin became a man. He wore deerskin breeches—oh, they became greasy in time, how difficult to clean—and blue woolen yarn stockings that his sisters made for him, and a speckled shirt. His white one he saved for the Sabbath. He slept in the attic over the shop and a family in town provided him with food.

Printing was labor Benjamin enjoyed. His strong hands worked the heavy manual presses, and his way with language helped him notice mistakes. He borrowed books from James and the local booksellers, and when a tradesman named Adams came into James's shop and took a liking to Benjamin, he gave him access to his private library. By then, Benjamin had read all of Josiah's theology books. His favorites were Plutarch's *Lives* and Dr. Cotton Mather's *Essays to Do Good*.

What did James print?

The New-England Courant, the first independent newspaper in the colonies. For four years, Benjamin seemed content with setting type, printing, and delivering. He enjoyed the feel of a well-bound book and the sights and smells of printing. In the evenings after work he practiced his writing, studied *Cocker's Arithmetick* and learned navigation from Captain Sturmy's writings. Even so, I saw a fly in the ointment.

What was that?

As Benjamin matured, he and James quarreled. Josiah bid me keep my distance, though I feared for Benjamin. I feel shame when I speak of it, but James beat him. To me, the blows seemed too frequent. I talked to James, yet their quarrels continued. His harsh treatment forced Benjamin to feel an aversion to a power more arbitrary than reasonable. Josiah later came to agree with me and took Benjamin's side, which James found unacceptable. He insisted neither his father nor his brother had a say.

Do you fault James in this matter?

Not entirely, since he had other troubles, ones that resulted from the dissent he encountered in his work. He stated and published strong opinions, and others disputed his views. Printers do not obey, they defy, and James enjoyed a challenge. Later his business suffered, but at the beginning, it flourished.

Were there bright spots in your sons' relationship?

Some. Benjamin wrote ballads on topics of the day and James knew his readers enjoyed them. One ballad told how the storm and the sea swept the local lighthouse keeper, his wife, and daughter to their untimely deaths. Another story concerned the killing of the pirate Teach, an unsavory man with the common name of Blackbeard.

Benjamin's best writing began as a secret, since he felt James would not print all he submitted. I disagreed with his deceit, yet understood his reasoning. He disguised his handwriting, wrote an unusual essay, and slipped it under James's shop door. In it, he pretended to be a widowed woman, a busybody with the pen name of Silence Dogood.

Where did he get his ideas?

He got some of them from essays in *The Spectator* and the *London Daily*. To practice his writing, he read the essays and rewrote the arguments to make them clear and simple.

What was James's reaction to the Silence Dogood essays?

When James found them under the door, he let the other men in the shop read them. His workers enjoyed them, and James decided to publish. Discussions swirled—who could the writer be? Many felt they knew.

"I know exactly," said the baker's wife. "She comes in here and talks the way she writes. She is fond of kerchiefs in a variety of color."

No one guessed Benjamin was this woman. In six months'

time, he wrote fifteen chatty Silence Dogood letters. Her cheerful advice became popular, and his secret stayed safe. Then he told James of his deception.

"You are vain," James declared with a sense of irritation.

When the truth came to light, people wondered how Benjamin wrote as a widowed woman from the country. How could he have knowledge of the female mind?

I have read some of the essays. Did he get any ideas from the family?

Our evening discussions could have mixed with Benjamin's imagination. Some ideas came from debates with his friend John Collins. John took the side of men—he had the better gift of arguing—and Benjamin took women's education and rights. Letters passed between them to help their writing, with Benjamin the better speller. Through his Silence Dogood essays, Benjamin helped others understand their biases and developed his wit.

"What an unusual character," my neighbors said.

Silence believed that women should have the rights and liberties that men enjoy. She made fun of women's hoop petticoats, chided the town drunkards, and ridiculed Harvard College.

She spoke in a positive manner for the education of girls and pleaded for freedom of speech.

Did her name originate from Cotton Mather's *Essays to Do Good* that Benjamin read as a child?

Of that, I am not sure.

How did it affect his precarious relationship with James?

As Benjamin wrote his essays, he gained confidence, yet it cost him his relationship with James. One argument concerned the price of Benjamin's keep. To feed his apprentices, James paid a family in town, yet Benjamin had a better solution. He took half the money James paid the family and fed himself. In time, James saw the new system benefited both of them. That was when Benjamin decided not to eat meat.

I do not eat meat, and it is uncommon.

Benjamin later changed that habit, but at the time he said it made him healthier and more clearheaded. Without the high cost of meat, he lived more frugally. With the extra money, he bought books.

Were there any other ways James and Benjamin helped each other?

James published articles in his newspaper that defied the authorities, and Cotton Mather called the writers at the *New-England Courant* the "Hell-Fire Club." He claimed they had a wickedness unparalleled anywhere upon the face of the earth. In one article, James suggested that Massachusetts's government officials had a casual approach to pirate thieves along the coast. The General Court considered James's attack a high affront, and they arrested him and sent him to jail. All this without a trial—an injustice, we felt. Benjamin managed the newspaper and in that way helped James.

Your father was jailed for his beliefs and then your son? Were you distraught?

I felt such distress during James's three weeks in a damp jail. I pleaded with him to relent. At last he made a statement that he was sorry and they released him. I understood James's feelings regarding the pirates, but I had a start when he published an article against hypocritical pretenders to religion. After this mockery of religion, the General Court made James stop printing the *Courant*.

That forced James to appoint Benjamin the publisher and thus release him from the four years left on his indenture contract. James had no real intention of freeing Benjamin, but Benjamin signed a new indenture to cancel the old. Later, when Benjamin spoke of leaving, James could not force him to stay. To make matters worse, Josiah sided with James. By then, the government people saw Benjamin as a freethinker and an infidel.

Had you begun to notice other changes in Benjamin?

He grew to six feet, with an open countenance and more of an ease with people. I valued his independent streak and his mechanical accomplishments, yet in other areas I felt strong disappointment.

Concerning what?

When speaking of religion, he lacked respect. I raised him to be pious, yet on Sundays he read in the printing house instead of worshipping. I hoped he would not remain at odds with our beliefs. Then came the last day, a Wednesday in September, when Benjamin was seventeen.

You sound discouraged. What transpired?

Before dawn, Benjamin crept away to board a ship for New York. He saw it as his only avenue. He sold some books to pay for his passage and his debating friend John Collins invented a story for the ship's captain.

"My friend has a girl in trouble," he said.

Benjamin left without his father's approval, since Josiah would have tried to prevent him from going. Much later, Benjamin admitted some fault and said perhaps he was too provoking and saucy. I worried. No mother wants to part with her youngest son. My heart emptied and froze.

What of his journey?

After he arrived in New York, he discovered the area had one printer with no work for another. The printer sent Benjamin to Philadelphia to work with his son in the family's print shop and newspaper. That did not suit Benjamin, so he found a job in another print shop. With Benjamin so far away, we worried and sent word through our daughter Mary's husband, Captain Homes, who sailed between Boston and Delaware. We urged Benjamin to return to Boston.

"All will be forgiven," we said.

Benjamin wrote us and stated he had done nothing that warranted forgiveness. He explained what he wanted for his life. His actions were hurtful, but I prayed to understand.

In Philadelphia, Benjamin took a room with a family named Read. They had a daughter, Debby. The mother was Sarah, and the father, John, was a carpenter, although John soon passed on. Benjamin wrote of Debby, an agreeable girl with a sweet countenance. Despite his feelings for her, Benjamin started to plan a London voyage.

For seven months we heard no word from him. When he arrived from Philadelphia to visit us, I embraced him with surprise and joy. Benjamin had money in his pocket and a new watch and fob, and he wore a fine suit. Josiah entreated him to make peace with James, yet Benjamin had his own concerns. He took Josiah aside and asked for money for his own print shop. He carried a letter of support from Sir William Keith, the royal governor of Pennsylvania, who promised to help purchase printing supplies upon Benjamin's arrival in London. Josiah told Benjamin he was too young to be trusted with the management of a business and refused his support. He wanted Benjamin to avoid lampooning and libeling.

"Work diligently, keep a rein on your rebellious streak, live frugally for three years, and save. If you fall short, I will make up the balance for your print shop," Josiah said.

Benjamin chose not to take his father's advice and wished us Godspeed. I kept my sadness in check, and this time I held him to my heart and bid him farewell.

Did London suit him?

Benjamin discovered William Keith was a dreamer with no money to back him, so the purchase of supplies proved impossible. In a letter, Benjamin said he drew great favor with his abilities in the water and others wanted him to open a swimming school, which held no interest for him. Instead he found journeywork with printers and saved for his passage home.

He returned to Philadelphia, although Boston would have pleased me more. A mother wants all her children nearby. I hoped he would reconsider, yet in a letter to Josiah, Benjamin made no mention of a return. Once again he requested his father's help. Josiah wrote that Benjamin's London adventure gave no indication of steady progress in his field and again refused to back him in a printing shop. To my dismay, Benjamin severed all ties with his father. I trust my husband in all things, yet I had a heavy heart.

How upsetting. How did you stay in contact with him?

Through our daughter, Jane. On his birthday, he wrote to her and said he missed her. Later, on a day close to her July wedding when she was fifteen, he sent a message.

"Be modest," he said.

Most of what we learned came in the letters to Jane that she shared, since she and her husband lived with us. Benjamin and Jane were close as children and shared a love of books. I taught Jane what little I know of writing, and Benjamin helped her before he moved away. Over the years apart, Jane read his letters to us and spoke of his deeds. In Philadelphia, he bought the Pennsylvania Gazette and became a Freemason. I knew nothing of Freemasons and tried to get an account of them. I found it to be a secret society only for men. When Jane felt discomfort over that, Benjamin assured her that Freemasons consisted of a harmless sort of people who had no principles or practices inconsistent with religion and good manners.

I know of Freemasons and I agree with that assessment. Did Benjamin renew his ties with Debby?

They resumed their closeness. Her life had changed considerably. While in England, Benjamin wrote her that he was not likely soon to return, so Debby married John Rogers, a good potter who turned out to be a worthless fellow. Benjamin heard rumors that John might have abandoned a first wife in England. What he knew for truth was that John took Debby's dowry, stole a slave, and ran from his creditors to live in the West Indies. He might have died, yet there was no way to tell.

Benjamin told us he married Debby. With the uncertainty over Mr. Rogers, Benjamin could not have a formal ceremony, for bigamy meant life imprisonment or thirty-nine lashes. In their hearts, and only in their hearts, Benjamin and Debby have been together as man and wife since 1730. With sorrow, I accept Benjamin's decision to live outside the law.

He must love her. Do you know what drew them together?

Debby was quiet and untaught and did not smile much, but she was sturdy, affectionate, and kind. Benjamin has since told me of her devotion, her sensible and careful money habits, and her attributes as a good and faithful helpmate.

What about William, Benjamin's first son?

I have no direct knowledge, and the circumstances confuse me. William came to live with Benjamin and Debby as their son. Surely that is their business, not ours. Let us not concern ourselves about these things.

And Benjamin and Debby's other children?

Debby bore Francis Folger Franklin on October 20, 1732. Benjamin wrote that he was a delight to all who knew him. When Franky was four years, the ravages of smallpox swept through the city just like when Benjamin was a child.

It was a terrible time.

Close to one in ten people died. So many argued on both sides of inoculation. Benjamin wanted to get his son vaccinated for the pox, but Franky took sickly with a bad cold. Poor Franky. Overcome with smallpox, he went to the Lord. Four years, one month, and one day together. So much grief. My nightly prayers went out to Benjamin. To lose a child.

My grandmother lost her first born, a son named Thomas, in an accident when he was six.

It is a pain from which many never recover. I worried for Benjamin. My mind eased when he visited us in the fall of 1733. His gray eyes held a steady gaze when he sat close and told me he had recovered from the shock. Jane arrived and greeted him warmly and remarked on his good health and correct path. James arrived and sat with Benjamin. With the two of them side by side, I could not help but notice the contrast between James's failing health and Benjamin's robust countenance. James spoke openly of his poor condition and asked Benjamin to raise his ten-year-old son, James Jr., and train him in printing. Benjamin agreed. Poor James lasted less than two years. We lost another son, and it tore our hearts.

How sad.

I must accept the Lord's will.

Was Benjamin able to help James's son?

He kept his promise, sent him to school, and then apprenticed him at seventeen.

How did Benjamin's visits affect you?

His visits were few and a mixed blessing.

How did you cope with your religious differences?

I had concerns that Benjamin seldom attended church. He felt truth was everything. In one letter, he explained but did not apologize for his religious feelings and then expressed thanks for our concern and asked us to pity and excuse rather than blame. I worry his good works will avail him for naught at his final judgment. Jane claims Benjamin's success is driven by God.

I enjoy reading Benjamin's *Poor Richard's Almanack*. Are you aware it sold ten thousand copies a year?

I am not surprised at the number, as our friends and neighbors speak often of his accomplishments. Benjamin sent a copy to me, and his wit and virtue impressed his father. One of my neighbors has a favorite quote.

"Early to bed and early to rise makes a man healthy, wealthy, and wise."

I am fond of one: "Fish and visitors stink in three days."

Jane often speaks of Benjamin's other work, his formation of a brigade to fight fires, the Union Fire Company. He proposed a property value tax to light the street and support a proper police force. Prior to that tax, too many constables spent time in taverns instead of their jobs.

With some other men, he formed the Junto to pave a small section of Philadelphia, and thereafter, everyone wanted clean, paved streets.

I am most fond of his work to provide schools since most children have only a little education at home. I think of my own limitations and wish I had learned more as a child. In that same vein, he worked to get the first lending library.

Benjamin is a clever man. He helped develop a system for removing garbage. He worked on lightning and electricity and invented words to make them understandable.

He devised a new candle made from whale oil with a clear, white light.

He invented the Franklin stove and sold it in his post office. The stove used less wood and gave off less smoke and drafts, and provided better heat.

Jane showed me a pamphlet that stated that women without this stove can get cold in the head, which falls into the gums and destroys teeth. Benjamin claimed bright fires damage the eyes, dry and shrivel the skin, and bring on the appearance of old age. Forgive me, I speak too proudly of Benjamin's accomplishments.

Did Benjamin have any more children?

In 1743, Debby gave birth to Sarah, named after Debby's mother. They call her Sally. On her fourth birthday, Benjamin wrote me that her love of books and school was greater than any child he ever knew. On her seventh birthday, he said Sally has industry with her needle and an affectionate temper and she is dutiful and obliging to all. Letters are wonderful to receive, though a visit gladdens me more.

When was his next visit?

In 1744, we had our third visit from Benjamin. He came for his father since every part of Josiah seemed to be failing. Throughout our lives, Josiah has seldom been ill, and his only problem came from the boiling lye that affected his sense of smell. Benjamin's visit cheered us both and Josiah made light of his troubles.

Did Josiah get his strength back?

In January of the following year, at eighty-seven years of age, my beloved Josiah went to the Lord.

My heart goes out to you. Were you able to find solace?

I fell spent with his passing and then sat by his grave and told him I would join him when the Lord was willing. I pray often and console myself with His reckoning. My family and my faith give me comfort.

Did others honor him?

The Boston weekly newspaper stated he had a constant course of the strictest piety and virtue and that he lived and died with cheerfulness and peace.

Was Benjamin able to attend the funeral?

He heard too late. He purchased a tombstone with the inscription *Diligence in Thy Calling.*

You spoke of differences between Benjamin and his fa-

ther. Did they have similarities?

They both had industry and intelligence, positive thoughts and independence.

You had a large family, which can be a broad mark for both pleasure and sorrow. You spoke today of another sorrow, your son Ebenezer?

You told me your grandmother lost a son in an accident. It pains me to remember the day my beloved Ebenezer slipped and drowned in a tub of suds. He was only sixteen months old.

Soap suds?

Suds need to cool after boiling the fat to make soap. By the time we missed him, searched, and found him, he could not be revived. The memory takes my breath.

Can you forgive whoever was responsible?

To look back fills my heart with regret, and I carry it with me forever. Sorrow colors how close one gets to the children who come after. Josiah never spoke of it. I chose to forgive and not dwell on it. I accept God's kind providence and His will. That acceptance was again tested when our son Thomas died at barely three years of age. He was an affectionate child, and I think of him often with sadness.

I wish my grandmother had been able to shake off her pain from the loss of Tommy. I never saw her smile.

It can be hard to find joy again. At thirty years of age, our daughter Sarah passed away in childbirth, and Mary died of cancer of the breast at thirty-seven. I mourn my lost children, yet I know I am not alone. We all have tragedies. We are pleased to have Jane, who cares for us. Benjamin continues to vex us from afar, yet he claims his opinions are not dangerous and his philosophy is to do good. We fear for his soul.

What do you hear of him now?

He goes easy through life. He has breakfast late; enjoys music-making, checkers, and chess; and visits the theatre. He likes some time alone in silence and thoughtful behavior. In 1748, he retired from printing to work on his science projects, his thunder gusts and electricity. He tells us of his experiments, his farm, his official duties, and charity work at the hospital. He continues to be generous and recently sent me funds to hire a chaise to ride warm to meetings this winter, since my health is failing. In my prayers, I thank God for my comforts.

Do you write to Benjamin?

I write short notes to him. I am a poor speller, yet Benjamin claims he readily understands every word. Just yesterday he wrote that he and his family are glad to hear that I enjoy a measure of health, notwithstanding my great age. He spoke of his son Will, a tall, proper youth and much of a beau, who has applied himself to business. Sally attends dancing school and delights in her books. Benjamin signed it, "your dutiful son."

You must excuse me now, for this has been a long afternoon. I hope I provided everything you need. Godspeed.

—— ❧ ——

INTERVIEW WITH BENJAMIN FRANKLIN ON THE DEATH OF HIS MOTHER

Our dear, good mother died at age eighty-four. The news arrived too late for me to attend her funeral. I know that my duty as a son was not what it should have been, and I thank my sister Jane for her care in those last days. Mother lived a good life as a discreet and virtuous woman. She is buried with my father in Boston.

4

Interview with Rose Bruskin Gershwin

MOTHER OF GEORGE GERSHWIN,
SONGWRITER, BORN SEPTEMBER 26, 1898

———— ⌘ ————

Why should I limit myself to only one woman
when I can have as many women as I want?
—George Gershwin

JAN HELEN MCGEE

I like this Russian tea. I've never had it, thank you.

ROSE GERSHWIN

Good. Now you can get on with the questions.

JAN HELEN MCGEE

Have you always known George had music in him?

ROSE GERSHWIN

Wait until you hear this. I wanted George to be an accountant. And before that I thought one of my sons should be a doctor, the other a lawyer. I had hopes for Ira and Arthur but not Georgie.

"What's the matter with you? You got no ambition," I used to tell Georgie.

"You'll grow up to be a bum," Morris, his father, said.

I guess we both got it wrong. But you know the end of that story. Georgie and his music. I must admit, the reason I wanted Georgie to be an accountant was to play the other side of coin from me. See, I love the racetrack. Rent a limousine, arrive in style, play the horses. And I love cards, at home or with my friends backstage at the National Theatre. They let me play there because of Georgie's music. Doors open, and that's good. The honors of his fame get me a special seat in a restaurant and my comforts. I get extra attention because no matter where Georgie went, he got noticed. That boy of ours was a good showman, and I'm the same. We both liked to talk and charm a crowd.

Are there any ways you aren't the same?

Some. I'm not one for affection, and that used to bother Georgie. When he reached for a kiss, I'd move my face away. It sounds unfeeling, but my upbringing didn't include public displays. That sort of thing makes me nervous. I can be a bit nervous about a lot of things, and sometimes I prefer things to people. For example, I'm obsessed with diamonds. I love your diamond ring.

It was my mother's. It's a little gaudy, but I think of her every time I look at it.

Never too gaudy with diamonds. Georgie got these for me. He was good with gifts and indulged me in that way. When he went on trips, he got me scarves and things. Morris got a phonograph and opera recordings. When I wanted a new mink coat, I got sable from the forests of Russia. And since I care about my looks, George gave me the money to help me be one of the first women in the United States to have cosmetic surgery.

In other ways I'm more like my son Ira. He's protective of his privacy. People see me at restaurants and the theater and think they know me, but they don't. My thoughts aren't out there for public consumption; they're mine. But today I'll tell you things you can pass on to Georgie's music lovers.

What was your role when your children were small?

I managed the household and watched over the finances. We had a maid to answer the door and clean, and I did the cooking. Georgie loved cornflakes—they're easy—but his favorites were my borscht and my double lamb chops. My cooking he appreciated, since he paid attention to good food. Lots of times, after he was grown, he brought vegetables and ice cream home for all of us. That's family. Georgie took care of us, and I took care of him. I had to, since he never married, which was fine with me. I never met a girl good enough for my Georgie. What did he need a wife for, anyway? When he had his parties, I acted as hostess and helped wherever needed. I encouraged his social life and gave him important advice.

"Get friendly with the famous and wealthy. They can do you good," I said.

I know the papers can be inaccurate, but I read somewhere that George was unhappy. Was that the case?

With all those parties, I don't understand why they wrote that. I guess they didn't know his true feelings. They didn't realize his poker face came from me. Anyway, happiness is overrated, but *interesting* is a different matter. Georgie liked things interesting, and he didn't waste time on anything dull.

Ira doesn't mind dull. Solid, careful—that's Ira. When the boys were young, we all thought Ira would be the musician, even though our family hadn't produced a single musician. Certainly Morris, my husband, wasn't one, though he claimed otherwise. He coaxed music out of the silliest contraptions. He blew through combs wrapped in tissue or tapped clothespins against his teeth, he made imitations of a cornet with his mouth, and he sang fairly. He whistled even better. Sometimes he went to the opera. That was his joke.

Oh, I miss Morris now that he's gone. Every day we had laughter. I miss him more than I thought I would. I got used to his habits in our long years together. You see his picture on that table? That's my Morris.

He certainly looks interesting. How did you meet?

We met in the old country in Russia. Morris's grandfather was a rabbi and his father worked as a mechanic for the artillery. Yakov Gershovitz was his name. Yakov is Russian for Jacob. He became an accomplished inventor and developed a model of a gun that he sold to the Czar's army. Because of that success, even though Jakov was a Jew, he could do any kind of work and go anywhere he wanted.

What was Morris's first job?

He started in a factory as a leatherworker, a cutter for women's shoes. Morris was easygoing, a funny man everyone liked. He took things as they came and rolled with the changes life throws at us.

"You have the soul of a wandering Jew," I told him.

We met after I turned fifteen. I was Rosa Bruskin then. He was nineteen and short, which I didn't like. I wanted a tall man. But Morris told me I was beautiful with a sensitive face and intense eyes, and he won me over. When I was a child, compliments didn't fly free.

What were your parents like?

I wasn't too close to my mother. She had her own way about her. My father was a successful furrier, so our family had money, but like many other Russian Jews, he gave up his business and moved us to America. We settled near friends and relatives on New York's Lower East Side.

Back in Russia, Morris faced twenty-five years of compulsory military service. Worse than that, his heart called out for me, so he followed us to America. On Ellis Island, the immigration officer turned Gershovitz into Gershvin. Here in New York City, Morris found a good paying job designing fancy uppers for women's shoes.

Did you get married in New York City?

I married him on July 21, 1895, when I was nineteen. The wedding was in a rathskeller on Houston Street. What a time we had, what a crowd. Even Teddy Roosevelt stopped by to have a drink. Back then he was president of the Board of Police Commissioners of New York City. Our party lasted three days. That Morris knew how to have a good time.

Where was your first home?

Right above Simpson's Pawnshop on East Hester Street. By then Morris got promoted to foreman in the shoe factory.

When did you have children?

In December of '96, Ira was born. We named him Israel, but we called him Ira for so many years that we almost forgot his real name. Like Morris, he's stocky and short. Ira's shy and gentle.

Georgie's our second son. His real name is Jacob, after Morris's father, but like Ira he never used that name. He was born September 26, 1898. About that time, we moved above Saul Birn's Phonograph Shop on Second Avenue, and then my third son, Arthur, arrived in March of 1900. About three years later we moved to Manhattan for good. By then Ira looked almost exactly like Morris. He was an excellent reader and a good student.

Was George the same?

Georgie couldn't have been more opposite. He didn't like to read and he had bad grades. What a handful. He stayed out for hours with his friends and came home with so much dirt on him that I gave up trying to keep him clean. He ran the streets and got so many injuries, like the day he got kicked by a horse on the bridge of his nose, which never healed. After that he had trouble with his breathing and tonsils. So much of Georgie's childhood was filled with petty stealing, minor things. It was just mischief, but we worried about his competitive streak and his street fights, even though he won most of them. Not only that, but he liked to play hooky from school. He tried to keep it a secret, but I knew. That boy, I knew. I could look at him and see right away he wasn't going to be like Morris or Ira. Even his physical features were different from both of them. Instead of short, he was tall with a long, thin face and movements like mine. That boy had lots of get-up-and-go.

You seem to have a lot of energy yourself.

I used my energy chasing after all three of my boys, but I didn't mind too much until my fourth baby came. It was Ira's tenth birthday on the day Frances arrived. We called her Frankie since I prefer sons. All my children were born healthy, and I'm thankful for that, but what I wanted most was education for them. If everything else failed, they could be schoolteachers. Education meant success.

Morris and I didn't have the chance for an education, so Morris had lots of businesses in his life: bakeries, a stationery store, a Turkish bath, a billiard parlor, and restaurants. Whenever he sold a business and started another, we moved to a different neighborhood, often once a year. One summer he ran a hotel. We didn't trust banks, so when times got tough I made Ira pawn one of my diamonds. I didn't worry, just made sure we got it back. Maybe once or twice I had to sell one. But don't get me wrong; Morris made enough money to take care of us. I remember one job I liked. For three weeks he was a bookmaker at the Brighton Beach racetrack. I helped out and kept an eye on him and his activities. He did what I told him to do. No matter what job he had, I did the books.

So you worked with Morris?

Oh sure, and he never minded giving me credit for the help I gave him. Our deal was *I do the books, I get a maid.* But it didn't matter how well I did those books; some of Morris's jobs turned sour. That racetrack job was a disaster, but while it lasted I enjoyed it. I love to gamble. Sometimes we even took the kids with us to the track.

I gather you and Morris spent a lot of time together then.

Don't misunderstand—we weren't together all the time like some couples. Pretty much we lived separate social lives. Morris had his lodge meetings and pinochle games. Every day I played poker with other women, and every Saturday night I hosted a poker party. My friends liked those parties, and that's how Ira got his spending money. He served drinks and food, supplied new card decks, and dispensed the chips. Not only Ira but also Georgie had an inventive mind when it came to making a buck. I guess he was about ten when he asked for money for a movie. I refused, so he went out on the street, took off his shoes and begged from strangers.

"I am a poor boy," he pleaded. He got enough for the movie.

While Georgie pulled his tricks, Ira followed the rules. That meant Ira studied music with my younger sister, Kate, on her piano. When he was fourteen, I bought a secondhand piano on the installment plan. I thought Ira's music would entertain my friends and bring some culture to our lives. As soon as they hoisted that piano through the second-floor front window and put it in our parlor, Georgie started to play. It turned out he'd been practicing at a friend's. Ira saw Georgie had all that music in him, so Ira quit taking lessons with my sister. To this day Ira can barely read music. His interest is lyrics.

It must have been a relief that George spent so much time with music instead of out on the streets.

I can't tell you how relieved I was when it kept Georgie out of trouble. He practiced all the time and took some lessons. After he heard the Beethoven Orchestra, he met the pianist Jack Miller. Jack appreciated Georgie's talent and arranged for lessons with his own teacher, Charles Hambitzer. A mild-mannered man, that Hambitzer, with sloppy-looking clothes, but we liked him. He motivated Georgie and, best of all, he refused to take any money for the lessons. Georgie repaid him by finding ten other boys for Hambitzer to teach for money.

"George is a genius who will make his mark in music if anybody will," Hambitzer said.

What type of music did he play then?

Hambitzer made him play Beethoven and Chopin and all classical music for a firm foundation. Then Georgie came home and played modern music and jazz. He studied popular music on his own, and then he visited Harlem and listened to the ragged beats and syncopation of the Negro musicians.

All the time that Georgie spent on his music bothered me some back then, but I see now it did him good. I'd stop his playing and insist he do some work on his school texts, but that boy didn't listen. He mastered his arithmetic skills, but he hated accounting, so I gave up hope for that job.

How did George start making money from his music?

That idea came in the summer of 1914, when he played in a Catskills resort and earned five bucks a week. He knew then that he could have a music career. At school he felt restless, and the only thing he liked was playing piano at assemblies. At fifteen, Georgie decided to leave high school. The suddenness surprised me since most of the time he came to me for advice on important matters. Not that day, though. He had his mind set.

So you had some concerns?

Concern? A whole lot of yelling from Morris and me. It didn't make him budge. Finally, Morris shrugged his shoulders and sat down. I kept at it. I suggested the fur business. Georgie said no, music would be his career.

"Uncertainty and disaster," I told him, "that's what music

will bring." Now you tell me, how wrong can a mother be?
**You're a funny woman. So where did he go to look for
work?**

Georgie put on a suit and tie to look older and got a job
as a piano pounder for the Remick Company, a publishing
firm on West 28th Street. Morris was relieved that he had
any kind of income. I decided to let him be, but I didn't want
him to be a piano player all his life. Looking on the positive
side, I ran it through my mind that Georgie was the youngest
pounder in that area they called Tin Pan Alley. I started to
change my thinking when I found out about the big money
in the popular music scene.

Georgie got paid fifteen bucks a week to demonstrate
Remick's songs. He played piano for singers called pluggers,
and in that way he pushed Remick's songs on vaudeville
performers and dancers. Chorus girls gathered around my
handsome son and breathed down his neck. As a musical
salesman, he played those songs eight to ten hours a day for
dance bands, restaurant orchestras, and music stores that
sold sheet music. As he practiced and changed keys, Georgie
pushed hit tunes.

What other musicians did he know?

He met Fred Astaire and his sister Adele, the vaudeville
song-and-dance team. It came about because Fred was hunting for new music at Remick's and heard George plugging
songs. Here's the interesting part of their meetings. Nor-
mally Georgie wrote songs and Fred danced, but when they
got together, they switched. Fred played piano and Georgie
showed him a few dance moves. Georgie told me he liked
Fred's piano playing, his knocked-out slap left-hand moves.

He had a dream to write a musical that Fred could dance in and be the star.

Georgie also admired the songwriters Irving Berlin and Jerome Kern from Tin Pan Alley. Irving was a Russian Jew who grew up on the Lower East side. Georgie called him America's Franz Schubert. At one point, Irving offered Georgie a job as his arranger and musical secretary, but with the offer came the odd request not to take it.

"You're too talented," Irving told Georgie.

Georgie could've used the money, but he turned it down and went after his own dream. As for Jerome Kern, Georgie heard his music for the first time at my sister Kate's wedding at the Grand Central Hotel. The orchestra played Kern's song from the show *The Girl from Utah*. Both of them had worked as song pluggers, so when they spent time together, Jerome gave Georgie help and encouragement. The music Georgie wrote during that time imitated Kern's in some ways.

Did any of you expect George would become a composer?

That surprised all of us. No one expected it; he just did it. When he felt blue, he wrote ballads. When his mood changed, he wrote lively tunes with outdoor pep. Georgie told me one time that some man told him he made the piano laugh. I agree. The beat and changes Georgie pulled out of his hat impressed everyone. I was honored to be part of it, and I even helped a little with his music. If I told him I didn't like a certain phrase, he'd listen to me and make a change. Some songs took a long time to write. I don't know the longest time it took him, but some days he wrote one in a few minutes.

Now look at me, I just talked past where I wanted to be.

At Remick's music company, pounders were not supposed to plug their own songs, so Georgie kept his ideas in a little notebook. Finally, in 1916, he sold his first song and made five bucks. After that he felt unhappy playing other people's songs, so he got a different job playing and cutting piano rolls for player pianos. He made twenty-five bucks for six rolls, and he recorded more than 120 rolls in all. That led to Broadway to a job as a relief player at a vaudeville house, but that lasted only a day. See, that's what relief means. Who knows when the regular guy will show back up?

Both Georgie and Ira were out of work a lot back then. With all his free time, Georgie took more lessons and pushed himself. He worked as a journeyman on the vaudeville circuit and soon made enough money to get us new furniture. Around that same time, Georgie changed his name from Gershvin to Gershwin, and later we all changed our names.

What did Ira do for work?

Ira enrolled in the City College of New York, but he stopped after two years. He tried a lot of jobs: the cashier at Morris's Turkish baths, then a darkroom assistant, then he wrote quips and verse for newspapers. That's my Ira, my writer, not a lawyer at all, but certainly a word man.

I love words in all forms, lyrics, books, talking. Did anything happen with romance for Ira?

Georgie made connections and got introduced to an older gentleman, Herman Paley, who invited Georgie to his regular Saturday night parties. Georgie liked talking to Herman's brother Lou about books, which helped him learn because he didn't read much. As friends do, they got to matchmaking. Lou's girlfriend Emily had a sister, Leonore, and one night

Ira went along to the party. Leonore and Ira hit it off, and nine years later got married. We call her Lee.

Anyway, back to the parties. After Georgie talked to Lou for a while, he'd spend the rest of the night playing piano. I told him what I thought about that.

"It's rude to arrive and play straight through until you leave," I said.

Georgie disagreed. "If I don't play, I don't have a good time," he told me.

When he played at parties, he worked out new ideas and tried out chord changes. That way he didn't have to practice as much at home. Georgie liked an audience, and it made him try harder. Even when we had parties here at home, he monopolized the piano.

Did your daughter Frankie have an interest in music?

I'm going on and on about Georgie and Ira, but they weren't the only ones with talent. Frankie had a sweet, small, husky voice. When she was ten, after a lot of dance instruction, I moved her into a stage career. We took off on a road tour in a show called *Daintyland*, and her performances got big write-ups in the papers.

What was touring like?

Here's a typical day on a road tour: Frankie danced the first show, and then we waited in the dressing room for the next show. She danced three shows a day, which took up a lot of time. After the last show, we went to a hotel and slept. Day after day, that was our life on the road. The grind exhausted us, so we didn't return the next year.

Did Arthur have any interest in music?

He plays by ear and wrote over one hundred fifty songs.

Like Morris, he has a good sense of humor. Here's what he says when someone asks him about music:

"I am a leading composer of unpublished songs," he says.

Songwriting didn't pay his bills, so he became a salesman of motion picture films and then a stockbroker.

You're lucky to have clever children.

I know I am. I told them what I wanted for their careers, and they did what they thought best. Georgie never deviated from what he wanted. He always wrote music. I remember the night he wrote "Swanee." Georgie and his friend Irving Caesar started it in a restaurant, continued it on the bus home, and finished it at our place. In the next room Morris's card-playing buddies yelled about the noise that Georgie and his buddy were making, but when the song was finished, Morris put tissue over his comb and joined Georgie for a duet. Let me tell you, that song "Swanee" had a trick. The key changed between the verse and chorus. That made it different from other songs.

When Georgie played "Swanee" during a show rehearsal, the girls from the Ziegfield Follies clustered around him and went wild. Can you imagine sixty girls dancing to that song at the Capitol Theatre, the largest theater in the world? What a hit, and what a surprise when nobody bought the sheet music out in the lobby. We never did understand it because later millions of copies got sold.

I like the line "How I love you, how I love you" in "Swanee." What happened after that?

When Georgie turned twenty, he got a lucky break and was hired to compose a Broadway show, *La-La-Lucille!* That show didn't work out, but because of it, he got a chance to play

"Swanee" for Al Jolson. Al sang it at a Sunday night concert at the Winter Garden and then recorded it. At last Georgie felt hopeful about his songs.

By the time he was twenty-five, he was famous. We never expected so much. By then I'd finally stopped thinking about an accountant job for him. Morris made the adjustment easier than I did. He liked Georgie's music 'cause of how Morris was a bit of a performer himself. With his offbeat comments, Morris loved to provoke laughter and spread his unique philosophy. As Georgie wrote "Rhapsody in Blue," Morris said an odd thing.

"Make it good, Georgie, it's liable to be important."

For that composition, Georgie got the beginning idea of a steely rhythm while riding the train. He finished "Rhapsody in Blue" more quickly than you'd expect, less than six weeks from start to finish. After a performance of the song, Morris said another funny thing to one critic.

"It's very important music. It takes twenty minutes to play," Morris told him.

Oh, we had a good laugh over that one. Another time, Georgie wondered what to call his second rhapsody, so Morris gave his idea.

"Call it "Rhapsody in Blue No. 2." Then you can write number three, four, and five just like Beethoven," Morris said.

One of Morris's favorites was "Embraceable You." It had that line, *Come to papa, come to papa, do.*

"That part, he wrote for me," Morris said.

George and Ira wrote several hits together.

Georgie wrote "Fascinating Rhythm" with Ira. Morris twisted it into "Fashion on the River." It could've been the little trouble both of us had with English, but I do know Morris loved to make jokes. Those jokes never masked the pride he felt. I can't tell you how it pleased Morris when Georgie and Ira worked together on the songs for *Lady, Be Good.* That's the show where Georgie finally got a chance to work with Fred Astaire.

As far as Ira goes, the *Lady, Be Good* songs helped him feel better about himself. For a long time before that, he used to say he belonged to the ranks of the Brothers of the Great. Never again did he talk that way. He found his place with good lyrics. I remember one night Ira and Georgie wrote a song together for the show *The Sweetheart Shop.* For that one, they got two hundred fifty bucks. The money pushed them to really start working together. First Georgie wrote the music, and then Ira wrote the lyrics. Georgie liked going first, but he appreciated Ira's ability to shape words around his melody line.

"Ira is a smart college boy with talent," Georgie said.

Were you ever close by when they worked on their songs? Do you have a favorite?

I watched and listened while I cooked. Of all their songs I have two favorites, "The Man I Love" and "Fascinating Rhythm." Let me tell you how the second one got its name. It came after Ira heard the music Georgie wrote.

"That's a fascinating rhythm," Ira said. The end.

Those boys worked together on songs, but their temperaments were black and white. Sometimes, like any other brothers, they didn't get along. Ira stayed well-behaved and spent very little money, not even on clothes. Georgie spent money and had a good time, but he had melancholy and thoughtful days. When they worked together, they had a lot of disagreements, but I tried not to interfere if I could stand it. I saw the results of their hard work and let them work it out the way it suited them. Songs took a lot of energy, and people are wrong if they think songwriting is easy. It's not. Georgie always said there's nothing more nerve-wracking than songwriting. He called it a mentally arduous task.

What were his writing habits?

He never wrote in the morning because he wasn't really awake. His best work was done at night. For hours at a time, he'd sit at the piano with no shirt on, smoke a cigar, and compose. He'd even write with people playing cards in the next room. Of course he had to, with all the card-playing we did. For twelve hours straight he worked, and it ended with nervous indigestion. To relax and unwind, he visited the osteopath. Sometimes he wasn't upbeat about his music.

"I'm a man with a little bit of talent and a great deal of chutzpah," he said.

Those doubts didn't keep Georgie from writing more songs, and neither did all the activity in our apartment. In the fall and winter, he worked the most. In spring and summer, he liked golf or tennis with his friends, but he never played other ball games for fear he'd hurt his hands. No matter the season, Georgie had energy. He ran when he could walk, and he liked when everything moved fast. He wanted to keep life interesting and full of gusto.

What else did George do in his free time, besides tennis and golf?

He went to concerts and listened to serious music, and for that he needed a date. Georgie liked women. For a year he dated Pauline Heifetz, the sister of Jascha, the violinist. His lack of interest in marriage put some women off, but he still had lots of girls. When he wouldn't settle down with Pauline, she married another man. Did it to spite him. I liked her sophisticated manner, but she wasn't right for my Georgie.

Then there was the scandal.

Can you address it?

I should, since people talk about it everywhere. I knew you'd ask me, so I brought it up first. It involved the chorus girl Mollie Charleston. She had a son, Alan, and claimed he was Georgie's, but I never believed it. Ira handled the arrangements. I won't say more on that.

There's another woman that people talk about, the songwriter Kaye Swift. She was married but later got divorced. She helped Georgie transcribe his work. Really, Georgie had dozens of gals who'd go with him to those Saturday night parties at the Paley's. He was fond of a college girl, Rosamund Whalling. Her mother was Jewish. Georgie said Rosamund had good sense like me. He also dated Mabel Shirmer, Julia Van Norman, the silent screen star Aileen Pringle, the Countess de Granny, and Simone Simon. He met Simone in Paris and helped her immigrate to America. Then there's Elizabeth Allan, Kitty Carlisle, and Paulette Goddard. Too many of them were actresses and married. I think he acted as their escort, or maybe he liked to pursue women courted by other men.

I didn't approve of many of those women. Neither did Ira's wife, Lee. The two of us would answer the door and try to control who entered the house. That way we kept the bad ones away.

But Georgie liked to be social. When he was about twenty-six, he hosted Sunday evening gatherings with friends from art and publishing. He'd ask Frankie to sing. She was only twenty and shy, with a husky soprano voice. Georgie liked her interpretations.

"She knows how to put over a song," he said.

He was protective of Frankie and not happy about her theatrical ambitions, but he paid for new dance routines, I guess because Georgie was a good dancer on his own. During the practice for *Lady, Be Good*, Georgie gave Fred Astaire hoofer advice.

Is there anyone in your immediate family who's not social?

We all liked people, especially Morris. When Georgie's friends came over, Morris made it all so much fun. After he retired, he hung around the house, so he loved to see people come and go. We'd open the door and watch Georgie's wire-haired terrier run out and back in, over and over, and Morris tried not to laugh. It's a wonder we didn't lose that little dog.

Did George get any of his song ideas during your parties?

He got some, but I don't know where he got the idea for his next hit "The Man I Love." I do know that in London, Lady Mountbatten made her favorite dance band play it over and over. That helped it become well known, and it led to Georgie's picture on the cover of *Time* magazine. He looked handsome, but the article was terrible. Georgie didn't care. He didn't trouble himself with other people's opinions like I did.

"Why do all the other composers get good reviews?" I

asked him.

I never got an answer because it didn't matter to him. He knew music and art had an interpretation different for each person. After that *Time* cover, he had success with "Rhapsody in Blue" and "An American in Paris." He called that one a tone poem.

Were there any other changes after his *Time* magazine cover?

We moved to a house for all of us on West 103rd Street. Georgie had a half interest, and Ira and me had the other half interest. On the ground floor, we had a kitchen and a large ballroom for ping-pong, billiards, checkers, and cards. An elevator took us to the second floor. That reminds me of a gag Morris pulled. He dressed up in a uniform and ran the elevator for Georgie's friends.

On the parlor floor of the house we had a dining room, and in the large living room we had two Steinways. The second floor had our bedroom and a sitting room. That's where Morris had his pinochle games and I played poker with my friends. Frankie and Arthur had the third floor, Ira the fourth, and Georgie the fifth. Up there on top, he had his bedroom, a study, and a music room with a third Steinway.

Throughout the house, Georgie displayed his contemporary art collection. One year Ira gave Georgie some watercolors he painted for his birthday. That pushed Georgie to paint, and they both made self-portraits. Georgie's work looked like Monet, and he called his style "modern romantic." When he painted my portrait, he talked about how he loved to sketch when he was young. Georgie said music is design, with melody as line and harmony as color. But painting was his hobby.

Writing and performing music came first. For a while, he liked conducting.

Did Ira continue with his painting?

He liked it, but that was when he got real busy with Lee, who was over at our house all the time. At first the newspapers linked her with Georgie, but that was only a one-sided feeling on her part. When Lee saw Georgie wasn't interested, she didn't let any grass grow under her feet. She went after Ira, reeled him in, proposed, and caught him. In that relationship, Lee plays boss, at least in front of people.

They married in a simple ceremony at the home of the rabbi. They stood under the chuppah while me and Morris stood side-by-side with the Sturnsky's, who own real estate. Georgie wore a tuxedo and yarmulke and acted as best man. It was a good day.

Where did they live after they got married?

Lee moved in with Ira on the fourth floor. I liked her, so I felt a little sorry for her when it turned out she couldn't have children. Not that I cared personally. Children are a lot of bother. To make up for that loss, she bought clothes. She has expensive taste. That, I understand. She did over the fourth floor and decorated it the way she liked.

A floor above them, Georgie wrote for a whole lot of shows, but sometimes they run together in my mind. I do know that the title song to *Strike Up the Band* came to Georgie as a dream.

I've heard that creativity presents itself in dreams.

George usually forgot when they came that way, but that time he got out of bed and wrote it out. Ira put in the lyrics and used words that told a story from part of Georgie's life. And my Georgie had a lot of life in him. He went out in the evenings, and he had plenty of musician friends who admired him. For his birthday, the composer Maurice Ravel wanted to meet him. When they got together, Georgie asked if he could study with him. That didn't sit right with Ravel.

"Why be a second-rate Ravel when you can be a first-rate Gershwin?" he said.

Flat out, he turned Georgie down. He said that if he studied with him he might lose his spontaneity and his unusual melodies. I have to tell you, Ravel was not the only one to notice Georgie's talent. Other people called Georgie's gift for rhythm and melody true genius. He never stopped playing no matter where he was.

Even on the ship over and back from Europe in 1928, Georgie spent a lot of time at the piano. The other passengers got free concerts I guess. Georgie told me that in letters. See, he always wrote to me when we were apart. That trip, he took with Frankie, Ira, and Lee. They went to London, where the four of them saw shows and met other musicians. Georgie, and I think Ira too, had interviews. In Paris, Frankie met Leopold Godowsky Jr., son of the famous pianist and teacher. But the trip wasn't all music, because I know my boys and their poker games. That put Ira's wife, Lee, and Frankie together, which caused a problem because Frankie got all the attention. That's how it goes.

How long were they gone?

About three months. When they got back to America, me and Morris and some others met them at the ship for a welcome-home party. Rosamond Walling was in our group. She was only seventeen at the time, with a beautiful face and fig-

116

ure. That Georgie. The women liked his music and his handsome face and his style with clothes. What a natty dresser. He carried a cane, and that set him off as different. Georgie fell in love easily, but he always said he was too damn busy to get married.

Have you ever thought about how you affected that decision?

I sometimes wonder if me and Morris soured him for marriage. Not that we were any different from any other couple. Sometimes I didn't treat Morris right. I talked down at him, but he was so slow. We had disagreements, but we were a family. I loved that we were all close and that our children lived with us, but I knew it couldn't last forever. When Georgie was in his late twenties, he decided to move out. I took to my bed with a terrible attack of asthma.

"Georgie, this move will cause my death," I told him.

His dog got all excited and jumped over me, back and forth from one side of the bed to the other. I wanted Morris's support, but guess what he said to Georgie.

"Why didn't you do it sooner?"

I coulda killed him. He knew how hard it was for me to be separated from him. I understood that Ira and Lee needed a place, but Georgie? One of my friends told me I should be grateful my sons stayed in New York City. They only moved over to Riverside Drive, where they rented adjoining penthouses. Georgie's had a spectacular view of the Hudson River, with rooms for everything: his mementos, a gym, and a studio.

It was after the move that his headaches started and life changed for Georgie. I didn't see it coming. We all thought he just worked too hard and had too much of a social life.

Will you talk about it?

I hate to get into all that sadness before I finish with all the fun we had. One December the family went to the Carnegie Hall performance of Georgie's *An American in Paris*. I wore my mink and diamonds, and afterwards there was a party in his honor. Not too long after that, Morris and I left for Florida, where we spent winters. In spring of '29, we closed our house on 103rd Street because summers in the city got too hot, and we moved to upstate New York.

Let me think what else happened during that time. Georgie had a show *Girl Crazy*, and he conducted the premiere. I'll tell you what stole that show. You should've been there. Ethel Merman sang "I Got Rhythm." We liked another song in that show, "Embraceable You." Ira wrote the lyrics for both of those songs.

Soon after that, Frankie got married. I didn't think anyone would ever marry her, but Leo did. For two years after they met in Paris, they dated, and I didn't approve. Just the thought of it made my asthma worse. Frankie said Leo was charming and handsome, but I saw a great pianist's son who lived in his father's shadow. He was a violinist with no money and few prospects, but she didn't care. Behind my back, she met him outside. They planned the wedding quietly, but suddenly one Sunday, Leo decided he wanted the ceremony that very day. It was crazy since me and Morris were about to leave for Florida, and Ira and Georgie were headed to Hollywood.

At the last minute they had to get a license and find a ring and a rabbi. Leo was tricky. A limo pulled right up to our house, and inside sat a jeweler with rings for Frankie to choose. Over at his apartment, Ira got the wedding celebration ready. I didn't know anything about it until the last minute. I thought they were giving us a farewell party. When I found out the truth, I took to the bed with worry. Morris paced and checked his watch while he waited for a rabbi they got from the telephone book.

First the rabbi arrived at the wrong apartment, but then he showed up a few hours before our six o'clock train to Florida. That rabbi sure did bring light into the ceremony. He couldn't have been more delighted to meet my boys. Meanwhile, at the last minute, I tried to get us ready. The day before, Kaye Swift sent me flowers, so I pinned some of them on Frankie's dress so she'd look special. With his big cigar in his mouth, Georgie played the wedding march and then a bit of "Rhapsody in Blue." The rabbi made music references, and Frankie beamed with happiness. We had to leave in a hurry to catch the train. Not that I minded.

That's quite a story. You have an unusual way of looking at things.

What surprised me was that Leo actually amounted to something. He made money with his partner by inventing the Kodachrome color film process. Proved me wrong. I guess I was wrong about a lot of things when I planned my children's future. They all turned out to be successful, so that's that, but I couldn't help but worry back then. Even when they were adults I had plenty of worry. One of the worst times was when Georgie, Ira, and Lee moved to California. I couldn't believe Georgie would go along with the plan since he didn't like the people in show business, but he hated to be alone.

The three of them rented a five-bedroom house in Beverly Hills where Greta Garbo once lived, and Lee ran the household. Georgie had famous cronies out there: Jerome Kern, Irving Berlin, and Harpo Marx. Those are important men.

I lived in California for several years. I had trouble knowing what month or season it was. How long did they stay there?

Some months later they returned to New York. Georgie had go-arounds with this girl and that, with one of them introducing him to someone who led him to endorse Lucky Strikes. But then he gave up smoking. Georgie liked to work, but he took time off to golf or visit Florida in the winter like we did. In the winter of '31, Georgie vacationed in Cuba for a few weeks. Besides golf, he liked roulette, nightclubbing, and the track.

Was Florida good for your health?

Florida was good for my soul. By then, me and Morris had health problems. I'll tell you, last year I had bad nights, and this year sinus trouble. But that was nothing compared to what happened to Morris. What a blow. Morris found out he had lymphatic leukemia. He didn't complain but I could hardly stand it.

I can tell you were upset.

You see me wringing my hands? No wonder I play poker; I need something to do with my hands. The end came at the Hotel Broadmoor. All the children were there with us. At one point Morris decided it was time for a joke. Oh, that man. Well, maybe it wasn't a joke. He took off his oxygen mask and started talking about the next man I would marry, telling everyone it would probably be someone tall. I shoulda told him one husband was enough. I shoulda said I loved him, but he knew it anyway.

Morris died soon after that. I took it hard, but the children took it harder. Getting over something like that takes a long time. I worried about Frankie and all of them, really. We did what we could to see that life goes on. No regrets. Look forward.

I'm sure you still think of him often.

I think of him all the time, especially when the big deals happen, like in November of '32, when Georgie was featured on the *Rudy Vallee Show*. That was one of Morris's favorite radio programs and mine too. Rudy had an all-Gershwin show, and George's friend Kitty Carlisle sang "The Man I Love." In the interview part of the show, Georgie told Rudy about his writing style. First he writes his music and then he plays it for Ira, who hums it and gets an idea for a lyric. Then they work it out together. Georgie told Rudy that Irving Berlin and Jerome Kern influenced him, and then Georgie stated a few of his ideas about modern music. He said it was normal for a piano player to want to use the sustain pedal all the time—that's the piano pedal on the right—but he thought they should guard against that. With his staccato style, he hated the pedal.

The pedal makes piano music sound ponderous.

"Rhythms must snap and cackle," George told Rudy on the radio program. And he told Rudy how important it was to keep studying music.

My Georgie never stopped learning. He took lessons in technique from Joseph Schillinger, a teacher and theory man from Russia, and after his trip to Cuba he experimented with the rumba and Cuban instruments. He wrote new shows like *Shall We Dance* with Ginger Rogers and Fred Astaire, and the *Porgy and Bess* folk opera, the all-Negro drama.

Did George work alone some of the time?

He never liked being alone, so he had Mabel Shirmer keep him company while he orchestrated. She sat there and did her petit point. After the day's work, the two of them took long walks to help what he called composer's stomach. A few weeks before he turned thirty-seven, Georgie, Ira, and Heyward finished *Porgy*. Someone told me Georgie cried at the last performance in New York. I don't know for sure. I never asked him.

Do you also have an emotional streak?

No, other things thrilled me more. When Georgie's friend Kay Halle talked with President Franklin Roosevelt at his inaugural ceremonies, the president told her he wanted to meet Georgie. I couldn't believe it when Kay got invitations from Roosevelt for them to attend a New Year's Eve party at the White House. Georgie told me they wheeled the Lincoln piano into the room and the president motioned for him to play. What an experience. Georgie only wished Morris coulda seen him.

Let me tell you another thing about Kay Halle. At the hotel where she lived, she made an arrangement with the man at the desk that Georgie could play the Steinway anytime he wanted. See, when Georgie spent time out in the country and tried to write music, the noise of the crickets, bees, and birds bothered him, so he liked to write in the city. Kay told me that one night she came in and there was Georgie playing an exquisite tune. It was "Summertime," the lullaby from *Porgy and Bess.* They both cried when he played it.

The minor chord changes and the sixths and sevenths in that song put me over the moon.

You know your music then, I guess.

I studied a long time. Didn't like my first teacher, though. She was mean. What happened next?

Hollywood came calling, and Georgie and Ira got a contract with RKO. During that year, Georgie gave concerts on the West Coast. That's when his terrible dizzy spells started. When he blacked out during a concert, the doctor said it was nothing serious. It didn't seem to affect his work, because Ira told me that one night in less than an hour, he and Georgie wrote "*A Foggy Day.*" Even the success of that song didn't stop Georgie's headaches, pains in his stomach, and a tired feeling all the time. I got mad at Lee because behind his back, she said he complained in order to draw attention to himself. I knew she envied Georgie and that frustrated her, but I forgave her because she loved him. Ira thought Georgie was just moody, with his depression and anxiety. We were so wrong.

You loved him and that's what counts.

I did love him. I did what I could. Georgie suffered a blackout and ended up at the hospital. The people there called it hysteria, so he talked to a psychiatrist. He quit that when a fainting spell on the tennis court made him know it was a physical problem. He wanted to forget that his body let him down, so he kept on. He started seeing Paulette Goddard, the big film star, even though she was married to Charlie Chaplin. Ira claims their song "You Can't Take That Away from Me" was written about her. Everyone liked that song. I liked Paulette.

I have to get back to Georgie's sickness and stick to it, but how does a mother tell this part of the story? I don't even know. But if I don't tell it, no one else will get it right. I can't even believe what happened. Telling it again and again barely makes it real, only more painful. Poor Georgie. Things got worse with his health. He dropped food, fell on the stairs, and kept losing his temper. Lee had him removed from the house and arranged for him to move into a smaller house, with a male nurse from Germany to attend him. The doctors found nothing.

One night Georgie called me. Three in the morning it was. All that money for a phone call in the middle of the night. Morris woulda hated that. I didn't know Georgie was that sick. I tried to explain all his symptoms away.

The worst day came on July 9th when Georgie had a nap and went into a coma. Ira tried to call me right away, but he had trouble reaching me because I was playing poker in the Rockaways. I told him I wasn't coming out to California. What good would that do? I could do nothing but worry, so I sat by the phone. I worried about that horse kick he got as a kid. I worried about the street fights with other boys. I worried about every single thing I could think of.

When the news came, it was terrible, terrible. Georgie had a brain tumor. That's why he smelled burning garbage when no one else did. Surgery didn't help, and my Georgie never came out of the coma. My Georgie, my poor Georgie was too young—only thirty-eight—too young to die. It was July 11, 1937.

That's far too young. When you have a child, you never think they'll go first. Where did you have the service?

Temple Emanu-El in New York. Close to twenty thousand people came. What a send-off. There was another funeral in Hollywood for his people out there.

This talk about Georgie's death has me in a state. I'll tell you one more thing. After Ira filed papers to be the administrator of Georgie's estate, I did too. Since I live in New York, which is Georgie's residence, I was named administrator. I became his sole beneficiary. That's only fair. I took care of him, and he took care of me.

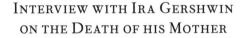

INTERVIEW WITH IRA GERSHWIN
ON THE DEATH OF HIS MOTHER

Life was never the same for my mother after George's death and her health deteriorated. In December of 1948, she died of a heart attack.

5

Interview with Allene Ganos Hughes

MOTHER OF HOWARD HUGHES JR.
AVIATOR AND MOVIE PRODUCER,
BORN DECEMBER 24, 1905

———— ❦ ————

Wash four distinct and separate times,
using lots of lather each time from individual bars of soap.
—Howard Hughes

JAN HELEN MCGEE

Your husband, Howard Sr., found a way to reach oil through granite, and he leases his rock bit to drillers at thirty thousand dollars per well. You must be so proud of him.

ALLENE HUGHES

Howard's successful. Three-quarters of the world's oil wells use his invention. Our son Howard Jr. is also destined to do great things. We call young Howard "Sonny."

JAN HELEN MCGEE

I'd love to hear about Sonny.

ALLENE HUGHES

You won't be able to meet my dear boy, the center of my world. What a shame. He's away at school.

You must miss him.

It feels odd. His care consumed me for so long. In letters, Sonny says life isn't the same without me. If his sorrow is akin to mine, then we are two lost souls. Maybe you can understand our connection if I tell you that, when I gave birth to Sonny, I almost died. I hemorrhaged, lost consciousness, and recovered only after four blood transfusions.

That sounds frightening, childbirth and its complications. I had a blood clot with my son's birth. I'm so glad you mended. Can you tell me about yourself?

I'd rather speak of Sonny, but I'll oblige your request and honor my own. I originate from the French Huguenots. My grandfather was a Confederate general and my father a social register judge. I have a brother, Chilton, and two younger sisters, Annette and Martha.

You look wonderful, so tall and thin. Do you favor any of your siblings?

I look similar to all of them, and we all have dark hair. I enjoy fashion and like to be clean. I was taught charm, which I used to become one of the most sought-after debutantes in Texas. My name in the Dallas Blue Book meant everyone expected me to marry a wealthy man.

Where did you meet your husband?

At a dance. I admired his name: Howard Robard Hughes.

Did his family meet with your approval?

Of course. His father, Felix, taught himself law and became superintendent of the local schools. After Howard was born in 1869 in Missouri, the family moved to Iowa, where Felix became a mayor and then a judge. I'd describe him as cantankerous.

Howard's mother is Jean, but everyone calls her "Mimi." She's a dreamer. Her family said she spoiled Howard, but I say, what's wrong with giving children everything they need? She was a good mother, and she encouraged all her children in the arts. Howard's older sister, Greta, sings so lovely; she studied opera. His younger brother Rupert writes, and he graduated from Yale. His youngest brother, Felix Jr., studied music.

Is your husband artistic?

Quite the opposite. He has no musical talent and no interest in writing. When he was young, he had a lot of spirit and he liked doing things his way. He fought local bullies and didn't do well in school. For one year he attended Harvard, and he studied briefly at Iowa State University, but tinkering with clocks and motors meant more to him. Let me change what I said before; my husband's thought processes and inventions are artistic.

What was the dance where you met him?

The 1902 Christmas Cotillion, where all the girls noticed a tall and handsome stranger. Who wouldn't notice my Howard? He stood against the wall with his lean slouch and impeccable clothes, and he charmed me from the start. I never had a beau with such an intense interest in my life and background.

How old were you?

I was nineteen, and he was thirty-two. I looked sophisticated but didn't feel it. Howard didn't notice my insecurities, he just swept me off my feet, and I fell in love.

When you met, was he well off?

He had potential and some money, but not a lot. He worked as a drillmaster and petroleum well owner.

When did he propose?

A few months later, in March under a full moon. I accepted.

I love to hear about weddings.

I wore a white gown of Bruges lace and mousseline de soie, and Howard wore gray tails and a white tie. We passed through an arch of pink and white roses with ornate ribbons, as Howard's brother, Felix, played the piano and his sister, Greta, sang opera selections. It was held at my parents' home on a gorgeous day in May. Everyone except Howard's brother Rupert was there.

The *New York Times* wrote about his divorce.

How messy that they splashed Rupert and his wife's problems across the front page, with those claims of infidelity on both sides. With all that swirling gossip, we understood his reluctance to attend. I certainly didn't want anything to blemish my special day, and nothing did. Our parents gave us ten thousand dollars as a wedding present.

That gave you a nice start. Where did you take your honeymoon?

St. Louis, then New York, then six months in Europe; a glorious time.

Did you return to Texas?

We arrived with just enough money to live in the barely tolerable Rice Hotel in downtown Houston, and then we moved to a four-room house on the east side of town in an area overrun with cats and unpaved roads. In the front of our house, a ditch bred mosquitoes and crawfish. I could never get things clean. What saved my sanity was finding out I carried a child.

Was it Sonny?

Yes, my darling boy arrived on December 24, 1905. My excruciating labor caused such damage to my body. Dr. Norsworthy worked to stop the hemorrhaging and Howard paced up and down the hospital halls.

He must have been beside himself.

He thought I wouldn't survive. Distraught is an understatement. We forgot all that with one look at our beautiful boy, Howard Robard Hughes Jr. His birth turned into a defining moment for Howard. When he saw his son for the first time, he decided to make something of himself. We sorely needed a change.

What did he end up doing differently?

He worked longer hours in the petroleum business. I took care of my fussy eater, my sweet Sonny.

My son never cared much about eating.

Isn't it difficult to feed a child who doesn't want to eat? I spent hours coaxing him to drink a little milk and take a bit of applesauce. I was so concerned. Every time I changed his diaper, I checked for tapeworms. My worry over his health didn't lessen when Howard came home and told me we were leaving for Louisiana and its stink of sulfur.

Our move to Oil City meant success for Howard, so I didn't dwell on my discomfort. I tell you now, I hated those grimy tent cities, and I detested the outhouse and the well-pump for water. My only comfort came from loving Sonny. I sang and read stories to him and slept by his side.

When Howard moved us to a suburb of Houston, I finally had a house with clean floors and shade trees. I rocked my baby boy and sang lullabies under a giant magnolia tree. I dressed Sonny in beautiful clothes, and we had him baptized. Luckily he didn't catch cold during the ceremony.

When did Howard create his drill bit?

Soon after Sonny's fourth birthday. It was a rotary drill bit that penetrated bedrock.

What was different about it?

It had 166 cutting edges on a series of bits that worked off a single shaft, and it changed oil drilling all over the world. Howard and his partner formed the Hughes Tool Company and then bought up patents for other rock bits and devised new drills. Howard wandered from oil strike to oil strike and hawked his drill bit, and at night he did what men do: he gambled.

Did you worry about those conditions?

Gambling meant easy women, but I chose a positive outlook. On the bright side, his absence meant I had a strong bond with Sonny. He slept on a trundle bed in my room so I could keep him close and well with my Victorian health rituals.

What do you mean specifically?

Daily, I bathed him in lye soap. I examined the contents of his toilet. Each morning I gave him Russian mineral oil and each evening he had Epsom salts. I took his temperature regularly. In the morning before he dressed and each evening, I checked his entire body from head to toe: his feet, ears, throat, teeth, and private areas. Most of the time I had to tell him to stand still, but it was the right thing. Some people called my rituals old-fashioned. I say, one can't be too careful.

What type of social life were you leading?

We joined Christ Church Cathedral and the Houston Country Club, and I gave summer garden parties and formal dinners. At last I lived as I desired, but only Sonny truly mattered. I made sure he looked fashionable, with white shirts and dapper knickers, and white socks to contrast his black patent leather shoes. I kept my eye on him, since I needed to know his safety and location at all times. I had a rule that Sonny could ride his bike around our circular driveway, but he couldn't ride dangerously free with neighborhood boys.

When he started school, our morning rituals took time, so the school administration had to understand our late arrival. After school I waited for Sonny, my only chick. I hated to see my little boy grow up.

Who were his friends?

He was shy and didn't have many, but he developed a close friendship with Dudley Sharp. Both Sonny and Dudley were mechanical, so in our workshop they built a radio transmitter and broadcasted their own show. Explorations and inventions kept them busy.

Did Sonny have any little crushes on girls?

One morning a mother of one of his classmates called me after Sonny gave my diamond earrings as a present for his sweetheart. They had to be returned, of course, so I suggested he give her some small stones in their place. I encouraged his little adventures but worried over his delicate constitution. To prevent him from getting sick, I took him on regular vacations far away from Houston's heat and humidity. One time we visited the seaside in Galveston with Sonny's cousins and other relatives. When the vacation ended, none of the cousins said thank you for all the fun they had; only Sonny, with his polite behavior. I cannot abide bad manners.

I agree. Etiquette is so important in this world. Did you ever think you overreacted in regards to his health?

Oh, never. Often I had to call Howard home from his out-of-town work to help me deal with Sonny's chills, bad colds, or hives. Many days I had to keep him out of school. At night, Sonny sleep in my room and Howard slept down the hall in the study. Even when we traveled to the East Coast, Howard took his own suite and Sonny and I shared a room. It wasn't until he turned ten that he slept alone in a room.

Sonny must have loved his workshop. Any boy would. Did he have outside activities?

I secured a coveted prize for Sonny. During the annual spring carnival at Christ Church Cathedral, my beautiful boy received the crown as King of the May.

I love May Day. One year at school, I wore a frilly white dress as a May court princess.

Sonny looked adorable on the throne with his paper crown and toga, but he refused to smile for the pictures. Other people made negative comments, but I ignored them just as I ignored their silly belief that we had an unusual attachment. They claimed Sonny seemed lonely and withdrawn, but I didn't agree. We had each other. What could be more important than the bond between mother and son?

I understand a strong attachment to your only child. Do you remember your first separation from Sonny?

It happened at age eleven when he asked permission to attend a six-week survival boys' camp in the Pocono Mountains of Pennsylvania. At first my answer was a resounding no. Sonny pleaded, so I discussed it with Howard, who said he should be allowed to attend. I worried terribly. Howard worked in Manhattan at that time, but I wanted to stay close to Sonny, so I took residence at a series of resorts in the Poconos. I missed my one and only little chick. When he told me the other boys at the camp teased him, I became almost hysterical, so each day Howard and I called and spoke with the camp director. He reassured us of Sonny's safety.

Before camp ended, we had grave concerns about a polio outbreak, so I removed Sonny from the camp and took him home. Sonny felt crushed, but we promised to allow him to return the next year. I overheard one woman say I was too protective, but every mother has her own way of raising her child. I didn't stymie his growth; I helped develop his intellect, and I read to him every chance I could. I introduced him to music and encouraged morning and evening practice on his saxophone until he produced beautiful sounds.

How did Sonny feel about school?

His attitude aligned with Howard's. Neither of them saw a need for that kind of learning. Sonny enjoyed mathematics, but he preferred to turn ordinary school games into experiments. In his workshop, Sonny had woodworking and electronic equipment, but he had to keep his work area spotless, and he did. Only two times he left the workshop in disorder, and both times we locked him out for a week. That cured that.

Sonny's experiments prove his genius, and I know he'll be outstanding in some field. Every year, he's more inventive, a mechanical wizard. At eleven, he decided to communicate with ships in the Gulf of Mexico, so he built the first wireless broadcasting set in all of Houston. Overnight he taught himself Morse code. He created a motorized bicycle from parts of Howard's steam engine. In our mansion, Sonny installed an intercom and a telegraph and connected it to Dudley Sharp's house. At fourteen, he took apart a Bearcat car that Howard had given him, and in less than a month he reassembled it.

Did he join any sports?

Sports? He joined the YMCA basketball team at South End Junior High, and he practiced swimming and diving. I couldn't forbid it, but being in the water with all those other boys bothered me. I made Sonny visit several doctors who reassured me he had good health, but I knew something would happen.

That day came when Sonny was nearly fifteen. He became quite ill. I summoned Howard, who had been gambling on the Mississippi, and he returned home immediately. I canceled all my social obligations and stayed by Sonny's side. We didn't know if he had polio or diphtheria, or scarlet fever or meningitis, because his legs barely worked. Howard offered the doctors any amount of money to cure our dear boy, but they couldn't tell what was wrong. For eight long weeks, we were in agony.

Suddenly the doctors decided Sonny had feigned his illness and claimed he had a hysterical paralysis. I never understood that diagnosis, especially since Sonny's illness affected his hearing. I know it did, because when I speak, he tunes me out and I'm not sure he can hear me. Howard's brother Rupert is hard of hearing, so it's possible Sonny's deafness is inherited. Those doctors didn't care what I thought. They stood firm in their diagnosis. I became more and more distraught, and to make matters worse, Howard decided Sonny would do better away from home. I nearly fell apart with grief when Howard sent Sonny off to the Fessenden Academy.

Where is that school located?

It's a private preparatory school outside of Boston. I fought and fought against the idea, but my entreaties fell on deaf ears.

How did he cope at Fessenden Academy?

He had good times and bad times. We provided him with all the funds he needed, so he played golf and made good progress with that. But there was a problem.

Was he still sick?

No, he felt better, but he had a crushing amount of homework. He complained every day. I pleaded with the headmaster to ease his school load, but the man said Sonny needed to do the required work. He said it's not easy for a boy who has been so indulged at home and has never attended boarding school. I fully disagreed with that man. I don't indulge Sonny. My concern is for his well-being. I felt sick with worry that entire year.

Then came the summer after middle school and more problems. When a baseball and basketball tutor arrived at our home, I highly disapproved. I saw no need for sports in his life, and I wanted him to be safe. Sonny and Howard weren't interested in safe. They wanted me to be less protective.

I guess that was a difficult situation for all of you. Where did Sonny go to high school?

Howard chose the Thatcher School near Santa Barbara in California. At first the school was full and we couldn't enroll him, so Howard offered to build a new gymnasium and thereby resolved the matter. At that point, Howard sat me down and insisted that Sonny no longer have special treatment. I didn't have a choice in the matter, so I promised to go along with his idea.

It can be easier to go along with a husband than to buck against him. Did Sonny like the Thatcher School?

Howard bought Sonny a horse so he could play polo, and Sonny liked that. I worried about accidents and about his social life, so I wrote a letter to the headmaster and told him of the difficulties present for an only child. I spoke of Sonny's adjustment to a new situation and the complexity of making friends. That might have helped a bit. What helped was when Sonny got a part in a school play. That production made him feel accepted.

My relief changed in late fall when Sonny got a boil and a scratch on his leg. A doctor rushed in to care for him. I was far away, but I kept close tabs on his progress. With Sonny gone, I felt lonely, which is a persistent problem. I should tell you, this interview has helped me.

Do you mean having company?

Not exactly. When I concentrate on the past, I feel happier in my connection with the present. Because of my distance from Sonny, I have to work at disconnecting myself from him, and I've done so. I write to him, but I know I don't write enough. I got a letter of admonishment from him where he reminded me he writes twice a day. He asked that I write at least once a day. I'm not sure why I can't. I have enough time, since I spend my day wandering around the house all alone. Howard's business puts him in demand, and he travels.

Have you heard anything discomforting about your husband during his travels?

I find it a bit of an affront that you ask such a pointed question.

I didn't mean to imply any guilt on his part. I just know that wealthy men are a magnet for some women. I'm curious how you cope with that.

I ignore rumors of movie star dalliances. What use would it do to acknowledge something so distasteful? I think instead of my dear Sonny.

Tomorrow I start my preparations for Christmas. This is a divine time of the year. I'll decorate the house and get ready for Sonny's arrival. Howard will be here, and my tall and handsome boy will be home for school break. Our time together will be ideal.

I must ask you to leave now.

I'm sorry I had to cut you off so abruptly during our last time together. Suddenly I didn't feel well. And today my time is limited.

You gave me so much attention when I was here. It's so kind of you to allow me to return.

I just received some terrible news.

Do you want to share anything with me?

I keep myself so isolated. What does it matter if I tell you? Women often share personal stories with each other. Two months after our perfect Christmas, I learned of my pregnancy. The doctors have concern for the risk since after Sonny's birth they advised against having more children.

Every child is such a gift.

It sounds wonderful, doesn't it? But quite the opposite is true. My life's about to fall apart. You must go as soon as I explain. My joy has become horror. I have a tubular pregnancy, and my life is threatened.

I am so sorry. What will you do?

The doctors suggest a termination. Only Howard and the doctors and you know, not my sister Annette and not Sonny. I can't worry my beautiful boy, so far away at school. He needs to concentrate on his own health. I love him more than my own life. He's my soul's existence.

I must go now. I have decisions to make.

INTERVIEW WITH HOWARD HUGHES, SR.
ON THE DEATH OF HIS WIFE

During an emergency operation, my darling Allene's heart stopped.

Yesterday, after she was admitted to the hospital, she wrote me a note from her bed. As I read it over and over, I'm touched by her tenderness and devastated by our loss. I find this to be an impossible situation. I should have been more attentive.

Only her sister Annette knows that Allene is gone, and she

vows to keep her silence. I trust you because Allene became so fond of you, but you too must keep silent for now. I sent a cable telling Sonny that Mother is ill. I have no idea how I'll break the news that he's lost her. I hope Rupert will tell him in the limousine when he picks him up from school, or on the train ride back here to Houston.

I plan to remove Sonny from his school, and Annette will postpone her marriage for at least a year and be a mother to him. The house I built for Allene haunts me, so Annette and Sonny and I will move to a hotel retreat in Southern California. I have no idea how Sonny's life can go on without his mother. They were so close. He will never be the same.

6

Interview with Nancy Hill Rockwell

MOTHER OF NORMAN ROCKWELL
ILLUSTRATOR AND PAINTER,
BORN FEBRUARY 3, 1894

───── ⚮ ─────

My ability was just something I had,
like a bag of lemon drops.
—Norman Rockwell

NANCY ROCKWELL

When Norman started his illustrations, I said, "Find a respectable way to earn a living. Keep drawing as a hobby."

JAN HELEN MCGEE

What led you to feel that way?

NANCY ROCKWELL

I knew about painting from my father, who painted and waited and let our whole family down.

JAN HELEN MCGEE

Did you have a trade in mind for Norman?

A trade, no. We never had tradesmen in our family, only gentlemen and artists. My mother had English royal ancestry on both sides. My brother, Tom, taught drawing and painting since he didn't have the technical skills my father possessed. Possessed—that's a good word for my father. Tom was the opposite. I admired him in every way.

How did your father learn to paint?

My grandfather, Thomas Sr., taught him.

Did either your husband or you have artistic talents?

My husband, Waring, taught both our sons to draw, and I made elaborate embroidery designs for my family and my church. Nobody noticed me though. I follow along behind my famous son.

I like the gold and yellow in this pillow. Is this your design?

One of many.

That must keep you busy. Norman is prolific with his work. How often does he paint?

Every single day, even Christmas. Everything he sees or does goes into his pictures. I love his illustrations that tell a story, but when I compliment him, he takes the other side. Some days he doesn't feel good about himself. He says he makes people too cute.

Do you think so?

Oh, I'm not sure. He has a style all his own. When I first noticed his talent, I tried to encourage and not push, but Norman claims I had his career planned since he was eleven.

You said Norman is descended from artists and gentlemen. What do you mean by gentlemen?

My father, Thomas Howard Hill Jr., had such promise. In

England as a child in short pants, he sang a solo for Queen Victoria at Buckingham Palace. My mother, Anne Elizabeth Patmore, descends from the Percevels, and as a young lady she was presented at Queen Victoria's court. Do you want to see the fur collar she wore? I have it here.

It's soft and beautiful, such a wonderful brown.

The color set off her big eyes. Mum had a smile to light up a room.

Were your parents the first in your family to leave England?

My grandfather and my grandmother, Susannah, left London for New Jersey, and then my parents and their first three children emigrated before I was born.

Tell me more about your mother.

A lot of charm, very little education, and religion played a big part in her life. She carried her beliefs with her when they settled in Yonkers, New York. I loved her, even though at times she acted distant.

How did your father make a living in America?

I don't know if you can call it a living. He knocked on doors, house to house, and offered to make portraits of people, pets, and outdoor scenes. That didn't bring in much money, so he did house painting. At first he called himself Thomas Hill, but after his mother died he used his middle name, Howard. I don't use Anne Mary, either. I prefer Nancy.

When were you born?

March 6, 1866.

You mentioned your siblings?

Three sisters—Amy, Kate, and Susie—and two brothers, Thomas and Percevel. That's six children, but my parents took in so many cousins that I consider myself one of twelve children.

Why are you so angry with your father?

He was dictatorial and reckless, and he squandered his talents and made us live in boardinghouses. Two faces, he had—one for us, one for others. His friends saw the wonderful face. They weren't privy to his drunken rampages, when he tipped over chairs and tables, lashed out at everyone, and screamed that my devoted mother was unfaithful. His fits made Mum anxious and weary. I never understood why she tolerated him. I assume she loved him. And only she loved him, certainly not his children. We called him a handsome street angel and a house devil.

Did that ever seem harsh to you?

No, I despise my father for his queer ways and inability to support us. He had everything backwards. After he sold a portrait, he never planned for the future. Instead, he relaxed until we ran out of money. Mum said the drink prevented him from painting.

Was he ever successful?

Only a few times. The National Academy of Design hung four of his paintings in their 1865 exhibit, and two prominent hotels own his oil paintings. Outside of that, he had no sense at all. One time he brought home twelve identical pairs of shoes, all the same size, as if all twelve children were the same age. People in the boarding house call him a lout.

Twelve pairs of shoes, that's amusing.

I'm glad you can laugh.

He does sound difficult.

I had a miserable childhood.

What were you like as a child?

I did things to gain attention, and I used everything to my advantage. When I read adventure stories in magazines and books, I fantasized about another life, and in church I soaked up tales I heard from missionaries. In my mind, only good things happened. At home, it was unbearable.

I remember only one contribution my father made—a skill he showed us that we passed on to Norman. He taught us to use small, careful brushstrokes to make what we called potboiler paintings. My father lined up all his children at the kitchen table to help him as we passed a painting in progress along the line. One child shaded leaves and another painted a stamp. I remember I formed a perfect moon. I use those skills in my embroidery designs.

Tell me about your brother Tom. Was he your favorite?

We all loved him best. He was the oldest and the most handsome. He whistled happy tunes to cheer us, but he too hated our father, so he escaped and sailed to Mexico and Cuba. We loved his letters about sharks and headwinds and his Sunday Bible readings. Our entire family, except our father of course, felt deeply religious, so my sisters' letters back to him spoke of Sunday school and church.

So he eventually returned from his travels?

Yes, he brought us tortoiseshell combs and spoke about the thrill of sailing. Even during his terribly ill years, when he coughed up blood and ran high fevers, he sailed any chance he could. When he decided not to wander anymore, he taught and did design work and sold easels to make a living. He married Lallie Newlin, and they had Little Harold.

Six months before their wedding, that's when tragedy

began its descent. My older sister Amy and her husband, Howard, died of consumption. Their three young children survived, but Mum developed the same problems as Tom. Both of them had lung congestion and a persistent cough. My sister Susie's two-year-old son died, and then both Mum and Tom died from consumption. I felt like I had knives in my stomach.

You poor thing. So many family members lost in such a short time.

The shock arrested me and made me feel I couldn't go on. Only anger sustained me. Their shameful deaths were my father's fault. He wouldn't earn a decent living, so our life of poverty brought on the consumption.

Who took care of Amy and Howard's three children?

Susie somehow found the strength to nurture the lost souls left behind. She and her husband Samuel adopted John, Amy, and Eva, who was slow. When Mum died, I had nowhere to live, so Susie and Samuel asked me to come to Rhode Island and live with them. I accepted but worried I might be destined for bad luck.

Thank goodness for family. Did you soon meet your husband?

Yes, my savior Waring, a steadfast man, sometimes stern and serious but always energetic. Jarvis Waring Rockwell. Sober and the exact opposite of my frivolous father. Waring was so handsome, with a full and neatly trimmed mustache. Actually, he looked an awful lot like Tom, and he carried himself like an aristocrat. He adored me from the start and we became engaged.

I had reservations about our three-year age difference—I'm

older—but to him, it held no concern. I worried that he married down by taking me as his wife, but Waring disagreed. He told everyone that I was pretty and small and ladylike. Even my strong will suited him, because he never minded when I demanded things and insisted I get what I want. He accepted my anxious state and bad nerves, and he looked at the world with positive eyes. He liked that I'd been raised in the church, and two years after our engagement, he converted from Presbyterian to my Episcopal faith.

You say he looked at the world with positive eyes? Isn't that the way Norman paints?

I believe that's true.

What do you know of Waring's background?

His mother Phoebe's family had quite a bit of money from the hat industry. Waring was her third and youngest child. Waring's father was John, an executive who supplied coal to the Union troops. Just two months after Phoebe and John married, John's brother, George, suffered a mortal wound in the final day of the battle at Stones River.

So many lives were lost on both sides, but that battle gave a boost to Union morale.

Waring seldom spoke of his brother. People with a solid background like Waring keep things inside. Everything about Waring was solid, and that kept our relationship on an even keel. About three years into our engagement, my father died at sixty-five of an epileptic fit.

How did you react?

I barely noticed his absence and felt no grief. I kept some of his animal paintings, and that's all. By then, Waring's love encompassed my whole world. I was twenty-three and felt young, even though others considered me an old maid. I couldn't understand their reasoning that I should hurry into marriage, since most engagements at that time were ten years. Mine was only five.

My big day came on July 22, 1891, at St. Philips Church in Rhode Island. Waring put palms and fragrant flowers in the church, and I carried a posy of duchess roses. I walked down the aisle to the tune of the "The Bridal Chorus." Waring's brother acted as best man, and my maid of honor was Frances, Susan's ten-year-old daughter. Frances wore white and carried a posy of white daisies. My brother Percevel gave me away, and Susan's husband performed the service. When I thought about how consumption claimed so much of my family, sadness came over me, but I managed to enjoy the ceremony and the wedding breakfast afterwards. Waring's parents and his sister, Grace, attended and commented on the lovely flower designs, and the local paper ran a nice article about the event.

We moved into a modest apartment bordering Central Park, and Waring clerked for a textile firm. Relatives lived within walking distance, and our social circle included committee members at our church. Except for my health, life seemed idyllic. The doctors never knew what was wrong, but Waring gave me unflagging devotion and never discounted my pain. I tried not to discuss my health problems with other people since he understood everything.

When did you have children?

We were a family of two until 1892, when I had my first, Jarvis Waring Rockwell Jr. We call him Jerry. After Jerry's birth, my constitution found no relief, as I soon discovered I was carrying another child. To make things easier for me, we sent Jerry to stay with my husband's sister. I strongly hoped for a girl, so I made miniature bedclothes.

That turned out to be useless when Norman Percevel arrived on February 3, 1894. He was a gangly baby and a bit horse-faced, but of course I loved him. Waring helped enormously and when I got my bearings, Jerry returned from Grace's. Since I was too worn out to do any housework, we lived in a shabby brownstone boardinghouse. I found it distasteful. I didn't like sharing living quarters with sad people with unusual habits. When little Norman turned two, I felt well enough for us to move to a fourth-floor walk-up railroad apartment. It had little light but I enjoyed the privacy.

Were Jerry and Norman similar to each other?

Quite different. Jerry was a masculine boy, and Norman was fearful and impatient—more like me, I guess. I thought little Norman's weakness harbored an artistic streak, and I knew he'd amount to something. I named him for Sir Norman Percevel and called him my sensitive nobleman.

"You have a valiant heritage," I told him again and again. "Never allow anyone to intimidate you or make you feel the least bit inferior."

I did my best to help him realize his vision, but some days I couldn't get out of bed. My niece, Frances, was nineteen by then, so she moved in to help care for the boys. For a time, my niece, Amy, lived with us. When she returned to my sister Susie's, I did my Christian duty and took in my sweet and slow niece, Eva. She drained me. Then life dropped cruelty into our laps once again.

What happened?

The consumption was brutal. My dear Susie and her husband Samuel died. My poor nieces moved in with us. I tried not to let all that death affect me, but it forced me to step away emotionally from my boys. As I look back, I understand Mum's distance. After all that tragedy, I thought death lived in my pocket.

You had more than your share of heartbreak. I can see how it caused concern.

I seldom worried about Jerry, but I felt anxious for little Norman. Every day I told him to be careful and stick by his brother's side. That worked fine until my nerves got so bad that I had to send Jerry to relatives in the country for the summer. I kept little Norman at home, but with Jerry gone, he resented his lack of freedom. That wasn't his only problem. He used to wet the bed over and over. I cured that by hanging his soiled sheets outside the window for all to see. Waring softly reassured me that he didn't wet the bed to spite me, and that made me realize that little Norman, with his warm heart, wasn't spiteful. During my resting time I'd call him into my room.

"Norman Percevel," I said, "you must always love and honor your mother. She needs you."

He liked our closeness. When he had bouts of illness, he'd crawl into bed with me. On those days, his color became so pale I called him Snow in the Face.

Jerry returned when school started?

Yes, and with everyone gone all day, I could rest. In the evenings, Waring sat quietly at the table with the boys and copied pictures from magazines. Do you remember that popular hobby?

It was good for anyone with artistic talent.

That gave Norman his start. When I felt well enough to leave my bedroom, I rested on the sofa and designed embroidery as the three of them shared magazines and made illustrations. I liked my family inside at home, and the isolation meant Norman developed his imaginative thinking.

Did your boys do other things together?

After Jerry started grammar school, he didn't want to spend time with his younger brother. Norman still wanted to gain Jerry's favor, so he worked harder at his drawing. When Norman was about six or seven, Jerry bribed him to make a fleet of ships that matched a story on the cover of the *Saturday Evening Post* about the Spanish–American War. Jerry liked the cardboard pictures of Admiral Dewey's various ship models that were included in cigarette boxes at the time, so little Norman reproduced cardboard cutouts of navy ships. He gave them to Jerry and his friends, who raced to see who could cut them up first. That took five minutes, but Norman became immensely popular.

The neighbor children loved the fire engine and lion pictures Norman made with chalk on the sidewalk. I liked outside play, but even that could be too noisy. Quiet play or time spent at other people's homes worked best, because company taxed my energy and my nerves needed hushed tones.

As soon as Waring came home from work, he came to me and asked how I felt. Most days I lay on the couch, tired and worn out. If I'd had a hard day, he got me a cold towel for my head. He made me his pet. For hours I tucked my head into his shoulder and relaxed on his lap. Waring was a perfect husband. He rose from clerk to manager of the New York branch of a cotton firm.

Was Waring close to your family?

My sister never felt the same as I did about Waring, and we had words. His dictatorial ways worried her, so I listened quietly and tried not to argue, since I wanted those traits in a man. I knew his inner side, our quiet pleasures, and his playful times with the boys. He understood that even though I rested most days, I sometimes burst out with fun. He liked my naughty humor and even suggested I influenced Norman in his illustrations.

The four of us had our little pleasures. When I had a bit of energy and we had nice weather, Sunday was family day. We each took our trolley pillow—I handmade them all—and we left all cares behind. As the trolley picked up speed outside the city limits, the ladies clutched their hats while the children and the men leaned back and relaxed. At the end of the line in the countryside, I spread out our second-best tablecloth and unpacked a picnic meal. You can see shades of those picnics in Norman's paintings.

How remarkable to hear where he got his inspirations.

Summer vacations meant a stay at a rural boardinghouse, usually a working farm, and I drank iced tea and talked with the other ladies. The adults played croquet. The boys roamed and wrestled. After a few hours, I told them to come inside. When they stayed inside for too long, I thought they should exercise. I wanted to guide them, but I know I seemed bossy. The boys barely noticed. Norman milked the cows and caught frogs and explored, and when he got tired, he sat and drew. He could draw anywhere, and he did it all the time. Later in his work, he painted our country summers.

Life was perfect on vacation, but at home we had trials. One day that stands out is the day of McKinley's assassination. Both Waring and I cried. National tragedies are something everyone remembers. A problem closer to home concerned our religious practices. The children said my church schedule was heavy-handed, and they balked when I insisted their free time be spent at St. Luke in the Field. Several times a week they had choir rehearsal, with a dress rehearsal on Friday and four services every Sunday. I loved the life of the church, and I acted as a delegate on the Women's Auxiliary and as a representative to a building drive. At home, I did my needlework to beautify the parish chapel.

Another problem came from a rule Waring made for the boys, and they hated it. On Sunday, he said no funny papers or toys, only church. He thought our church schedule kept them out of mischief and out of my hair. On the Sundays that I missed church to rest, I made sure we sang hymns in the parlor.

You said Norman and Jerry played outside. Did they have any other physical activities?

Jerry had his athletic involvements, but little Norman didn't have that strength and agility, with his thin arms and shoulders. He felt self-conscious about his long neck and prominent Adam's apple, his pigeon-toes and orthopedic shoes, and his thick, round glasses that caused the other children to call him "Moony." I diverted those negative thoughts with talk of his beautiful, curly, reddish-brown hair.

Most of the time Norman kept a good attitude, and he used pranks to get past his looks. Over and over, he practiced a crooked limp to generate sympathy. He did this trick where he stretched the sleeve of his coat, walked down the street, and pretended he didn't have a hand. It was easy with the coat he wore: a man's size and too big. Since I knew my clothes would last, I spent money on them, but the boys grew so fast. Jerry especially detested the old clothes, since he had those athlete friends who judged him. Norman's solitary nature meant he preferred drawing over everything, even school, which he hated.

What part of school didn't he like?

The confines, the rigid classes, he couldn't see the advantage of it. When something didn't serve his purpose, he refused to exert himself. The only part Norman enjoyed was lunch at home. I watched out the window for them to come into sight on their speeding roller skates. Norman timed it from school to home: ten minutes. I praised him for his skating exercise, just as I praised him for his attention to details in his drawing. I felt a kinship with Norman, who stayed home while Jerry ran free.

I did my best at the time, but now that they're grown I realize I acted withdrawn. I lost so many loved ones, and detachment felt familiar since that's how Mum raised me. That made me uncertain with life and most days weren't good. My nerves suffered, even though the doctors couldn't find anything wrong with me.

We did have wonderful evenings, though. After dinner, Waring read out loud from a chapter of a Charles Dickens novel. We believed in learning and high culture, and I liked anything British. Dickens became our family hero because of his life lessons. When Waring read, Norman sketched characters. He did the Artful Dodger and Oliver Twist, and he impressed us enormously with his Mr. Micawber from *David Copperfield.* When he had trouble drawing a character, he asked Waring to read that part again and made quick pencil sketches. Norman loved Dickens's twists and turns of daily life, and the humor and romance inspired his imagination. After Waring finished reading, Norman studied the illustrations in the books. Those family times meant a lot to us.

Were you close with any other family members?

When Waring's mother, Phoebe, died, his father, John, asked us to move into his large Manhattan brownstone to ease his loneliness. It worked out fine, except for a short and uncomfortable time when Father Rockwell wanted to marry my niece Amy, but that passed when she chose another man. After that, Father Rockwell went back and forth from the city to his home in the country.

Another family member, Phoebe's brother-in-law, Gil, visited us often. What a character, with Christmas presents on Easter, fireworks on Christmas day, and chocolate rabbits for Thanksgiving. Norman loved his humor. His backwards look at life influenced Norman, who used Uncle Gil's likeness for one of his *Post* covers.

Another character who visited was Waring's brother Samuel, a charming rascal who played guitar, piano, and banjo. Samuel had a nervous attitude toward women, and he ended up getting a horrible illness called locomotor ataxia. Norman claimed the illness came from too many ladies. Poor Samuel, his waist-down paralysis led to a long, agonizing death.

After Samuel died, we moved to Father Rockwell's three-story country house in Mamaroneck. The boys transferred schools, and Jerry starred in football, but Norman had trouble with his grades and scored a 70 percent in drawing. Only one teacher appreciated him, a Miss Smith from his eighth-grade year. At Christmas, she asked him to draw colored chalk murals on the board, and she gave him an A in her class. That year he also got first in algebra. Later, when Norman was grown, he corresponded with Miss Smith, and she inspired his 1935 *Post* cover tribute to schoolteachers.

What an honor for Miss Smith. Did your sons like Mamaroneck?

Both boys seemed content. They even liked our new church, where Waring acted as vestry clerk. Every Sunday, Norman was crucifer.

I'm sorry, what's a crucifer?

He bore the cross aloft and led the procession down the aisle.

Oh, yes. Did Norman like church then?

He disliked when the sexton spat and grumbled as he polished the crucifix, and he hated the choirmaster's heavy drinking. It disillusioned him about his faith.

What changed for Norman when he became a teenager?

He transformed as they all do and scorned his sissy name. I disagreed. I held on through that turmoil, and finally his attitude changed when he got work on a mail route. He delivered on his bicycle in an area where the millionaires lived. Mrs. Constable from our church lived along his route, and she gave him cake and ice cream and taught him proper ways to do things. She commissioned Norman to design four Christmas cards to send. Best of all, she recommended him as an art instructor to her friends, so every Saturday afternoon Norman helped the wonderful Ethel Barrymore with painting. In turn, Ethel told him stories and developed his love of the theatre. The endorsement of these ladies of society meant so much to me.

Did he continue to study art?

When he turned fourteen, he asked us if he could study at New York City's Chase School of Art on Saturdays, and I approved. The worst parts were the trolley and the four-hour-round-trip subway ride. When Norman showed us he could go alone every week, we convinced his regular school principal to let him skip school on Wednesday afternoons for art classes. When that same principal realized Norman couldn't abide the structure, they expelled him for misbehaving during his second year of high school. His wisecracks kept people in an uproar, and he had trouble sitting still and concentrating on things that didn't matter. I have that problem myself. We have so many similarities. We even look alike and get what we want from others.

After the Chase school, Norman went to the National Academy of Design. He enjoyed the anatomy work but refused to complete tasks he didn't like. Next, he attended the Art Students League, the most liberal art school in the country, where he found his niche as an illustrator. As a result of art commissions like Mrs. Constable's, he won a scholarship and became a class monitor. That meant he had his tuition fees paid, but he also had to work, so he auditioned and instructed the models who posed for anatomy class. For spending money, he worked night shift at a restaurant.

Were you still living with Waring's father?

No, Waring resigned from the vestry and we moved to a

boardinghouse in the city. I couldn't accommodate caring for Father Rockwell any longer, and I had cancer of the breast. Today it's discussed more openly among women, but back then it wasn't. I didn't want to bother Waring or the boys, so I took myself to the doctor's office and got myself home after the operation. In that first operation they gave me ether, removed the breast and the surrounding tissue, and sent me home with antibiotics. Later I had the other breast removed.

I feel so badly for you. How could you handle that burden alone?

I gathered my courage, took the bravery I learned from my mother, and decided the operation wouldn't kill me. I'd seen enough of death, and I wanted to shield my family from pain.

You put their feelings ahead of your own. That's caring. Tell me about Norman's career.

He illustrated the *Tell Me Why* stories and a Scout hiking book, and one summer he studied easel painting in Cape Cod with Charles Hawthorne. In the winter of 1912, he came down with the same thing that has always afflicted me— problems with his nerves. We suggested he recover at a farm in the countryside, and that helped Norman pull through and return to work. He became the art editor for *Boys' Life* and sold two paintings and a sketch to the *Saturday Evening Post*.

How did his success affect you and Waring?

Norman generously moved us to a family hotel in New Rochelle, where we joined St. Paul's Episcopal Church. Norman chose not to attend with us, but he sponsored our dancing lessons, where the women in our social circle noticed Waring's attentions towards me. They said I was lucky, and I made a point of looking my best. Norman gave me shopping trips for new clothes and beautiful shoes, and after his first cover for the *Saturday Evening Post*, he piled hundred dollar bills on the table in front of me to show his success. He had hundreds of *Post* covers.

Did Norman and Jerry find women who became special to them?

Jerry fell in love with Carol Cushman and got engaged to her. At the hotel where we resided, Norman noticed a boarder, Irene O'Connor, an Irish-Canadian schoolteacher three years his senior. He quickly proposed and, before Jerry could even marry Carol, Norman and Irene had a quiet wedding in the pastor's study at Blessed Sacrament Catholic Church. Jerry acted as best man and Irene's sister was maid of honor. Irene wore a blue silk suit with a large white hat, and the sapphire ring and gold watch Norman gave her. They had a wedding breakfast and then honeymooned in the Catskills.

After only two weeks in their tiny apartment, Irene moved back home to her parent's house for two months. I had an inkling something would go wrong, since Irene didn't attend church and didn't want children. I often wondered if she married Norman for social reasons, but then she didn't even attend Jerry and Carol's wedding. By the way, Carol's job as an actress led Norman to draw a Hollywood-related cover for the *Post*.

What effect did the Great War have on their lives?

Both boys did their part. Jerry joined the National Guard, and Norman joined the Navy when the war was almost over. At six feet, he barely weighed 130 pounds, so he stuffed himself with donuts and bananas to pass the physical. After he got posted to South Carolina, he drew cartoons and made layouts for the camp newspaper, *Afloat and Ashore*. After three months of service, Norman had his discharge and the war ended.

After the war, Norman made more patriotic paintings while Irene gave parties and answered Norman's fan mail. Other times, her treatment bordered on mean. I could never understand how he tolerated her, but he worked hard to give her everything she wanted.

Both Norman and Jerry worked hard, a trait they learned from Waring. Jerry traded on Wall Street, and Norman had his magazine covers. His portrayal of people doing ordinary things with a humorous twist led to the *Ladies' Home Journal* reproductions of his oils. After that, we didn't have to watch our budget so carefully, and Norman got us a nice apartment and a Chevrolet sedan. Norman was as kind as Irene was shameless.

What do you mean?

Irene led the life she chose. When Norman went to Europe three times, she stayed home and spent all his savings in shady business deals. When Norman was in the hospital, I heard terrible gossip about her behavior with his chauffeur. I told Norman what was proper, but he held on, even when Irene's mother, sister, and two brothers moved in with them and disturbed his evening quiet. When Norman insisted her family move out, she refused to live alone with him.

Finally, Norman took a place in Manhattan and separated from her, but my relief didn't last. Norman entered the hospital for tonsil problems and felt lonely, so they reconciled. He told her if her family moved out, he'd buy her a big house in the society district, so she agreed. They played bridge, golf, and tennis at the country club and they started a jazz-age open marriage that didn't meet with our approval.

Seven long years we were estranged from Norman, and I blame it all on Irene. Even Jerry and Carol and their sons, Dick and John, backed away from him. I know it affected Jerry, who had his own bond trading company until the 1929 stock market crash sent him into a business designing toys.

You stayed close with Jerry?

Yes, but then Carol wrote a revealing and embarrassing article for *Cosmopolitan*.

I know that magazine. How did you react?

We felt uncomfortable, but Carol bordered on sainthood compared to Irene's misbehavior. One time Irene even checked into a hotel with another man and put the room under Norman's name. After fourteen years of misery for Norman, Irene asked for a divorce and Norman accepted it.

A wonderful thing happened next. Norman took an extended trip to California and, through his friends the Barstows, he met Mary Rhodes.

What is Mary's background?

She graduated from Stanford and worked as a mathematics teacher. Her father's a lawyer, and her mother's from a well-established steel family. A few days after they met, Norman and Mary got engaged, but to satisfy her father they waited three months to get married.

Their wedding was held in the Barstow's gardens, and a Presbyterian minister officiated. Mary carried beautiful flowers, and since she's almost as tall as Norman, she must have looked regal in her pretty dress. She's so right for Norman, with her willingness to put Norman's welfare first.

Norman and Mary left New York City and moved back to New Rochelle, and Norman quit the big parties and country club activities. A quiet life meant more time for him to paint. Mary read aloud to him like Waring did when he was young.

When did things change in your estrangement from Norman?

We tried to make it right but couldn't. Six months after their wedding, we heard the awful news that Waring had stomach cancer. It was so odd the way it happened. The doctors came to attend to my nerves, but instead they examined Waring. It turned out he had cancer, and I wasn't sick at all. He took the news better than I did.

Did you come together after that news?

A few weeks later at Christmas time, we set things right with Norman. What a relief to be together for the holiday. I can hardly discuss the rest of it. I loved Waring so deeply, and he took such good care of me. I must try to stop shaking.

Should we stop for a while?

No, I'll finish. After Christmas, Waring wasted away. We took one last trip to Florida, and there he died. I wanted to get out of bed but felt so sad without him. Those weeks were a blur. I do remember that not long after, Norman had a son named after Waring. They call him Jerry, but his full name is Jarvis Waring Rockwell.

Oh, Waring, my wonderful Waring. I miss him. After he died, I couldn't face being alone, so Norman loaned Jerry and Carol money to buy a new house and I moved in with them. They gave me the large bedroom in the front. All the grandchildren call me Baba.

Waring's death affected Norman's nerves, and he got melancholy. Ideas didn't come to him, so Norman, Mary, Little Jerry, and their German shepherd moved to Paris so Norman could study there. When Mary became pregnant, they moved back to New Rochelle, and Thomas Rhodes Rockwell was born. He carries on my brother's name.

Did you get along with Carol?

She couldn't abide my pacing. I just couldn't stay still. After a year, I moved to a boardinghouse. The people there caused trouble and didn't get along with me either, so I lived with my cousins in Rhode Island. That didn't work, so I moved in with Norman. I know Norman loves me, but when I lived with him, he couldn't work. I stayed right outside his studio, perched on the steps, but he said I distracted him. Within a year, I had to move back to Rhode Island.

Were you able to stay in touch with Norman after those complications?

Too much of what I knew about Norman I learned in the papers. In the summer, Norman and his family came to visit me in Rhode Island, and then Norman's third son, Peter Barstow Rockwell, was born. After Peter's birth, I had to be hospitalized, but the doctors insisted it wasn't serious. Norman says I'm always sick and complain too much, but if he could live in this body for just one day, he'd understand.

Now Norman lives in the Green Mountains of Vermont where the colors are brighter and the people leave him alone. Mary enjoys the North, and I'm glad she's happy. She shapes her life around Norman's needs and helps me when I visit them.

Good, so you're able to go to Vermont.

Every week that I'm there, Mary takes me to the doctor to see if it's something other than my nerves that's bothering me. She's been a dear, with just one little problem. As Mary drove me back to Rhode Island one time, she kept swigging from a flask to settle her nerves. It was only that one time.

Norman paints well in Vermont?

He does. It comes from a private place inside of him.

One last question. Can you tell me how you influenced Norman?

Norman had a solitary childhood, and that made him yearn for more. My condition probably inspired him to paint life the way he wanted it to be. Yes, now I'm sure of it. Here is my final thought. Norman might not have lived it, but he paints the perfect world.

INTERVIEW WITH NORMAN ROCKWELL ON THE DEATH OF HIS MOTHER

My poor mother died at eighty-four. My cousins organized her funeral and a relative of my uncle Samuel conducted it. I arranged for a special funeral train car to stop in Yonkers to deliver her to be buried in the family plot. She lies next to Dad.

7

Interview with Mattie Womack Slye

MOTHER OF ROY ROGERS
SINGING COWBOY AND MOVIE STAR,
BORN NOVEMBER 5, 1911

———— ❧ ————

When my time comes, just skin me and put me up there on
Trigger, just as though nothing had ever changed.
—Roy Rogers

JAN HELEN MCGEE

I love Roy's music. I read he was the top–money-making Western movie star from 1943 to 1954.

MATTIE SLY

We're right proud of him, and we love listenin' to him sing. But I gotta tell you straight up: I don't call him Roy Rogers. I named him Leonard Slye.

JAN HELEN MCGEE

Do you want me to call him Leonard?

MATTIE SLY

That's up to you. Doesn't matter a bit to me what you choose.

When did he change from Leonard to Roy?

After his first picture came out, he said he needed a new name. First he used Dick Weston, then Roy Rogers. He said it sounded more rugged, but it didn't work for me.

"Honey," I told him, "I just can't call you Roy." His answer to that didn't surprise me.

"Well, you can call me Leonard," he said, so that's what I do. Some of his friends call him Buck.

Today I'll call him Leonard. Do you play music?

As far back as I can remember my family played music. Same with my husband Andy's family. We left our mark there for sure when we encouraged our children with singing, guitar, whatnot. My girls didn't want a career of it, but they stood by Leonard and supported his dreams. Since we all play by ear, I couldn't teach any of them to read music, but that didn't stop Leonard. That boy is smart even without much book learning. Of course, he went to school longer than me, and I wanted that. When I was young, my parents was just too poor for me to be staying in school long. But now, music, it don't demand much in the way of formal learning. Well, now I'm rambling on.

I want you to ramble on! I admire Leonard, and I want to hear as much as you can remember. Start by talking about yourself.

I was born Martha Womack, but I use Mattie. We hail from Beefhide, Kentucky, with its low hills and tall trees. One thing that strikes people was all the unusual names in our family: Farina, Possum, Blanche, and Phineas.

I don't know anyone with any of those names.

They don't use names like that nowadays. At two years

old, my life changed some when I got stricken with the white swelling. That's what country people called it; now it's polio. After that, getting around was hard for me with my weak leg all crippled. I had to grab hold of it in order to walk right. But I didn't let it bother me much, just grew up ordinary. I didn't grow up real tall, though. Only got to five feet. But I'm tough.

I met Leonard's daddy, and my head got turned all around. What a good lookin' man, I said to myself. A man like that gets used to a lot of attention, but it didn't seem to affect him much. He just acted like an easygoing feller who played guitar and mandolin same as me and loved his music.

Andy's real name is Andrew, and Leonard calls him Pop. He's part Choctaw Indian and a bit on the small side, but right off I noticed the strength of him and I liked it. Now I gotta tell ya, Andy's a dreamer and that can be hard on a wife, but his dreaming sometimes worked for us. Then again, other times it didn't.

What did Andy do for work?

When he was young, he tried a lot of jobs, played music for traveling folks, and then worked in a carnival as an acrobat. I guess Leonard inherited Andy's muscles and sense of timing and balance, and that helped him do those tricky moves on Trigger.

What did Andy like about you?

He saw his opposite side in me. Some people call me shy, but I tell 'em I just keep to myself. What with my leg and all, I don't get around like others do, so I have my limits. That's one reason I'm private. Speaking of my leg, Andy never much noticed or cared about it unless I was hurting that day. Then he took a bit of the load off me to make sure the kids was fed and clean. Most times he appreciates me and knows all I done. I see those things now, but back when we met I couldn't figure what Andy seen in me. I gather he liked it that we both play music. I loved his friendly nature. He talked to others so easy and performed in front of crowds. Well anyway, for some reason he married me instead of some other girl.

Is Roy, I mean Leonard, your first-born?

First I had my girls, Mary and Cleda. Then Leonard made his way into this world, and after him, Kathleen. Leonard came on a cold day—November 5, 1911—and I gave him the full name of Leonard Franklin Slye. That day, Andy came home from work all surprised he had a son. After two girls, he couldn't believe it.

"Prove it's a boy," he said to me.

I pulled those blankets off and showed him, and Andy took to whooping and hollering. Adding to his pleasure was Leonard being the splitting image of Andy with that handsome face and those squinty eyes. Whenever he could, Andy'd brag on the similarities between the two of them. He loved our girls, but a man holds a special place in his heart for his son.

Where were you living, and what job did Andy work at that time?

Back when Leonard was a baby, we lived in Cincinnati, Ohio. Now that was a scrappy time. We lived near Andy's work at the United States Shoe Company, in a four-story, red-brick tenement building with fire escapes in the front and some stores down at ground level. I didn't mind it, but Andy didn't like it there because he got enough city life as a child. He liked change, so he had a saying he'd use over and over.

"Greener pastures are out there," he'd say.

I understood. Cincinnati's cold meant a short growing season, and we had trouble gettin' vegetables out of a garden. So we could move on, Andy teamed up with his brother Will and started to build a houseboat. Maybe that sounds right easy to you with two grown men involved, but what you don't know is that Will's blind. Not that it mattered one whit. The two of them just got about their work and rounded up heaps of scrap lumber and salvaged what they could. I worked alongside them and stitched bedsheets together to make sails. When we finished and whitewashed that houseboat, we could see it was sorta squatty and looked like a barge. The neighbors couldn't stop talking about it, having their fun. "There's Andy's Ark," they'd say and laugh. It didn't matter to me since I never did care much what any of my neighbors was thinking.

So your new home was a houseboat. What was your destination?

We put all our things on that boat and headed down the Ohi' River for Portsmouth. All along that river trip, people had a kindness towards us. When that durned river flooded, we watched out for each other, and when the water got low, they helped push or pull us. When we needed a tow from fishermen, Andy worked odd jobs for them. Then the little money he made got taxed to pay for World War I.

I took it day to day, but we had a hard life. Imagine, seven of us on one little boat. Today I can't even think on it. That was some close quarters with squalling children. Now mind, they was all sweet, but every minute some kind of trouble reared up and splashed me but good. One time when Leonard was about two, I don't know, he must've been playing a game or having a fit or something. Well, he threw every bit of my silverware into that river. I got hot on that one, but lucky for him, when the water went down we found those forks and spoons sticking up outta the sand. That day he escaped my fury but plenty of other times he didn't. You know how boys are.

Yes, I have a son, but it was my daughter who fired me up with her shenanigans when she was really young. What happened next?

We finally made it to Portsmouth, but then we hit a terrible flood that lasted thirteen days. Houses rose up off their foundations and floated away as we waited in the rain and felt lucky. What a pitiful sight to know that folks' lives got turned upside down. We did what we could to help, just like those that helped us.

How were you able to recover?

After that flood cleared, we moored the houseboat and Andy got a decent job in the shoe factory nearby. I enrolled Leonard at the Union Street School.

So Leonard looked like Andy—handsome.

He got many a remark about being pretty, with his hair white as cotton. That talk didn't make him act up though, 'cause even at a young age Leonard acted respectful. Both me and Andy taught the children that.

How long did you live on the moored houseboat?

Until Leonard was about eight, but Andy's brother, Will, stayed on it for the rest of his life. Living on that boat with all them people was too tight a fit, even though you'd think with my big family I wouldn't'a noticed. I liked when we moved to dry ground and had a yard. Then the children got on much better. Having somewhere to run off to improved their dispositions.

When we scraped together enough money, we moved out to the countryside twelve miles from Portsmouth and settled in a little area called Duck Run. We lived at the end of a holler where the foot-deep ruts in the road filled up with mud after every rain. Because of those rough roads, we didn't travel much. Leonard suffered the most, asking all the time to go to the picture show. We only got there maybe once a year.

What did Leonard do with his time?

Leonard and Andy took to building our house. After they finished I sure did compliment them on all my extra space. Mhm, I liked it fine. I enrolled Leonard at the Duck Run School. When he wasn't in school, he kept busy with hunting for food, and that freedom put him in a good mood. I did inside work with the girls 'cause problems with my leg kept me from helping outside. Leonard plowed with our old mule, and that was a sight, what with Leonard's little arms reaching up to get hold of those plow handles. Me and the girls laughed at him when he wasn't looking. Leonard had a lot of jobs. He gathered eggs and shoveled chicken droppings, but he didn't like that kind of work and sometimes he got an attitude on him. He could be ornery as a mule, so he got his bottom blistered more than once. But he knew from age seven that he had to be the man of the family, even if he was a little small for some of them farm chores.

Why did he have to be the man of the house?

He just had to. Andy worked over at that shoe factory in Portsmouth and only got a chance to come on home once every two weeks on the weekend. That little bit of time together meant it was hard for him and Leonard to get close, but Andy taught him it never hurt to dream. I did my part with Andy gone. I worked on harmony with the girls and Leonard and helped them on all their strings. Andy gave them pointers when he could.

What did you do after sundown?

Since we lived way back in the hills, there wasn't much to do at night, and that houseboat was the same. Rather than arguing, we worked on our singing and playing. With singing, we mixed it all up. Andy started with the low tone and we built harmonies onto it. After some of that, either Andy or me called out a chord and the children played it. Leonard got a lot of practice that way and it helped with his career.

Some nights the neighbors came over and we'd square dance in the old barn. By the time Leonard was ten, he did the calling. He was good at it, moving those words fast out his mouth, same as singing. Those are just muscles, you know, there in your mouth. He'd do the allemande lefts and do-si-dos, and in between he'd sing a few western ballads for the folks. I'd sit back and close my eyes and enjoy his sweet voice. We had good times.

But I do remember something that wasn't so good. Leonard had just turned eleven when he fell out of a cherry tree and tore up his shoulder. Since we lived way out in the country, we'd only go to the doctor if we thought someone was gonna die. So we put Leonard's arm in a sling and it healed up, but when he got older it pained him on hard days.

I broke my shoulder when I was two. Luckily I don't feel pain now. So you lived on a farm, did you have a lot of land?

A small farm, but enough to grow food and have critters. Andy bought Leonard his first horse, a little black sulky named Babe. He loved that horse, and not much came between them. Leonard rode Babe everywhere, to prayer meetings and square dances. Leonard can be bashful like me, but he sure felt comfortable around animals and he knew what to expect from their behavior. To learn more, he joined the 4-H Club at school and entered shows. After his pet pig won the grand prize at the Scioto County Fair for rapid growth, Leonard got a trip to the state capital.

That's a thrilling adventure.

I could tell by his excitement as he kissed us goodbye that he'd be doin' something special in his life. Other than clarinet in high school and an acting role as Santa Claus in the school Christmas play, he didn't have a lot of excitement. In Columbus, he loved the elevator in the Old Neil House Hotel, and he rode it over and over, up and down.

What changed for you when the Depression hit?

That was serious hard times. Leonard said he needed to bring money home, so two years shy of graduation he quit school. He wanted to be a doctor or dentist, so he felt a big disappointment when he had to go on down to the shoe factory alongside Andy. Lots of times the smell meant Andy came home with a terrible headache. It was a headache day when everything changed. I was in the kitchen with a damp cloth to Andy's head for the pain, and out of the blue Andy looked hard at Leonard.

"Let's head out to see Mary in California," he said.

Mary, which daughter is she?

That's our oldest girl. She moved out there with her husband.

Were any of you upset with his decision?

Well, Leonard liked the idea, and I felt fine with it. I never minded going along with Andy's adventures. We piled all our rickety junk into the old '23 Dodge we had back then and took off. Leonard had about ninety dollars in savings, so that went to gas. At night we put blankets out by the side of the car, played and sang awhile, and then hunkered down and checked out the stars. By day, we saw other families like us, hungry and tired, thinking of the Golden State.

When we arrived, Mary fed us good and then found Andy and Leonard jobs loading and driving gravel trucks. Andy liked it out there for a while, but after four months he decided we should head back to Ohio. Leonard came with us but didn't stay long. He left again for California with Mary's father-in-law.

That's a lot of moving. What did Leonard do when he returned to California?

He built roads and picked peaches. Food was hard to come by, so he caught rabbits and shared the meat with the people that worked alongside him. Other times, the farmers fed the work crews. After supper, they sat around the campfire. Leonard played the fiddle and learned Jew's harp and harmonica.

How long did you stay in Ohio?

Not too long. We sold the farm at Duck Run and went off to California again. Out there, Andy did fruit-picking work with Leonard. In the evenings we played our instruments and sang, and people listened and joined in some. Life didn't come easy, but we found the joy we could.

How did Leonard's music career get its start?

Leonard was about eighteen. He did harmonies with his cousin, Stan Slye, and they played guitar and mandolin. After they got some confidence up, they performed for a few dollars here and there. Mary did some hard talking to Leonard and pushed him to try out for *Midnight Frolic*, an amateur radio show. Since the show ran from midnight to six, anybody could go on it. He was scared to death, but Leonard went ahead and did it, and Mary stood by him for support. Mary's good like that.

A few days later he got a call from a guy who asked him to join his group, the Rocky Mountaineers. After that group, he joined up with the International Cowboys. That suited Leonard just fine because he loved to perform and make people happy.

Music and traveling make it hard to find a steady romance. Did Leonard find someone?

When he was twenty-one, he met and married Lucile Ascoles. It happened fast, but it didn't work out because of Leonard's touring. They got divorced right quick. I didn't have time to make any judgments about her, but anyway that's not for me to say.

Next thing, Leonard toured with the O-Bar-O Cowboys, and in New Mexico he met a girl named Grace Arlene Wilkins. Arlene was tall, soft-spoken, and nice. We liked her right off. The way he met her went like this: it started on some radio show down there. Leonard liked to talk a little in between songs.

"I sure do have a taste for some lemon pie," he said to the listeners.

I don't know why he was wantin' some pie that night. I guess because after hunting rabbits and shooting hawks off telephone wires in order to eat, he wanted something a bit sweet to add to it. Arlene and her momma heard Leonard on the radio, and they requested that he sing "The Swiss Yodel." So he did, and they appreciated it.

The next day Arlene and her momma came to the stage door and delivered two big lemon pies for Leonard and the boys. It turned out, just like me and Andy, him and Arlene had music in common. What a lovely singing voice on Arlene. She played piano too, but her mind was solid that she wasn't going to perform. She just did it for her own self and the enjoyment she got out of it. The two of them got on real well, and Leonard treated her good like he does me. Oh, that boy of mine thought of my welfare. Around that time, Leonard did a real special thing for me. Well, he did lots of them, but what I'm talking about is the brace he got for my leg so I could get around better. That helped a whole lot.

For the next three years, Leonard toured with the Sons of the Pioneers, and him and Arlene kept in touch with letters. In July of '36 they got married in New Mexico. Once a week after that, all the boys in the Sons of Pioneers came over to Leonard's house for Sunday supper and poker playing. Arlene cooked and they all called her Sis.

I read that Leonard stayed with the Sons of the Pioneers for three years. What happened after that?

Leonard changed singing groups again. That's how music goes and all. He did some more radio shows and sang with

Gene Autry. I spent some of my nicest evenings listening to the two of them on the radio. That show turned out to be a boost for Leonard, who always thought and planned what he wanted.

When he heard about singing cowboy screen tests going on at a movie studio, he went down there to see if he could land a job. Even with his sweet tongue, he couldn't get past the guard at the gate. He tried to sneak in with some extras, but that didn't work. Luckily, he spotted a music friend, who talked the guard into letting him in. Sure as shooting, Leonard got that cowboy part and signed a contract with Republic Pictures.

Did that work change your life?

When Leonard got his career going, he brought me to the UCLA hospital and got me fixed up with a wheelchair. Another time, he gave Andy and me a big surprise. Leonard acted like he needed a new house, so he picked us up and took us out to San Fernando Valley. He showed us a pretty white bungalow set in a little chicken ranch.

"What do you think of it?" he asked.

We told him we liked it just fine, and to our surprise, Leonard handed Andy the key.

"Welcome to your new home," he said with a big old grin.

He paid nine thousand for the place but planned to spend ten thousand. When we refused to take the extra thousand outright, Leonard hid the rest of the money in my pantry. Finding that money was like mint tea after a summer thunderstorm. We had a good laugh over that one.

That sounds fun. He's a generous son.

I tried to give something back and help Leonard out where

I could. After his first publicity tour, he got a boatload of fan mail that I helped Arlene answer. Most of his fans were between six and fourteen years old, so we sent out penny postcards with a picture of Leonard and Trigger on them. Leonard wanted to be kind to people that supported him. Those little things helped, and his career took off in a big way. Between '38 and '42 he acted in thirty-six pictures. In each one, he'd sing five or six songs. He ended up buying his movie horse Trigger. You heard of Trigger?

Sure I did. I had a pretend horse named Trigger.

That's a good one. I guess everyone's heard of Trigger. Well, he got second billing, but there's something you should know about Trigger. See, Trigger acted as a movie horse, while Trigger Jr., no relation to the first Trigger, went on as his show horse. Leonard loved Trigger as much as any of us and ended up buying him. I accepted it, but I still had to go and tease him a whole lot. I guess you know that when Trigger died, Leonard had him mounted like at those museums. Couldn't put him in the ground. Besides that horse, he had a colorful sidekick, name of Gabby Hayes.

Leonard was called the King of Cowboys, wasn't he? And he was on the cover of magazines?

He got that nickname from his rodeo appearances all over the country and all the things that happened. What a hoot to see him on the cover of *Life* magazine. What a thrill when Leonard told me he met the president.

I would love to meet a president. How did it happen?

It was on Franklin Roosevelt's sixty-first birthday, a March of Dimes Ball held in the White House. But that was a while later.

Let me stop a minute and think where I am in the story. Oh, I know. After we got that chicken ranch, Leonard and Arlene moved onto a six-acre place not too far from us. They wanted babies, but none came, so they adopted a sweet little girl they named Cheryl Darlene. Funny thing, right after that, it turned out Arlene was carrying Linda Lou. She came in '43. Arlene had another baby in '48, this time a boy named Roy Rogers Jr.—called Dusty. Leonard was so happy, he took time off in the middle of a movie. He talked of all the things him and Dusty could do, hunting and riding and all.

Then just six days after Dusty's birth, a dreadful thing happened. Arlene had a blood clot go to her brain and she died. Awful, awful, awful time. I didn't know what to do to help. Leonard grieved so. He took her death hard, and my heart ached for him. I helped with the grandchildren as best I could, but with my leg and all, I had limits. Besides, I couldn't replace a momma. Our healing came on slow. Leonard cared for those children and worked too, but being a widower puts a lot of pressure on a man.

Dale Evans came into his life then?

She was his costar in a movie they worked on. Her real name is Frances Octavia Smith, but the studios called her Queen of the West. The movie meant they was together all day and they got close.

Six months after Arlene died, Leonard bought a ranch called Sky Haven, and months later he proposed to Dale. I could see Dale was a good person, but another mother coulda worried about the match. Poor Dale had a hard life early on. Her daddy owned his own nursery in Texas and liked to gamble. Dale's momma, Betty Sue, stood not too tall but had a strong personality, and could she cook.

I can let you in on the reason another momma mighta worried. The story went like this: When Dale turned fourteen, she got married and had a son, Tom. Back then, people hid young births. Dale had big dreams, so her momma raised the boy so Dale could be a movie star. Because of how it was back then, Dale pretended Tom was her brother. She got divorced that time and another time, but she told me those mistakes only made her try harder after she married Leonard. It was New Year's Eve of 1947 when Leonard and Dale had their marriage ceremony in Oklahoma.

Marriage often affects women's careers. What was the backlash for Dale?

According to the movie studio, getting married meant Dale's career was over. The studio didn't want married girls in their pictures. Dale's life became real different, God love her. Instead of attention and excitement, she stayed home and made clothes for her and the girls and did a lot of cooking.

Did she miss movies?

I never asked. In our family, we talk more about business than feelings. I know she was good for Cheryl, Linda, and Dusty, those poor children. After their momma died, the change came down hard on 'em, especially Cheryl and Linda because they was older. They missed their momma so much. Andy tried to cheer up the girls, so he made a cute playhouse for them and their dolls out by the pond. Dale got real interested in church, and that helped her get past the disappointment I know she must've felt after she left the pictures. All that changed when Dale found out she was carrying.

Then they had a scare. Dale got the German measles and

had to stay in bed so she wouldn't lose the baby. In '50, Robin Elizabeth was born, and that made them real happy. But things didn't sit quite right. Don't get me wrong, Leonard and Dale looked on the positive side. What happened was, little Robin had mongolism. Other people said to put Robin in an institution, but they said, nuh uh, we ain't havin' none of that. They loved that baby as much as any child.

It must have been difficult nonetheless. Did it affect you directly?

Some things happened that affected me quite a bit. Little Robin got a slight case of polio, and I felt bad for her. I didn't want her going through it like I did. For two long years, Dale and Leonard nursed that girl through all kinds of problems. Since Robin had to keep healthy, she had to stay away from the other children, so Andy and Leonard built a little two-room house on their property for Robin and her nurse. That poor baby struggled so much through her short life. It was right at her second birthday when her little heart gave out. Leonard and Dale couldn't stop crying. I hated to see their heartache. The other children came to stay with us so they wouldn't have to go through the funeral with their parents all broke up like that.

"Robin's gone to heaven to be with Jesus," Dale told the children.

It helped when Dale and Leonard adopted two little ones, Harry John David Hardy—called Sandy—and Mary Little Doe. She's part Choctaw Indian, and they call her Dodie. Next they adopted a Korean girl named In Ai Lee. They call her Debbie. Then came Mimi, a girl from Scotland. Leonard and Dale were her official wards. That's a lot of children, but each of 'em had jobs. They cared for the thirty hunting dogs, the horses, and the pigeons. By then, Dale got back to working on pictures, a happy change.

Did they travel a lot?

Leonard and Dale left for the studio set before sunup, and they'd be gone for weeks at a time for personal appearances. When they took to traveling, women they trusted helped with the children. I helped, too. I love my grandchildren. They call me Mammy, and they call Andy Grampy. We had such a time. They loved the pond Andy and Leonard built for them.

What else did Andy do to keep himself busy?

He cared for the pigeons and chickens and sold the eggs. After a time, he got tired of that and just wanted to garden, so we moved to a smaller place in Van Nuys. The children visited for a day or two and slept in a little cottage out back of the main house, where they pretended they lived on their own.

Did any of the children sing with Leonard and Dale?

All of them performed real nice in their shows. Cheryl and Linda sang so pretty, but Cheryl liked it best. Dale did a lot of songwriting, and she wrote their theme song "Happy Trails to You."

I love that song, so positive and sweet. Anything else you can think of?

I guess I'm winding down. I didn't say much about Andy and me, but we have a marriage that's lasted through the tough times and the good times. We got through the bad times by keepin' our own counsel and doin' some things together and some not. Andy has his little projects, and we both watch *The Roy Rogers Show* on television. I felt proud when Leonard and Dale got invited to the White House for Ike's grandson David's birthday party. They sang Western songs for the president.

It sounds like Leonard's been pretty busy.

He is, but he finds time to be good to us. I'll tell you one more story. I'm a simple woman and don't need much, but I always had one kind of emptiness. As a child, I never had a store-bought doll. I must've talked about it a lot in the old days, and I guess it made an impression, so Leonard started a doll collection for me. On his trips all over the world, he bought dolls and sent them to me. The grandchildren tried to hold them and play, but I caught them.

"You get near my dolls and I'll snatch you bald-headed," I hollered.

Have you been to any of Leonard's movie sets?

We like being asked, but it don't mean we go.

Why not? I would love it.

We just don't want to get in anybody's way.

I kept you so long. Can I ask about your health?

I'm just gettin' old. My heart's not quite right, and I worry 'cause Andy feels poorly. At times like this, we think about what went on before. I remember Thanksgiving dinners at Leonard's house with the family, but sometimes my leg gave me trouble and they'd come over to our place. Leonard is a good son and a good daddy to all his children. He worked hard for his success.

It's a long way from Duck Run.

Sometimes I miss the holler, but time passes fast. We had the ride of a lifetime.

INTERVIEW WITH ROY ROGERS
ON THE DEATH OF HIS MOTHER

The good Lord took my mama on November 3, 1958. She died of a heart attack. My first fan, she helped with my music and she believed in me. Not a day goes by that I don't talk to her in my heart.

8

Interview with Martha Bulloch Roosevelt

MOTHER OF THEODORE ROOSEVELT JR.
PRESIDENT OF THE UNITED STATES,
BORN OCTOBER 27, 1858

———— ⁓⁓ ————

Whenever you are asked if you can do a job, tell 'em,
"Certainly I can!"
Then get busy and find out how to do it.
—Teddy Roosevelt

JAN HELEN MCGEE

I appreciate that you found time for me today. Theodore Jr. is so accomplished. He graduated *magna cum laude* from Harvard College with a first in his class in zoology and political economy, and he became the youngest man ever to be elected to the New York State Assembly. Can you tell me how you influenced him?

MITTIE ROOSEVELT

With my Southern upbringing, it's only polite to mention

all my children. We call Theodore Teedie, Anna is Bamie, Elliott is Ellie, and Corinne is Conie. I do believe they have all
been shaped by my family and my background. To give you
an example: my sister Anna is the reason Teedie loves history. Her stories of naval battles made him love the history of
war. Have you read Teedie's book, The *Naval War of 1812*?

JAN HELEN MCGEE

**The *New York Times* called it excellent, but I regret to say
I haven't.**

MITTIE ROOSEVELT

That is too bad. I imagine as a reporter you have more
interest in the here and now than in history. I understand,
since I try to live in the present.

Southerners like nicknames, how did you get Mittie?

It's a derivative of "mighty little," or a combination of my
given name, Martha, and "little." It fits me since I'm five feet
tall. And you are right; Northerners never understand that
most of us in the South have two names.

Where did you live in the South?

I was born and raised in the sand hills of Georgia, above
Atlanta, in a lush valley on the Roswell plantation. Our
charming home, Bulloch Hall, had white columns and was
patterned after a Greek revival mansion.

You have such pretty blue eyes and beautiful, pale skin.

Why thank you. I used to have silky, black hair. Age affects
all of us.

It does. On the plantation, what did you enjoy?

I loved riding parties and picnics as my uncles played flute
and violin. My sister Gracie had a pretty soprano voice, and
I sang alto.

It sounds lovely. Did your family have slaves?

Yes, it was typical of the South, although my husband's family lived in the North and didn't have any. Our Southern family included nineteen slaves. My sister Anna and I had a sweet nurse named Mom Grace, and we each had a slave child our age that we called our little black shadow. From the time I was a little girl, Toy slept at the foot of my bed and we did everything together. She was all mine. When my husband met her, he seemed bothered by her presence, but I let him know she had always been important to me.

I first met Theodore, whom I call Thee, when he came south in 1850. Even though I'd just turned fifteen, I'd been taught to hide my unease and carry myself with confidence.

"Full of herself," others would say. Momma called it self-assurance.

At parties I felt quite gay, but melancholy often overtook me. At first, Thee barely noticed my moods. You might call him besotted.

How did you meet?

Thee's oldest brother, Silas, and my half-sister, Susan, introduced us. Susan is married to Dr. West, and his sister is married to Silas. All of them, including Thee, shared dinner together one night at Silas's home. As they told stories, Thee became entranced with our plantation and way of life, so he wrote my family a letter of introduction and mentioned his business trip to the South. We invited him to visit, and he sent a letter with the date, although he arrived before the letter. We had retired for the evening, and all the slaves had gone to a corn shucking at a neighboring plantation. Imagine our surprise.

What were your first impressions of Theodore?

He had beautiful eyes and a direct gaze, and he was talkative and cheerful and wonderfully dressed. I had some reservations since I hadn't been fully prepared for the implications of his arrival. Thee knew exactly what he was doing and hoped to be enchanted by more than our plantation. He claims our first meeting captivated him.

Thee stayed with us for several weeks. Our days felt both short and long, with quiet walks and never-ending conversation. On horseback rides and the hunt for fox and deer, I noticed his strength and coordination. In the evenings, we had parties and theatrical presentations. After the parties, we sat alone in the parlor and read aloud to one another. Thee loved poetry, which impressed Momma. When she approved the match, Thee beamed. With my head in a spin, I felt young and silly compared to Thee. I liked him anyway so I gave him my gold thimble to cherish. When he finished his business and returned north, we corresponded by mail.

Letters can be so intimate and such fun to reread. What did you discuss?

I told him my background so he would fully understand me, and I opened my heart about my daddy's passing, which occurred only one year before Thee's visit. With Daddy gone, our life turned upside down. Momma had trouble leaving her room, and when she did, she looked at me and cried, since I favor my Daddy. Now let us move to a lighter note.

Tell me about your parents and their courtship.

James Bulloch and Martha Stewart. For a brief time they courted, but Momma's daddy preferred the United States senator John Elliott. She didn't want to go against his strong wishes, and she was unsure of her feelings, so she married the senator.

Momma and the senator had three children, a son and two daughters, one of them Susan. This is the unusual part, although in the South people do things differently, my daddy married the senator's daughter Hester. Daddy and Hester had a son, and then, sadly, both the senator and Hester passed on.

After a proper amount of time, well, proper to Momma and Daddy but maybe not to some, my parents married each other. A lot of tongues wagged and some people said scandalous things, but I think it's terribly romantic how their lives split apart and came back together. The backlash did not abate, so Momma and Daddy moved away from Savannah to the Roswell plantation. At Roswell, Daddy planted and worked hard, and he and Momma gave lavish parties and had heaps of fun. Momma had another son and two more daughters, and I am the youngest.

Then came the horrible day that my daddy passed on. Oh, it was a wretched day. Oh, it was so sad.

How did your Mother cope?

Momma had great reserves of strength, so we didn't see the enormity of her hurt, but it pained her desperately. After the brunt of her pain eased, she realized her predicament. She had a lot of children to raise alone.

Then you met Theodore?

Yes, and two years after that, I took a visit to my sister Susan in Philadelphia. Thee stopped there to see me on his way back from a European business trip. Since I was seventeen, I felt more of an inclination to pay attention to such an important man. Momma instilled that virtue in each of us.

She spoke often of Daddy's pride in his heritage. He was of Scot descent, and his grandfather was the first Revolutionary President of Georgia. President or governor, I have heard it called both, so name it what you will. Our family's past and Momma's thoughts about the future propelled me into a relationship with a good man who could care for me in all kinds of ways. That man was Thee.

After a charming time at Susan's, I left Philadelphia for New York City to be a guest of her husband's sister and Thee's brother, Silas. I learned quite a bit about Thee's family during that visit. Thee's father, Cornelius Van Shaack, was a commanding, red-haired man, not too tall. Cornelius's father, James, had opened the first Roosevelt & Son to sell hardware, but Cornelius had more interest in imported glass for windows and mirrors. Thee's Quaker mother, Margaret, had arrived in Pennsylvania on the boat with William Penn.

How did Cornelius and Margaret meet?

I don't know for certain. I can tell you other things I know about them. Most people saw Cornelius, called CVS, as a strong-hearted merchant, but with Margaret his sunny disposition held strong. He adored her and wrote her beautiful poetry, especially during their engagement. When she passed on, he wrote a poem dedicated to her. Ten years later he joined her in heaven.

How many children did they have?

Soon after they married, Margaret got busy and bore Cornelius five boys. Imagine her terror.

"Horrid children," is what I have heard, although that seems harsh.

Poor Margaret. I feel so blessed that I had two girls and

two boys. Even with all those energetic boys, Margaret was a good mother to Thee. She sang songs in Dutch, which she learned without any knowledge of the language. Thee enjoyed her songs, but he preferred mealtime, where everyone talked at once and affection and nonsense ran rampant. And he just loved summers on the north shore of Long Island on Oyster Bay.

What else can you tell me about Cornelius?

He had great interest in the societies to prevent cruelty to children and animals, and he taught a Sunday school mission class.

How did Thee and his father get along, if Cornelius was so dominant?

Fairly well, although they had a difference of opinion when Thee came of age to attend college. Cornelius declared it a waste of time, so Thee went along with his father's notions. After a tour of Europe, he entered the family business.

What happened after you left New York City to return to Georgia?

I missed my Thee. I enjoyed his cheerful nature, and I felt confident in my own deep love. Thee came to visit me again at Bulloch Hall, and we became engaged. When he left, I cried. With my eyes all swollen, I felt dreadful. Everything seemed associated with him. I tried to remember the poetry he quoted during our horseback rides and the books he read. Thee loved to read, and it showed in his letters. I treasure his precious words of devoted love.

Did you marry in Georgia?

Three days before Christmas in 1853, I had my beautiful wedding at Bulloch Hall. Before it started, I felt entirely nervous. I worried Thee would arrive too early, and I worried what could go wrong. But nothing did. As evening fell, my bridesmaids entered in white muslin dresses with full skirts. I descended our curved staircase in a white satin dress with a long veil. In my hands I carried a prayer book that Thee had given me. With small measured steps, I entered the dining room where an altar had been set. Flowers and candlelight gave it the perfect touch. I missed my daddy, although my family surrounded me with love.

Our wedding stood forth as the social event of the season, an exciting time with every imaginable festivity. My mother sold four slaves to pay for it. We had hams and turkeys and cakes of every conceivable kind, and ice cream made with ice hauled from Savannah, two hundred miles away! When the time came for dancing, my brother Dan played the flute, since it was the only music we could engage in because of our strict beliefs. Thee's mother and father were there and it was their first trip south. They couldn't understand some of our customs, but how kind of them to travel so far. Every little thing turned out just right. When it came time to set off for our home in New York, I shed too many tears, but I never regretted leaving with my husband.

Where did you live in New York City?

In a connecting house at 20th and Broadway, right next to Thee's brother Robert. His wife, Lizzie, kept a menagerie of animals, including a monkey named Topsy that she dressed in trousers and brocade shirts with gold studs. I found that amusing.

It must have looked so comical. Did you have difficulty adjusting to your new life?

I adapted well, with rounds of calls, Assembly Balls, and our dinner parties. Thee ordered dozens of yellow roses, put one in his lapel, and always ended our parties with dancing. Even after our children arrived, the parties continued, although I needed to rest for a long time after their births.

Tell me about your children.

Bamie came in 1855. I named her Anna after my sister. Bamie is short for bambina, which is Italian for "baby girl." The poor child had spinal trouble and wore an instrument for four years to strengthen her back. We found a physician who prescribed exercises and gave her a lighter harness so she could lead a more active life and not feel so much pain.

After her birth, it took me years to recover. Thee thought country air would restore me, so he took us to Georgia to visit my family. After he paid his respects, he returned to New York and Bamie and I stayed on. In my letters, I sent him rose petals and all my love. I kept his letters, and I read them so many times that they're tattered to bits and the writing has faded.

Can you quote from any of them? Is that too much to ask?

" . . . darling, you cannot imagine what a wanting feeling I have." That one is my favorite.

"You know how I love you, darling, and what an intense pleasure it would be now to carry you . . ." That one might be too private to continue.

Did he return for you or hire someone?

He returned for us. It was so hard to leave Momma and my sister Anna. A year after I left, they had to give up Bulloch Hall. When they came north to live with us, their arrival made my life complete.

When was Theodore Jr. born?

He came into this world on October 27, 1858, a blond baby in good health. Before he arrived, I worried since Thee was away on business. Momma and I had just finished shopping when I felt unwell. She sent for the family physician, who couldn't come. Bamie went to look for a relative, and the servants dashed everywhere to search for a doctor or midwife. A doctor neighbor came to help, and at a quarter to eight that night, my eight-and-a-half-pound boy arrived. I didn't need chloroform or instruments.

Why do you call him Teedie?

As a toddler, he was beautiful, but at first he looked like a terrapin.

My daughter looked like an old man until she was two, and then she blossomed. I had a challenging birth with her.

I am pleased you recovered. The difficult part for me wasn't having Teedie, but afterwards. All I wanted to do was lie alone in my bedroom with the shades drawn. My sadness lingered for months. Elliott was born in 1860. What a pretty baby. He calls me his Sweet Little Dresden China Mother. A year after Ellie, my sensitive Conie arrived.

Thee and I loved our children deeply, with our hearts and with gifts of books and toys. My Br'er Rabbit stories and my mimicking accents were in high demand, and my sister Anna and I told stories from our childhood that the children called slave tales.

Where did they go to school?

They spent their time together, tutored in our home. Anna

taught them art and literature in exchange for Thee's hospitality. For history, math, and science, they had a separate tutor, and Thee and I taught them languages. I could go on and on about all four of my children, but I will return to Teedie.

Our Teedie had his own way about him and had many solitary pursuits, yet he was a most affectionate and endearing little creature. He enjoyed reading and wrote long curious letters to me when I visited in Georgia. He wrote that he loved my long letters and then proceeded to tell me about bugs and birds.

Who fostered his appreciation for nature?

Thee and I loved dogwoods and azaleas and the music of the wren and thrush, and we encouraged Teedie to roam through the woods to collect rocks, bugs, leaves, and nests. He loved taxidermy and bird identification and drew accurate pictures of wildlife during summers at our country home. Thee taught the children to ride and swim at an early age, so every spring my babies had a wild eagerness to go. What a sad group they became when I dragged them back to town in late fall.

Did you prefer the town or the country?

I had pleasant times both places with my painting and sculpture, and I filled our houses with fine furniture and porcelain. In the spring, I surrounded myself with precious violets. Both summer and winter, I dressed in silks and white muslin. Thee liked me in white, and it makes me feel clean. Each day I take two baths, one for cleaning and one for rinsing. I have such delicate health that my baths are a necessary part of my life.

What else did you do at your homes?

Art and socializing took precedence over meals since I think the help should have a say in what they serve. After our noon meal and a rest, I received guests for lively conversations.

Mornings could be complicated. Some days I had difficulty getting out of bed. When the children bounded into my room, I didn't know how to greet them or how to greet the day. Before I was diagnosed with attacks of neurasthenia, Thee said I had melancholy one day and gaiety another. He encouraged me to be happy, and I did try. Have you experienced that feeling? Wanting to fade into the bed?

I seem to have the opposite. I used to feel as if I couldn't slow down. Did your melancholy cause a problem for you and Theodore?

My darling Thee accepted me and all my ways. He was an understanding man and few problems existed between us. One that did exist didn't have to do with my emotional state, but rather the War Between the States. It's beyond grim to have family and friends on two different sides.

I have family in Alabama. A person feels divided when a loved one has dissimilar views.

It helps to know other families suffered in the same way. My brothers fought for the Confederacy, while Thee's parents were abolitionists. Dinners at their home were a trial for me, and uncomfortable silences and dissimilar beliefs meant indigestion during our Sunday waffle lunches with them. In my own home, when we had strongly Northern dinner guests, I stayed upstairs and ate with the children in the nursery rather than defend my Southern sympathies.

You believed strongly in the South?

During the war, on the days when Thee left on business trips, my mother and sister and I unfurled our Confederate flag, rolled bandages, and packed supplies. We secretly sent medicine, clothing and money to our friends in the South. During our picnic lunches in Central Park, we passed relief packages on to sympathizers. The packages got shipped through Confederate agents in North Carolina to the Bahamas, and blockade runners took them to Georgia. Our soldiers needed our help.

I never knew such a thing existed. Did Theodore fight in the war?

I could not bear the thought of Thee being killed by or killing my Confederate brothers, so I begged him not to fight. Against his own judgment, he agreed. When he paid a substitute to shoulder a musket in his place, it pained him. It was common among our friends, but he felt he should have served. I say he did his duty when he gave time to charitable causes. He taught a Sunday school mission class like his daddy before him, and he did a lot of relief work. For months during the war, he worked with President Lincoln's secretary, Mr. Hay, to persuade the president to pass a law that sent an allotment of soldiers' pay home to their families. He visited troops in the worst kind of weather and gave talks to convince them to join the plan. The children called him "Greatheart."

Did he enjoy Washington?

Yes, he did. At dinners with Mr. Lincoln, he became a favorite of his wife. She is of Southern background. Mrs. Lincoln found Thee charming, so she asked him to accompany her on afternoon carriage rides in the countryside. One day he escorted her to town to give her advice on which bonnet suited her in the most becoming manner. Thee told me everything, every moment he spent with Mrs. Lincoln, and I accepted his account. I knew too well my husband's proper manners and his fondness for the President. And his fondness for me.

How did you both deal with the President's death?

When Thee learned the President had been shot, he drew a deep breath and the color washed right out of him. As we watched the funeral procession from our window, we kept our arms around each other and said blessings for our untroubled lives. I say untroubled, even though every family has its difficulties.

Can you be more specific please?

Thee spent a lot of time in Washington after Conie was born, and Teedie was a handful. He had to be watched every minute, and his energy taxed my delicate health. I just could not join Thee in Washington.

Changing moods can be so trying.

Some days I had happiness and others I felt cut off from life. I tried so many cures, and one summer the doctors gave me ether. When I had my melancholy, Thee cared for me. He said he thought of me as one of his little babies and implored me not to become a strong-minded woman. That brought me to laughter and in turn, I called him my loving tyrant. Bamie helped enormously with the younger children, which eased my mind. Teedie called Bamie a little feminine Atlas.

When I felt gay, I had parties at both our homes. I tried to instill Southern hospitality in the North, and I achieved more success when we moved uptown near Central Park.

Thee said I wore him out with my gaiety. I made conversation come alive, and I loved to quote Dickens and Shakespeare.

Did you take the children on outings?

I insisted they attend the theater and galleries, which Bamie especially enjoyed. Not many people feel this way, but I believe children should be allowed to mingle with adults. When Teedie came of teen age, we hosted delightful Friday evening dances for his friends, and when my husband was home, we attended.

Thee was a loving father. On the children's birthdays, he gave them his attention for the entire afternoon to do whatever that child wished. At our country home, Thee lined the children up on their stomachs on our raised deck and then stood below and fed them. Before every breakfast, Thee read morning prayers aloud, and in the evening he read poetry.

My children have such different personalities. My oldest is full of energy and my youngest takes life easy. How are your children different?

Ellie has charm, with a strong and handsome countenance. Conie often talks with enthusiasm and commands everyone's attention with her sense of fun. Other days, she has volatile outbursts and tears. Bamie has a sunny disposition and a mother-hen attitude. Teedie has a huge imagination and craves knowledge like other boys crave food.

When he was young, Teedie had problems with poor eyesight until he got glasses and he had terrible asthma. When he suffered horrible headaches and had trouble sleeping, Thee and I became overprotective and nervous. Six or seven times a night, I got up with Teedie and tried to relieve his anguish with chivalry and adventure stories. He used his illness to keep me up late sometimes, not that I minded. On the bad nights, he gasped, choked, and wheezed and then trembled and sweated until he was soaked. Thee walked up and down the hall with Teedie in his arms. We tried everything the doctors suggested: black coffee, tobacco, ipecac, mustard plasters, and hard massages. Thee put Teedie in our horse-drawn carriage and drove through the dark streets of New York City for hours in hopes the fresh air would help him breathe. As he grew, Teedie experienced some relief.

I'm happy to hear that. My children's breathing problems lessened as they grew older.

Thank goodness they had a respite.

Did your children have close relationships with other family members or friends?

We considered Edith Carow a part of our family. She was Conie's close friend, and she shared an interest in books with Teedie. Edi and her parents lived with her father's older sister in a house behind Thee's parents. Later, Edi went to Miss Comstock's school, but early on, my sister Anna included her when she tutored the children. After history lessons, Anna told stories. I believe she was even better at it than I am.

How did your mother deal with the end of the war?

When Sherman's men burned and looted Bullock Hall, she lost her will to live. Then she passed on. Without her, I felt empty. Events happened and I wanted to tell her. I shared my life with her and suddenly, no more. The children missed her almost as much as I did.

Losing a mother is devastating. When my mother died, I moaned until my daughter pleaded with me to stop. How did you cope with her death?

I thought about the cycle of life and about my children. I wanted to be strong for them and I needed a diversion for my mind, so I asked Thee to take us abroad on a tour of Europe. I wanted to see my brothers, James and Irvine, who were granted amnesty after the war and lived proudly in exile in England. Jimmy had been a Confederate navy agent, and he commissioned the war vessel CSS *Alabama*. In just two months in 1862, the *Alabama* burned and sank twenty Union ships with supplies for the Yankees. Jimmy chose Liverpool because of his business associates, and the *Alabama* warship had been built there. Irvine had been a midshipman and fired the last gun in the fight with the *Kearsarge*.

Thee thought a trip would benefit Teedie's asthma, and he wanted the children to learn about the world. Teedie couldn't understand where we were going or why, so he cried in the carriage all the way to the dock. We began our yearlong grand tour.

In Liverpool I had a wonderful ten-day reunion with Jimmy. My children loved their Southern cousins, but they weren't accustomed to all that kissing. After England, we toured some more and then sought out higher elevations to help Teedie's breathing. At night, I told stories and delicately rubbed his back. During the day, the children played outside while Teedie read. When they came indoors, Teedie repeated my stories. Slowly he regained his ability to breathe and could join in their outdoor fun. With longer and longer hikes, his stamina improved.

The mild weather during our two months in southern Italy helped his breathing the most. Then it was on to Rome for the holidays. At 6:00 a.m. Christmas morning, Thee and I dressed in beautiful clothes for the children's arrival in our room. The glorious day began with stockings and presents.

At the end of our trip, we said a tearful goodbye to Bamie, who stayed in France for a year at an English finishing school known for its liberal arts education. I didn't want to part from her, but another fortnight with my family in England cheered me. Teedie looked forward to going home.

So hikes and outdoor activities helped Teddy?

The entire trip taught us the importance of exercise for Teedie. We never worried about Ellie, with his strength and agility, but Teedie had a smaller stature. He must have been about eleven when we started his visits to a gymnasium operated by John Wood. Thee wanted Mr. Wood to expand Teedie's chest, improve his breathing, and make him stronger. Teedie worked hard with weights and made such progress that Thee hired Mr. Wood to set up a private gymnasium on our second-floor, out-of-doors piazza. We had swings, bars, and seesaws. The boys adored it, and Teedie never stopped exercising after that. He boxed and lifted weights long into the night.

In the country, Teedie rode, swam, hiked, and rowed, although he didn't care for sailing. Exercise helped him embrace fear and it stimulated taking the lead in life rather than hiding back. We encouraged physical and mental activities to promote positive feelings in all our children.

My son had a rebellious stage when he was thirteen. Did Teddy go through changes?

After he learned to use his double-barreled shotgun, he became an excellent hunter. He collected specimens and donated the skull of a red squirrel, a turtle shell, and four bird's eggs to the American Museum of Natural History, which, along with the Metropolitan Museum of Art, was founded with my husband's help. I had to hold my shawl over my nose, since every day he reeked of arsenic from his work with animals. His laugh became a sharp, ungreased squeak that almost crushed the drum of my ear.

You continued to live in New York City, correct?

Yes, but our house felt too small and the area became commercial, so construction began on our new home on West 57th Street, just off Fifth Avenue. To ease the move, we embarked on another European tour. We visited my family in England and then traveled on to Germany. Then came a two month cruise up the Nile, with each of us in staterooms on a chartered houseboat. I loved the air on the deck. On that trip we met Ralph Waldo Emerson—such an interesting man—and his daughter, Ellen.

After the Nile, we visited the Holy Land and North Africa and studied the culture, language, and arts. Teedie stared in awe at the pyramids in Egypt. The Arab women's life stories fascinated me, and I drew great strength from Bethlehem. In every country, Teedie shot, collected and prepared his bird specimens. Every morning, the children had two hours of lessons and Bamie helped with French.

None of the children knew German, so Thee sent Teedie, Ellie, and Conie to live with German families in Dresden to learn the language. We put Conie in a different home from the boys so they wouldn't speak English, but Conie got so upset we had to let her return to them.

Bamie and I went off to Carlsbad to take the cure with mineral springs and sulfur baths, and we shopped for fur-

nishings for our new home. When I received news of Teedie's awful time with headaches and wheezing, I worried, but
then he settled and had a wonderful experience. Suddenly,
we learned Teedie had the mumps.

How frightening!

I raced to his side. Fraulein Anna, who was the German
mother where the children stayed, suggested I needn't be
anxious about him. She predicted that one day he would be
a great professor or even the president of the United States.
Her good wishes didn't lessen my concern one bit. I bundled
him off to the Swiss Alps, where he got better and then worse
again. Finally he felt well enough to return to New York City
and our new home.

When summer came, we moved to a new house in Oyster
Bay named Tranquility, with white columns and a wide ve-
randa that reminded me of Bulloch Hall. Bamie, with her ca-
pable mind, managed both houses. She encouraged the boys
with their ambitions and helped me handle the money since
I had headaches and my horror. It is a delicate subject, intestinal trouble. My entire disposition became affected. I had
trouble with appointments, since by the time I felt ready, it
was too late to go. I became terribly concerned with cleanliness and insisted that clean sheets be placed on the furniture.

Ellie had troubles of his own with concentration, head
pains and nosebleeds. The doctor prescribed morphine and
other painkilling drugs, but they couldn't find the problem.
At night he had fears, and he couldn't sleep alone. He thought
a change would help, so he approached his father and asked
to attend boarding school in New Hampshire with a friend.
Thee agreed, but first sent him out West to Fort McKavett to

rough it for a few months. What an adventure, to camp and work on the prairie.

Did Teddy go with him?

Teedie stayed home and studied Latin, Greek, and math with a tutor in order to be ready for the entrance examinations for college. That was the year Teedie fell on his head while skating at Central Park and got knocked senseless. For hours I worried myself sick, but he recovered quite nicely. In September of 1876, he left home to attend Harvard College.

All of us wrote long letters. I told him to keep up with his studies and asked about his health and his schedule. Thee stated his anticipation in passing over his responsibilities as soon as Teedie's shoulders were ready to bear them. Teedie wrote of literary coffee parties in his room that featured the work of Edgar Allan Poe. On his eighteenth birthday, Teedie wrote that because of his family, he never spent an unhappy day unless by his own fault. He kept a picture of me on his mantle. What a sweet boy. All my children are sweet.

Then tragedy struck. Oh my, can I make my way through it? When Teedie was a sophomore in college, my beloved Thee collapsed with terrible intestinal pains. He was only forty-six. The doctor said it was acute peritonitis. By the time Teedie came home from college for Christmas, Thee had improved some. I tried to hide my fright. We nursed Thee with tender devotion and wished we could take away his agony.

On February 9, 1878 my beloved Thee passed on to heaven. I cried alone in my room. Even now, a flush of pain travels through me whenever I think of his suffering. Teedie traveled home quickly but arrived too late to say goodbye. He felt overcome, but I told all my children that their daddy was safe in the arms of Jesus, and I tried to be strong for them. The flags in New York City were lowered to half-mast.

What an honor.

Teedie called his father the best man he ever knew, a man who combined strength and courage with gentleness, tenderness and unselfishness. With the support of my children I got through that unbearable time, although I never recovered the strength of body and will I had with Thee beside me. My sadness lifted a bit when my children found love.

Love makes everyone hopeful. When did Teddy find love?

The summer after Thee passed on, Teedie came home to Oyster Bay and continued his friendship with his childhood friend Edi. When they quarreled and had a falling out, Teedie's heart opened to another. This is their story.

Teedie had a friend named Dick Saltonstall. His family lived in the Chestnut Hill part of Boston. During a weekend stay with them, Teedie met their cousin, Alice Hathaway Lee, a girl with gray-blue eyes, honey hair, and a willowy figure. She wasn't as deep intellectually as Teedie, but he gloried in her and called her Sunshine. Alice's father had a banking and investment firm.

At first, Alice didn't know what to make of Teedie, with his studious nature, thick glasses, and his faint smell of formaldehyde, but that winter they skated and went sleighing and read to each other. Teedie had luncheons in his college room for Alice and her mother, and on Class Day in June, Teedie proposed marriage. Alice refused him, but he continued to ask. My stalwart boy wouldn't give up, so I invited Mr. and Mrs. Lee to New York to visit. They came with Alice and

Dick's sister, Rose. I liked Alice, who reminded me a little of myself, with her flirtatious manner and all-white clothes. I liked her even more when she called Teedie Thee. In private she called him Teddykins. To return the kind favor of their visit, Bamie and Conie called on the Lee and Saltonstall families, who gave dinners in their honor.

Teedie had a bit of a setback when Alice paid him little mind at her coming out party, so we were surprised when Alice, Rose, and Dick arrived in New York City to spend a week with us. On New Year's Day, Ellie had a splendid luncheon, and Teedie and Alice danced.

In January of Teedie's senior year at Harvard, Alice accepted his proposal and he ordered an engagement ring. I felt so happy for them. In a letter Alice wrote me, she said she loved Teedie deeply. A small problem occurred, a bit of a row about the wedding date. The Lees thought Alice too young to be married the following autumn, so my darling Bamie came to the rescue and suggested the newlyweds live with us for their first winter. The Lees agreed to that arrangement.

I imagine Alice appreciated your introductions to New York society.

I had teas, parties and at homes not only for Alice, but to find a match for Bamie. James Roosevelt, a member of the Hudson River branch of the family, had been newly widowed, but Bamie declined since he was as old as her father. Then Bamie turned out to be the matchmaker when she invited James and the tall and stately Sara Delano to dinner. James was immediately smitten with Sara, who told Bamie the visit was one of the most important events of her life. Sara visited James at his estate at Hyde Park, and they later married.

I love matchmaking. Tell me about Teddy's wedding.

First, Ellie and Teedie took one last trip together out West. Ellie felt much stronger, so he outshot Teedie, and that caused banter. Brothers like competition. They loved the frontier and had a marvelous time, except when a snake bit Teedie. They told me well after the fact.

On Teedie's twenty-second birthday, he and Alice married, with Ellie as best man and Conie a bridesmaid. It was a late October Indian summer day and guests crowded the Unitarian Church in Brookline. We returned to the house for a champagne toast, and the young people danced the soles off their shoes.

They had no official honeymoon, just quiet time at Oyster Bay, where Bamie had stocked the larder. Teedie wrote that he wished their honeymoon could last forever. They rode, walked, played tennis, and read aloud to each other. They only stayed a fortnight because law school was about to start.

When they returned, they moved to our third floor. Teedie took Thee's place at our family charities, the Orthopedic Hospital and the New York Infant Asylum. Alice accompanied me on drives, shopped with Conie, and made social calls.

What about Conie and romance?

Conie married a well-to-do, young Scotsman, Douglas Robinson, a large man with a large voice. Ellie set off on an around-the-world adventure, but he wrote and said he'd return and always care for me. When he came back after a year, he brought me a lion-skin trophy.

Did Teddy and Alice ever take an official honeymoon?

At the end of a term at law school, Teedie took her on a four-month honeymoon to Europe. It started badly, with Alice seasick the entire voyage, but they had a wonderful time after they arrived. They went to Ireland, visited my family in Liverpool, and traveled on to London and Paris. From Switzerland, Alice wrote me a pretty letter while Teedie scaled the Matterhorn.

What precipitated Teddy's interest in politics?

After they returned home, Teedie acquainted himself with the political interests of our district and decided not to be an attorney.

Did they continue to live with you?

Teedie, Alice, Conie, Douglas, and I took a house in the Catskills for a wonderful vacation, and then he and Alice moved to their own home, a small brownstone not too far from me. Teedie bought more land, for a total of 155 acres at the top of a rise, and in his mind he designed the house he wanted for Alice. He took another trip out West and bought land in South Dakota to partner in a cattle business with some other men.

Did Ellie find romance?

He wed a beautiful nineteen-year-old debutante with big, blue eyes, Anna Rebecca Hall. Her family's charming country home lies along the Hudson River. Anna's father thinks so many things are sinful, but we believe Anna's upbringing and stability help Ellie. The papers called their wedding a brilliant social event. The bride looked every bit a queen, and her bridesmaids were worthy of her. Teedie acted as Ellie's best man. After their marriage, Ellie gave Anna a small coupe automobile to drive to social engagements. Women driving—now that is a novelty—but Anna is adventurous.

What do you see when you look back at your life?

I see a richness of love and family. Teedie and Alice moved back to my home so she will be more comfortable when their child is born. I love my children close by. They help ease the pain from the loss of Momma and Thee. Who would have known I would be the strong one? The one left when others have gone to heaven?

I hope I haven't pressured you in any way or increased your sorrow.

You have been kind. I appreciate the skill with which you ask delicate questions. As women, we are stronger than we know or believe. Now, you give my best to your family in Alabama.

INTERVIEW WITH BAMIE ROOSEVELT ON THE DEATH OF HER MOTHER

Teedie is too distraught to be interviewed, so I will speak on his behalf. While working in Albany, he received a telegram that his daughter had been born. As his fellow assemblymen congratulated him, he received a second telegram to come home immediately. He arrived at 11:30 that night and found poor Momma dying of typhoid fever and Alice comatose from kidney failure. He held Alice in his arms, but she barely knew of his presence. He left her only to see Momma for her final moments. Our Sweet Motherlings died at 3:00 a.m. Alice died the next afternoon.

9

Interview with Louisa Van Velsor Whitman

MOTHER OF WALT WHITMAN,
POET, BORN MAY 31, 1819

The best part of every man is his mother.
—Walt Whitman

JAN HELEN MCGEE

I read Walt's *Leaves of Grass*. His poems made me contemplate love. How did you feel about his book?

LOUISA WHITMAN

I didn't understand most of it at first. George sat down with me to help, but it seemed like another world, not one we knew.

JAN HELEN MCGEE

George?

LOUISA WHITMAN

That's my son who inspects pipe. He cares more for pipes than poems. At first, I told George that Longfellow's *The Song of Hiawatha* and Walt's *Leaves of Grass* seemed pretty much the same muddle as the other, so if *Hiawatha* meant poetry, then *Leaves* did. Do not misunderstand me, my whole self believes in Walt.

When I found poems in *Leaves of Grass* that I liked, I had to read them several times to comprehend them. I thought my mind wasn't working correctly.

I try to see Walt's poems as other people do, and each night before bed, I read a little bit of *Drum-Taps*. All those poor boys who suffered in the Civil War.

Did any of your other family members read *Leaves of Grass*?

My husband Walter never had the chance to read it, but he didn't care for poetry, so I don't think he would have liked it. My daughter Hannah boasted she was the only family member who liked it.

"Walt's poetry is like the saying he has. 'Everything important is personal,'" Han said.

I keep my favorite, "Whispers of Heavenly Death," at my bedside. I enjoy the calming way it looks at death. A friend wanted to lend it, but I couldn't let it go out of my hands. It reads like the Bible.

Did you hear the negative comments about Walt's poems?

That attitude affected Walt the most. When he had an appointment in the Indian Bureau of the Interior Department, they found out he authored *Leaves of Grass* and discharged him for obscene poetry. He moved to a clerkship in the Attorney General's office where the men didn't mind what he wrote.

I was once discharged from a school for my outspoken beliefs.

It's important to state your opinions, and it takes fortitude to find your own path in life.

I appreciate your views. How did Walt do his writing?

He did it the same way in his newspapers and his verse. He wrote on a few sheets of good white paper, then folded and fastened them with a pin or two. He loved words, the shape and sound of them, and he had perfect tone and a sensitive ear. At home, on the beach, and from the top of the omnibuses, he recited Shakespeare and Homer verses. He loved Italian opera and hoped he'd find a human voice with perfect tone and delivery. The opera helped him write verse since music is close to poetry.

Did he sing?

In public, no, but everywhere alone, he sang in an undertone. He sang in the bath, and that meant quite a bit of singing. Walt takes more baths than anyone. He's not orderly, but he loves to be clean. When the season was right, he swam, and when the cold came on, he visited the baths. After his baths, he took care in his dressing and sang again.

How did he dress?

When he walked the streets, others took notice, since he changed with the fashion of the time. He was fond of a gray frock coat with a boutonniere and his polished cane. When he went out, I looked for his wavy, auburn hair to shine in the sun before he stopped to don his high black hat. Next, he wore only black, and I remember a dark, wine-colored suit I admired. Now he wears looser clothing like a workingman. Whatever he wore, his manner stayed shy and slow moving. Walt cannot be hurried.

Was he vain?

Don't think Walt only cared for himself. The opposite is true. He cared for others' plights. He helped stop the flogging of seaman, helped improve mental institutions and prisons, and worked to raise wages for artisans, mechanics, and sewing women.

Now come settle with me by the fire. I put a blanket up at the window to keep out the wind and bustle of the city.

Thank you. It's cold, yet I feel comfortable.

Here's an extra quilt if you need it. One's sufficient for me since I don't feel the cold today. We all have our spells of good and bad. Some days I'm lame in one of my knees, but two things help: cold weather and bathing my limbs in cold water.

The price of ice is very high.

It is. Now don't look at my old sleep shoe. I have a troublesome bunion on my foot. I should stop with my complaints and be cheerful, which Walt reminds me of so often.

"Mother, you put the worst construction on it," he says.

What's your daily routine?

I get up early a little before daylight, make a fire, sweep out, and get some coffee, bread and butter. Butter is monstrous dear, ain't it?

Butter is too dear for use in all my meals.

I love it so. After I finish eating, I don't rest content until I write to my children. Walt is the most regular with his letters. After I write, I bake, but not when I have the distress in my head or when the pain in my legs and the rheumatism keep me from sleep. A friend said put a potato in each pocket and wear them until they're hard, and then the rheumatics will go in the potato. I told her I'd carry half a dozen if it did me any good. Would you like a fresh egg and bread and butter?

No thank you. I'm content. Please tell me about Walt's and your early years. Weave his tale of words.

The love he has for language came from his ancestors, men of fire and women like water. Sea tales, militia adventures, and the women who directed slaves formed pictures for his imagination. I don't know that I helped in any way. Walt is the special one. I ain't. I live one day at a time by the lessons of the Quakers, with respect and love for the individual, in whom God moves and speaks. I learned this from my Mammy, who told me not to press my demands and to quietly wait for what God gives me. And God gave me a rich life and a son full of sweet words.

Everything I have a little of, he has a lot. Like strength, storytelling, and feelings instead of facts. I can't spell and my writing is uncertain. What I do best is keep peace in the family, which is true for most mothers. I do it through stories, and I mime and impersonate. Mammy and her father passed the tales down to me and I spun them for Walt. He added his feelings and made his verse.

As far back as I remember, the women in my family used stories to keep our minds off chores that never ended. We made clothing and household items, we harvested and preserved vegetables for winter, and we made bread and cider for mealtimes. We laughed and rolled out tales and mimicked anything we could to try to best each other. I held my ground.

Did your daughters join you?

Of all my children, Walt loved the kitchen the most. When the others played and caused mischief, he sat and listened to the women talk. He only spoke up to tell us what story he wanted to hear again and again. He liked my mother's tales the most, with their Dutch and Welsh influence.

I would love to hear some of the stories. Tell me about her.

Naomi Williams, called Amy, with a round face and blue eyes like mine. Mammy had a gentle and sunny spirit, with no unkind words for anyone. I'm similar in temperament, though I'm not good at holding my tongue. Mammy had seven sisters and one brother, and her mother was Mary. People back then called my grandmother Mary shiftless, but I don't abide by that. Her family liked to roam, so she had it in her nature.

Mammy's father was John, agreeable and well-liked he was. Mammy told story after story about him. Then she thought about his sad fate and a cloud came over her face. Her father and brother, lost at sea.

How scary. I would never stop wondering what happened.

Mammy hoped for a return that never came. She imagined a death by drowning or worse. She was burdened by grief, with no brother or father and a mother who couldn't stay home. It was Mammy's seven sisters that saved her. She told me that my father, Cornelius, took the place of her own father.

When she met Pappa, he seemed bigger than life. His father was a weaver and he descended from an English baron. Pappa had a booming voice, a ruddy face, a big appetite, and an open heart.

What was his job?

Early on, he was a sea captain and part-owner of a ship that conducted West Indies trade. Pappa loved to tell adventure stories of sea fights and tragedies, British ships, and John Paul Jones. I don't know how many were true, since a fine line existed between those he witnessed and the tales told to him. I do know his sea tales helped Mammy remember her lost father.

When Pappa tired of the sea, he traded and bred horses of blooded stock. Everyone called him "the Major." He raised and bred sheep and cattle, cultivated peach trees, and grew carrots, turnips, oats, wheat, and barley. He had the energy of a young man and for over forty years he drove a stage and market wagon filled with produce to the Brooklyn ferry, a distance of forty miles. When he had animals ready to be sold, he tied them to the back of the wagon and set out like a caravan. I loved the horses he bred, and so did Walt. When I was younger, I rode daily and others considered me a daring rider since I had no fear. On Saturdays, when Walt grew old enough, he rode until he tired. We loved the peacefulness of riding, with birdcalls and nature's bloom.

I love to ride a horse and sing.

You are like Walt, singing all the time. I did my riding at my childhood home in Cold Spring Harbor, in the center part of Long Island. I remember the first time I got on a horse alone, right at the turn of the century. I was about five. We had all those horses, so I had freedom and independence that other young girls did not. My lack of restrictions became part of me, and my liberty planted itself in Walt's writing.

When were you born?

September 22nd of 1795.

Anything else you remember from when you were young?

As I moved out of girlhood, I got compliments about my figure, though I cared more about the workings of my mind. I had a gift of strangely knowing things before they happened, and I had dreams of those I loved. I remember clearly the morning a mystical Indian woman visited us. Over and over to Walt, Mammy spoke about the woman's beauty, purity, and visions. He turned that story into a poem he calls *The Sleepers*.

What led you to choose your husband, Walter?

There was so much talk in my childhood, so I sought a man of reserve. When I met Walter, his quiet nature and intense eyes drew me in. After we married, I felt the heat of his quick temper when he took a drink, though I feared more for the children than for myself. He acted so glum. Without the drink, Walter loved children and cattle. I admired his open mind and his belief in the rights of the workingman.

And your husband's family?

His great-grandfather exchanged his grains for West Indies sugar and rum. After he died, he left five hundred acres to Walter's grandfather. His grandmother was a big woman who smoked, chewed, swore, and used opium like so many women at that time, and she worked hard. She split wood and heaved it to the house slaves, who stacked it and carried some into the house. She rode up and down the fields and directed the slaves who tilled the land. Their land passed to my husband's father, a militiaman during the Revolutionary War.

And Walter's mother?

Hannah taught school and had a real lively way about her. She had an attractive countenance until the day she passed to the Lord. Her father was a patriot, and Walt loved her stories of how the British camped and foraged, back at the time when they held Long Island. Poor Hannah ended up an orphan, so her aunt raised her on a large farm. She taught Hannah how to care for a home and the sixteen slaves on her property.

When was your husband Walter born?

Bastille Day, July 14, 1789. When he turned fifteen, he hired out to a cousin for woodworking and carpentry in New York City. At eighteen, Walter returned to West Hills to chop wood and build houses. In the evenings, he whittled. Too often he complained about the idle rich, but he believed in the rights of all people and universal education, and he spoke his mind.

When Walter's father died, his children sold most of the land. On some leftover acreage, Walter took up farming. His plans included taking a wife, so he built a sturdy and simple house.

Did you live nearby?

A few miles away, in a rambling house with a great barn and pens full of cattle and horses. Walter drove over the narrow road to court me and soon grew fond of my pies and blue eyes. I'm not one to reach out to strangers, so his attention pleased me. We sat under shade trees and spoke little. Our shared belief in the rights of others brought us closer as we settled into each other's company. My family consented and the date was agreed upon.

When did you marry?

I was twenty-one. It was a June day with frost in the morning. By noon the sun sparkled off the grass like twinkling fairies. After the wedding and a little party, we rode to Walter's house. I sat down under his great oak tree and stared at his apple orchard and decided I could be happy there. I started my chores and began my new life.

And you had children.

My first, Jesse, named after Walter's father, came easy in March of 1818. Like other farm families, a man's first son is important, so Walter and Jesse had a steady bond. My son Walt was born on the last day of May in 1819. Walter Whitman Jr., with hair black as tar and eyes a bluish kind of gray.

Who did he look like?

He had the ruddy complexion of his father, but he looked like me and my Mammy's family. From the start, we shared a sensitivity. I suffer from an abundance of emotion, and his mind is a bubbling pot of feelings with a stew of gathering senses.

My next baby—Mary, after my grandmother—was born in February of 1821. She's a beautiful girl and has full awareness of her appeal. Two years later, I had Hannah, named for my husband's mother. Her fair skin and delicate movements caused Walt to call her his blossom.

Does Walt have his faults?

I can say that some days find him intense and strange. As a child, he took to himself to observe the world, and other times he went off with his older brother, Jesse, to gather seagull eggs, fish for eels through the frozen ice on the bay, or walk to the highest point on the island. Walt loved flowers and newborn animals, the still fish in ponds and the movement of plants in water. My stern husband couldn't understand the boy, but to me, he felt like my skin.

The problem with Walter and Walt is they had opposite ways. Walt didn't like physical work and had a dreamy side, while Walter spoke little and had outbursts of anger. Walter's physical work eased that anger, but he decided farming was too dependent on the weather. Not long after Hannah arrived, Walter sold our house and moved us to Brooklyn, since the number of stores and houses went from fifty to over one hundred fifty in one year. Walter's friends claimed he could find work with no trouble.

Did you like it there?

I liked the activity, the people to observe. Walt loved the East River. The ferry became his favorite, since the gatekeeper allowed him to climb aboard the horse team boats to ride to New York City and back. Once a week, Pappa came into town with his produce and animals, and we visited. Walt loved to hear those sea tales over and over, and Pappa could hardly break away from Walt when it came time to warm himself at the tavern and talk with other drivers.

In summertime, Walt waited outside the tavern and then rode along back to the country to live with his grandmother. He loved the shore, where the water meets the land, and he loved my Mammy. In return, Mammy held a sweet fondness for him. When she passed on in '26, I believe it hit Walt even harder than the blow I suffered. He claimed her death became his greatest sorrow. I know it was one of mine. Pappa lived on until he was eighty, so we had more of him.

How long did Walt stay with your parents?

We moved six times in ten years, so when summer ended and Walt returned home, it often meant a new location. The moves made me suffer anxious thoughts, but our family grew closer with the changes. Every move had a pattern: the purchase of a lot, then Walter built a house, and we lived there until it sold. Some of the houses he lost to creditors, since Walter had a trusting nature and swindlers preyed on his innocence.

"It is some comfort to a man if he must be an ass anyhow, to be his own kind of ass," Walter said.

He tried his best, and even in hard times he made sure we had necessities. Only the drink inflamed a pessimistic attitude.

"Keep a good heart; the worst is to come," he warned. His anger tightened my stomach.

You had more children?

I had Andrew Jackson in 1827 and George Washington in 1829. Walter liked heroes of the Revolution and the War of 1812, so he chose their names.

I want to tell you something quickly. I don't like to speak of it, and I don't know how to do it without tears. Before Andrew, in 1825, I lost a little baby boy who was not even half a year old. From the first he was sickly. We never even gave him a name or a christening. I wept and wept, then went on with my work. Now I will dab my eyes and recover.

I am so sorry for your loss. To relieve your burdens, did you ever take time away?

Later in life, I took a bit of rest when Walt provided trips to Saratoga and Newport. The children still at home loved the change. I liked those trips, since staying home meant I had to face my struggles. At home, to escape, I lost myself in cakes and pies. Walt appreciates my cooking so. He even talks of writing a cookbook to include my taste in pickling recipes. All my children claimed I was a good cook, that is, in between their fussing. I tried to hold the peace but they never let up. Now Walt, he acted different from my other children.

How so?

I remember one day when Walt was six years old. We waited with a group of people to see General Lafayette, the French hero of the American Revolution. The General picked Walt out of all the children in the crowd, lifted him, and carried him on his shoulder for quite a ways. The General sensed Walt's good nature. Walt never forgot it.

And I told you, Walt was my only child who sat and talked to me in the kitchen as I worked. When he went out, he loved lectures, libraries, and museums, and he chose his own path without following anyone else. Only a few of my prayers had to be for him. I prayed more for my other children to find strength and a way of their own.

What church did you attend?

Some days I prayed with the Baptists, but I had no set church. When Walt was nine, he attended Sunday school at an Episcopalian church. He didn't stay long, since they had no music. My husband never attended church, but he had his own strong beliefs, and he liked to argue. One of his beliefs came from the circuit rider and Quaker leader Elias Hicks. Mr. Hicks preached openly about human truth and private ecstasy.

My husband didn't read much, only his subscription to the *Free Enquirer*, a Wednesday revolutionary paper with articles about power and passion. He liked to read about the rights of the workingman. He hated slavery, which was legal in New York until Walt was eight, and he taught Walt to value democracy and think for himself. I taught Walt to have respect and to honor women in every way.

"They are not one jot less than you," I told him.

You have an open mind and solid opinions. Was Walt any different at home than at school?

At home, he spoke freely. In school, he stayed quiet and serious with no trouble. He attended the only public school, which had plenty of books but never enough for Walt.

When he turned eleven he needed money, so he ran errands for two attorneys he met at church. After he proved himself as an office boy, they helped him with handwriting and composition and gave him a subscription to a circulating library. Out of all my children, only Walt and Han read. Books fly through their fingers.

What other jobs did he have?

After the attorneys, Walt helped a physician. After that, he learned the printing trade as a journeyman for the *Long Island Patriot*. The job suited Walt, but all that ink and dirt troubled him. He wasn't legally bound, but he stayed with the apprentices at the typesetter's house next door to the shop. I missed him.

Did he care for sport?

Very little. Instead, he enjoyed what he called "first-rate aquatic loafing," a float on his back. That gave him time to think, compose his verse, and plan edits for his writings. After his floats, he did as he pleased. Some days he arrived late to be with us, and some days he left as dinner got served.

I have more children to tell you about. In 1833, Thomas Jefferson was born, fat and rosy-cheeked. You know that's a good sign with babies. Jeffy thrived, but I had an illness that started after his birth and worsened in the winter. I don't know if my nerves affected me, or if all those babies took a toll. My habits changed. Baking meant nothing, and I couldn't keep the house clean. Walter decided country air would improve me, so we left Brooklyn and moved back to Long Island, not far from my father.

Was your father alone then?

After Mammy passed on, Pappa quickly married another. Walter claimed the woman wasn't a good investment. I tried not to judge, though I never felt close to her. No one can take the place of a mother. Walt was fifteen, so he stayed behind and boarded with a family when we moved. He had his own interests, the theatre and the opera, with free tickets through newspaper offices where he worked. Walt loved oratory and singing.

"Wisdom can be conveyed not only through words but through the musical tones in the mouths of singers," he told me time and again.

Walt liked to take Jeffy to the opera. Around the house, he whistled and sang, and in the afternoons he read. I remember a book of mine he read until it almost turned to dust. *Consuelo* by George Sand. The way his brain worked seemed so different from my other children.

Was Thomas Jefferson your last child?

I had one more, my ninth child, Edward Whitman, born in the summer of 1835 when I was almost forty. My poor baby had a malformation of the left hand and left leg, and as his body grew, his mind didn't. Along with that, Eddy had a stubborn way about him. He tried to help out, but he stayed a child all his life. Walt wanted to help care for Eddy, but I told him he had his whole life ahead of him and his own interests.

What were some of Walt's other interests?

After he turned sixteen, he joined two debating societies. In one, he took the minutes. Walter thought he should work more, but Walt disagreed.

"Living is more important than making a living," he said.

They often had words, but I loved when Walt visited. He came after big fires destroyed the printing shop where he worked in New York City. That visit ended when he argued with his father over his refusal to push a plow or feed livestock.

Instead of that dirty work, Walt took a job teaching in Norwich. He taught one term at a country school and boarded with the family of a student. At that job he had four terms of thirteen weeks each. For the next term, he rode his white horse, Nina, on to another school. He worked nine hours a day, with Sunday to rest, and he taught as many as eighty students from ages five to sixteen.

What was his teaching style?

He read his own verse to his students, and instead of recitation he wanted his students to think aloud. He loved to teach music and wanted music education in all the schools. I thought the job suited his restless nature, but he preferred daydreaming over teaching.

Was there anything at the school he disliked?

He hated how long it took to line paper and split and shape goose quills, and he hated how the other teachers ran the class with a heavy hand. He supported a system. Let me think how he said it.

"A philosophical system that repudiated lashes, tears, and sighs," he called it. Walt used gentle words in place of the paddle.

At day's end, he didn't use tobacco or overindulge in liquor. Instead he wrote verse. For a time he liked teaching, and people admired his skills. Even my son George, who had Walt for a teacher, claimed it to be so, but Walt decided to move on. After he turned nineteen, he became an editor. In his editorials, he praised domestic virtues and clarity of thought.

When Walt decided to start up a publishing venture, we mortgaged our house to help. He rented space above a stable to publish the *Long-Islander* and hired George. After ten months he sold it and then went back to teaching and got busy with politics. When he acted as a stump speaker for a Democratic rally, I couldn't attend, but I imagined his slow, quiet voice, pitched a little high. He had ten thousand people listening, and his speech got reported in the *Evening Post*. Even more people knew him after his writing was published in the Hempstead weekly, the *Long Island Democrat*.

When did he find time to see you?

He stayed with us on his annual leaves of absence. He took his meals with me and tried my patience with his lateness. When I took offense, he said he inherited his firmness and endurance from me, but his willfulness and obstinacy from his father. In late summer of 1845, when we lived on Prince Street in Brooklyn, Walt moved back in with us.

What precipitated that stay?

Walter no longer felt hale and couldn't build and sell houses anymore, so Walt joined George and Andrew in that trade. True to his nature, Walt got bored of carpentry and physical labor and started to write for a newspaper. That brought in enough to help pay installments on our house. I remember a beautiful carnelian pin he gave me, the boots he got for the boys, and the furniture he bought us. And he planted a garden of vegetables and flowers.

When he left again, he wrote to me. I like letters, even if there ain't anything particular in them. I wrote back in my little scribble. Mine spoke too often of family frustrations, but Walt gave consolation to me. In turn, when he needed me, I welcomed him home and kept his manuscripts safe. One of my favorite letters came when Walt nursed those poor wounded soldiers in Washington. I have it here. It mentions his poems, letters, and manuscripts.

"I want them all carefully kept," he wrote in his beautiful hand.

Now, I slowly reread his letters. Walt knows how to say things in a way no one else can.

Have you kept all of his letters?

We burned the letters with his most private thoughts. Not for display.

Can you tell me anything that was in those letters?

I won't speak on that. I can tell you that Walt wrote some letters to me and directed them to Jeff. When Jeffy was small, Walt raised him as I struggled with Eddy. Walt even bought

Jeffy a piano in hopes that he'd love music like Walt, but it didn't happen.

I love music, but you can't make someone else care about it. Did Walt keep traveling after he stopped teaching?

In '48, Walt went down to New Orleans to write and edit a new daily newspaper, the *Crescent*, and the owner found chores in the shop so Jeffy could go with him. They left by train and then boat. After they arrived safe, Walt wrote about the filth in the boardinghouses, with dirt even in the food.

"We never wanted your cleanliness so much," he said.

What else did he say about New Orleans?

He didn't like the locals' large consumption of juleps and ale, but his financial prospects seemed bright and he loved New Orleans. During the day, Walt took in the sights and studied the French people and then wrote about it for the *Crescent*. In the evenings, he read and went to balls and the theatre, and that was when he stopped using his full name, Walter. Then Jeffy got dysentery and became homesick. Walt never said so outright, but I think he had homesickness himself.

"O how I long for the day when we can have our quiet little farm and be together again," he wrote.

Then the editors of the *Crescent* expressed their dislike of Walt's male friendships, and he resigned.

He calls his manly friendships "adhesiveness."

Yes.

What did he mean? Can you make it clearer for me?

He claimed his personal attachments with men were stronger than ordinary friendships, and he said the love of comrades fed his soul.

When they returned from New Orleans, did Jeffy recover?

They arrived in perfect health. By then, my children had scattered. Mary married Ansel Van Nostrand, a shipbuilder, and had five children. He provided for her and she seemed content, though she complained about his habit of drinking.

I have family members who have that habit.

Drinking is a sad compulsion. My oldest, Jesse, had a liking for it. When he went off to sea as a merchant marine, I worried.

Worry is part of motherhood, I believe. How was your husband feeling?

He got worse and worse. When he knew he had only a little time, he asked Walt to take him to visit his birthplace. Walter got so bad that he bought us a plot in the new Cemetery of the Evergreens, high up on a hill to watch the coming and going of ships.

Then came a bit of trouble. Walt brought home a landscape painter and musician named Charles Heyde. Soon after, Charles boarded with us on Myrtle Street. My daughter Han adored his artistic side and enjoyed him right off. He liked her delicate nature and fair skin, and they fell in love and married. In time, Charles's odd habits and hostility changed our opinion of him. When they moved to Vermont, Walt called him "the bed-buggiest man."

My poor Han, she never told of life as it happened. Instead, she boasted that in the old days, our family owned Long Island from neck to neck. I worried on her and tried to keep it from Walt, since he needed to concentrate. At home, he tried to write but couldn't because of the street vendors, the boys with firecrackers, and dozens of hogs running loose in the streets. He wanted to lecture, so he wrote and filled barrels with ideas, though I knew little of what he wrote. I fed him and kept his life clean.

How was your husband's health at that point?

On the eve of his sixty-sixth birthday, my poor husband died. With his bad spells, which run in the Whitman family, and his paralyzed legs, we knew he didn't have much time. Mary stayed and helped me. I was sad and then kept on with a solid spirit. One has to go on.

After the funeral, Mary fell ill and Walt took her back home to rest. I let Walt go without a fuss, though I needed him at home. By then, Eddy was grown and hard to handle, and Jesse's rages got worse. We all suffered so. It broke my heart, down the road, when we had to let Walt commit Jesse to the lunatic asylum. I held steady and baked my cakes.

It must have been so hard for you. Did Walt have his own set of friends?

He started a life with different ways and younger, working-class friends. For a time, his friend Fred lived with us, and then Walt met Peter Doyle, a Rebel soldier and streetcar conductor. I enjoyed all his friends. I like to talk with Fred at cake time, though Fred said Walt was lazy and I denied it. Walt muses and writes. I tried not to worry what people thought about his manly friendships and his writings. He wasn't like anyone else.

"Never mind what they think," he told me time and again.

Walt's brothers and sisters called him a mystery, and I agreed. All my children made their own choices, so I tried to go along with them. Jeffy grew up and married Mattie and moved out of the house.

I remember May of '56. May is my favorite month. We moved to a five-floor brownstone, and I took in boarders. One of them was a butcher. They have such an odor, but I'd rather have six butchers than one soap-maker. Our family lived in part of the house, and Walt shared an attic bedroom with Eddy. I worked even harder to keep the house nice for Walt. Then Jeffy and Mattie and their new baby moved back in with us. I love them, but they can be wild and annoying. We had no quiet. For a time, Walt moved to Boston.

Did he like it there?

Yes. Then in '60, he came to live with us in Brooklyn. He worked on his articles and poems and helped me in the house, and he went out for pork and poultry and brought back fruit. I liked his help, since Eddy got more lame and couldn't do much due to his rheumatics.

What changed after the start of the war?

George joined up. I felt solemn when he had to go.

What about Walt?

He visited the sick in the hospitals in New York City.

How did George fare in the war?

In December, 1862, we saw George's name on the war wounded list. So many unfortunate fellows lost limbs, so I begged Walt to find him. He left for Washington and the front. When he changed trains, his pocket got picked on the platform and he had to borrow money from a writer friend to keep on. After Washington, he traveled south through the battlefields and looked all over for George. He searched through forty hospitals, and finally, in Fredericksburg, he found George alive with only a gash in his cheek from a shell fragment. Walt telegraphed the good news, but it saddened us to hear about all the other boys in the hospitals.

Walt wrote you letters during that time?

Walt wrote, "All my difficulties seem trifling."

He tried to be encouraging but found it difficult. He said being on the battlefield with George was the worst three days of his life. After he saw those boys in bad shape, he started visits among the camp hospitals in the Army of the Potomac. For years, he dressed wounds and held the hands of the dying. He read verse to them, but never his own, and gave a few words of cheer. When he assisted in an amputation, a scalpel cut him, and that gave him a bad infection in his arm as well as dizziness and trembling. To cheer him, I sent him parcels, sometimes with cake. Every week, he sent rent money, but I got fidgety for fear of theft since he put it in with his letters. I have a letter here.

"Mother, I have real pride in telling you that I have the consciousness of saving quite a number of lives by keeping the men from giving up, and being a good deal with them," he wrote.

How did he support himself as he helped those soldiers?

He wrote for the *New York Times*.

How did you keep from worrying?

Some days, friends of his would stop and give me news, and that helped. Sometime later, after *Leaves of Grass*, Bronson Alcott and Henry Thoreau came to talk to me of Walt, his poems and beliefs.

"Walt has always believed in the weaker against the stronger. He is my umpire in all disputes," I told them.

I enjoyed company, but it got cramped with our boarders.

I dreamed of a house of my own. Eddy, Jeffy, and his wife, Mattie, didn't like the house where we lived. It had fresh air but the cold winter winds came in. The boarders' rent gave us income, but Jeffy and Mattie fussed about money and spent a lot of it.

Then Jeffy got a good job in St. Louis, and George and his wife, Louisa, returned to help me care for Eddy. Poor Louisa, her only child died in infancy. We get along fine, except George and Louisa act a little too saving with their money. George broods like Walter did, but he's noble and clever.

I had so many burdens. At one time, Andrew and his dirty, lazy wife, Nancy, lived with me. I gave Nancy one of my gowns and a quilt petticoat, but they said I was stingy with my bank book when I wouldn't give Andrew money for a drinking spree. He bought expensive lamb and got things on credit at the grocery, and the two of them tended to their own cares and let their children, Hattie and Jimmy, fend for themselves. Those poor little objects of misery. I did what I could.

Did Andrew serve in the war?

He served for three months until he fell ill with a throat ailment, and he was very bad with the pleurisy. They cupped and blistered him. When my children are sick, my world collapses in on itself.

I too feel helpless when that happens.

What's worse is for a mother to bury her child. I was called upon to do it more than once. I know I'm not alone, but my heart fell when my poor Andrew passed on at thirty-seven of tuberculosis and the drink. Before Andrew was gone forever, another tragedy came to pass when his son, Jimmy, got run over and killed on Hudson Avenue by a brewery wagon. No child should die before his parents. The grief takes your breath and leaves little in its place.

It's a part of life that none of us wants to face.

Andrew's death caused so much trouble. Nancy goes it in the streets and never took notice of her daughter. You would think her Hattie belonged to someone else if you looked at Nancy's ways. Then Jesse threatened Hattie and attacked me. I told you about the asylum. I wrote to Walt, and with his clear head, he knew we had no choice.

That's a terrible shame. At least you can rely on Walt. Tell me more about his health problems after the war.

He had aches and a bad humming in his head, some deafness, colds, and hot weather faintness. The doctor said Walt's malaria and the poison he absorbed in the war caused it and told him to rest six months. Walt started to feel a little better, but then George and his regiment got captured and put in prison for six months. When George got lung fever and almost died, the Confederates put him in a military hospital. I gloried when he was part of the prisoner exchange in '65. After he came home, George acted haunted and moody and distant. He had rheumatism real bad, but recovered enough to start a small building business.

So many people had problems during those longs days, and then President Lincoln was shot. Where was Walt?

At home with me. We felt so sad when the news came. Walt visited the White House one time after Lincoln's second inauguration, and almost every morning one summer, Walt watched the President pass by in his barouche on the way to the White House. John Hay, the President's private secretary, told Walt that Mr. Lincoln enjoyed Walt's poetry. That made it even harder for us when he was shot. The day it happened, Walt read the newspapers while I cooked breakfast, but our food turned cold. We ate not a mouthful. We barely drank our coffee and talked only a little. Throughout the day, Walt read me the extras that arrived. It was lilac time, so we always associate the odor of lilac blossoms with that tragic day.

The two of you were so close. Were you sad that Walt didn't have children?

It pains me. He treated women like sisters, yet he claimed matrimony to be the ideal state for men and women. I sometimes think Eddy and me put too much of a burden on him, what with the time and money he gave us. Walt sends us more than he can afford and our dependency bothers me. I console myself with one of his sayings.

"Your welfare is my dearest concern," he tells me. Walt has a giving spirit.

Earlier you mentioned Walt's friend Peter.

They're comrades. They met when Peter was eighteen and Walt was forty-six. At first, Walt tutored Peter, who couldn't read or write. Now, they live in Jersey City, and they walk every day to aid digestion. Walt speaks often of good health, and he drinks water all day. When they dine here with me, they take walks. Walt had clothes made for Peter and speaks of him fondly, and he sends him flowers and takes care of his money for him. He acts as a father to Peter, like he has for all of us. We call him our old standby. When poor Jesse died of a rupture in the asylum, I wrote many letters to Walt.

"Ain't it sad," I told him in between tears.

In Jesse's last moments, the poor soul had no friend near

him. To think he was buried in a pauper's grave. He'd done some wrong, yet he was my first-born. To lose a child is almost too much to bear. I hope he's better off.

I am so sorry for your loss. You live here in Camden now.

Last year Eddy and me joined George and Louisa here. George used to be generous, and now he does all right money wise, but he's so saving. He's hospitable though.

Is George feeling better now?

He's well and looks too fat.

How did Eddy adjust to the move?

He misses his Brooklyn church. I worry more about Walt. His letters look shaky because his left arm and leg got paralyzed from apoplexy. He calls it a "whack" and says he'll recover. We heard from Jeffy in St. Louis that his wife, Mattie, died. I never understood her prescribed diet of whiskey and raw oysters. I liked Mattie, and I could tell her so much. She was good to me when I couldn't find kindness from my own daughters, with their different ways.

Eddy is a very good boy lately, and he says he hopes I won't die. Someday, we'll all find our final resting place. The two of us drift along. I can't read much. My head gets confused. I take the sleeping draught once in a while and that lulls my pain. I get by with a dream of going back to Washington to live with Walt and care for him like in days past. It's a great consolation to get his letters. They're nearly all the comfort I have. When I turned seventy-six, Walt pleased me with one comment.

"You look young and handsome yet," he said.

I know you accept his comments with a kind heart. You've given him so much love. Which of your virtues

rubbed off on Walt?

It may be my reserve and my interest in observation. And my Quaker beliefs, with faith, hope, and charity as my watchwords. He's a mix of color, a blend of our family's past and his interest in the future.

When I'm told he has talents beyond ordinary men, I nod and agree. I don't tell them Walt can be a little cold and secretive. I don't tell them he has a stubborn streak like his father or that he does things at his own notion. I tell them and I tell you, here at the end of our time together, that my sweet-tempered son has a wistful, quiet nature, and that his inner visions and strong emotions suit a life of writing. I love my good old standby, Walt. With words, he gives his soul to the world.

INTERVIEW WITH WALTER WHITMAN JR. ON THE DEATH OF HIS MOTHER

When I heard my mother's health failed, I left for Camden. We sat together for three days and then my dear, dear mother passed away on May 23, 1873. I have not reconciled to her death and I refuse to let anyone remove her gray dress from the wardrobe. Over and over, I read the last letter she wrote.

> *"Farewell my beloved sons farewell. I have lived beyond all comfort in the world. Don't mourn for me my beloved sons and daughters. Farewell my dear beloved Walter."*

Mother's death is my most staggering, staying blow. My physical sickness, bad as it can be, is nothing compared to this. Here is part of a poem I wrote to ease my dark cloud.

I sit by the form in the coffin,
I kiss and kiss convulsively the sweet old lips,
the cheeks, the closed eyes in the coffin.

I cannot imagine life without her. She was the rarest combination of practical, moral, and spiritual and the least selfish of all and any I have ever known. She has been my deepest emotional attachment. My dearest, perfect mother. I sleep on the pillow she made for me.

10

Interview with Anna Lloyd Jones Wright

MOTHER OF FRANK LLOYD WRIGHT,
ARCHITECT, BORN JUNE 8, 1867

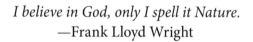

I believe in God, only I spell it Nature.
—Frank Lloyd Wright

JAN HELEN McGEE

I hope we can talk in an open and honest manner about Frank's childhood and how it shaped his life.

ANNA WRIGHT

In the past, I lowered our ages and substituted good stories for real ones, but the truth was nobody's business. Now I'll be honest with you, so people can understand Frank's true genius as America's greatest living architect. That was my vision for him. Did you know that between 1894 and 1911 Frank constructed 135 buildings?

JAN HELEN MCGEE

That's impressive. Which is your favorite?

ANNA WRIGHT

The Unity Church in Oak Park, Illinois. It stands as proof of his intellect.

I'd like to hear about your background.

I was born Hannah Lloyd Jones in Wales in 1838, the fifth child of Richard Lloyd Jones and Mary, known as Mallie. My parents met when my mother heard my father preach, and they married against her wealthy parents' wishes.

A rebellious streak that you and Frank inherited?

Possibly.

When did you come to America?

When I was small, my father's brother, Jenkin, and his sister, Rachel, arrived here and wrote about the inexpensive land, so my parents came with their seven children.

Where do you fall in the lineup?

The oldest is jolly Mary, then Thomas, John, and peacemaker Margaret. I'm next, then Nannie and Jenkin, named after my uncle. In our family we use "Sister" and "Brother," so I was Sister Anna. For our parents we use the Welsh Tad and Mam.

Can you recall the ocean crossing?

I was barely six, but I remember it was difficult. On our first voyage out, a heavy gale carried our mainmast away, and back we went to England for repairs. After our second start, we lived six long weeks on that small, uncomfortable boat. After we arrived in New York, we took a canal boat and lake steamer to Wisconsin.

On that long journey, my three-year-old sister, Nannie,

fell ill with a cold and a high fever. She died in my mother's arms. What an abysmal time. Mam's sobs kept me awake all night. The next morning Tad prayed for Nannie and we buried her in strange ground. Mam stopped crying, gathered her strength, and helped us move forward. Even with her strong attachment to *yr hen wlad*, the old country, she had a deep conviction for a new life.

Tragedy imprints on our brain. No wonder you remember it so well. Why were you headed for Wisconsin?

Many of our relatives lived there. We eventually moved to Hillside, in the isolated Helena Valley, where my relatives had 1,800 acres between us. The neighbors called it "the valley of the God-Almighty Joneses." We never ceased to surprise them.

Did your father preach in America?

In the old country, he'd been a fine lay preacher, hatmaker, and a tenant farmer. In Wisconsin, with the help of Mam and us children, he became a prosperous farmer.

"Add tired to tired, and add it again," Tad told us, as we cleared land and helped with field work.

Tad was resourceful. He exchanged tobacco with the Indians to get venison, and he and my brother Thomas, a carpenter, built a small house. It had two bedrooms and a loft for eight of us, so the tight quarters meant a physical closeness to my siblings. I also felt an emotional closeness to them, but Mam meant the most to me. To stay with her, I did the indoor work of spinning, weaving, and cooking. I loved her gentle spirit and her knowledge of medicinal plants. Her care strengthened me, and in return I helped her cope with the loss of Nannie.

The birth of Ellen and then Jane—we call them Nell and Jennie—helped ease her pain. I felt such admiration for both of them, and as adults they followed me into teaching. Neither married. Poor Nell was engaged, but a bout of smallpox scarred her face and turned her hair white, and her despicable fiancé called off their marriage.

"He has lost," I told her. She took the love she would have given a husband and put it into devotion to her work.

At least as a teacher, she was admired for her intellect.

It's a calling that is sometimes respected, sometimes not.

Are your sisters the youngest?

Mam had two more, James and Enos. I assisted as midwife for both of them, and by the time I was fifteen, I helped in over a dozen family births. Midwife duties and caring for my five younger siblings took work. The worst was Enos and his difficulties with reading, but that prepared me for teaching. Later, I taught my students what I learned at home, books, and poetry. My brother Thomas liked Shakespeare and Longfellow, so he read them aloud in the evenings. He grew up to become the county architect.

Another architect? All of you are intelligent.

I give credit to my parents' love for learning. Both were freethinkers who admired Abraham Lincoln and opposed slavery. We had a family motto: "Truth against the world." Mam found her truth in fairy tales. In a soft voice, she told tales in Welsh, her only language and the one we spoke at home. Mam's nurturing spirit soothed us and drew other people to her. Most astounding was her gift of clairvoyance. One prophecy came true about my brother, Jenkin. She predicted that he'd be wounded in the Civil War, and he was.

I believe in clairvoyance. I like to study it. Since you spoke Welsh at home, did you have trouble with English in school?

Spelling, at first, but now my grammar is perfect. In school my teacher said I was her most promising student, so I became an assistant teacher, and then a full teacher. I rode from one country school to another as a man might, on horseback with no fear. And like a man, I had a stubborn and impulsive streak. I might have been mistaken for one, with my tall frame and broad shoulders. On cold or wet days, I wore a military style jacket with brass buttons, and I walked with a free stride. I doubt I fooled anyone. If they looked closely at my hair in this waterfall style with curly ringlets, they knew.

Your hair is beautiful. Mine is so thin.

Mam said nature's most precious gift to mortals is a beautiful head of hair. It was one concession I made to femininity, since I refused to wear corsets or any color in my dress. In my garden, I loved color and I still do. My passions today are the same as then: knowledge and nature. Mam said plants and flowers had a link to religion.

"Nature and wisdom," she said, "the keys to life." I gave that advice to Frank.

"Link the perfect home to truth, beauty, simplicity, and nature," I told him.

I understood Frank so well, even more than I understood my sisters and brothers. I loved them, but like all large families, I enjoyed some things and others not so much.

What did you love most?

I loved the support, but I yearned for freedom from the tribe, so I sought a new teaching position. That's how I met that short, little William, Frank's father. I cannot abide that man, and I hate the part he played in Frank's beginnings.

Was William a teacher?

County school superintendent. He interviewed and hired me to teach.

What about his background?

William Russell Cary Wright, born in Massachusetts, father a Baptist minister. He attended college and then worked as a piano forte teacher and organist. Married his student, Permelia, and then he studied law.

Did they have children?

Their first child died in infancy. Next came Charles, George, and Lizzie. After they moved to Wisconsin, I boarded with them and started my teaching job. After Permelia gave birth to a dead child and succumbed to childbed fever, I moved out of the house for a time and then returned to help William care for his children while he lawyered. That job pitted rich against poor, and he didn't like it. He preferred the ministry and speaking. When President Lincoln died in 1865, the townspeople chose William to deliver the eulogy in ceremonies on the courthouse lawn. That's why he wanted Frank's middle name to be Lincoln.

How long were you there before you married?

Two years. I taught and cared for those children and cultivated my moral attributes like a garden.

In the early years, what did you find appealing about him?

I hate the ground he walks on, but at first he seemed ideal, with fine features and a jaunty way of dressing. He was well educated, with wonderful manners and elocution, and he wrote waltzes and polkas. He played six instruments and had a fine bass voice. One of his instruments was a violin he made. I'd never known a violinmaker. His knowledge of sound impressed me.

How did your parents feel about him?

He gave concern to my family for many reasons. One, we are Unitarian and William is Baptist. Two, they didn't like that he moved so often. And three, he had held so many jobs. At first, I disagreed. I found him good looking, musical, and intelligent, and I wanted to pass those attributes on to a son.

That seems sound. What happened to change your opinion of him?

When I met him, I didn't notice how much attention he paid on the three children not my own. What a burden. Lizzie was five and the boys seven and nine, with minds of their own. I was saddled and yoked with their care. The boys kept their distance, but Lizzie had a mean streak. When she looked at me with that face like Permelia's, I couldn't control my outbursts. Her beauty disturbed me, and William's rapt attention to her enraged me. My siblings claim I have a tremendous temper, and with Lizzie it erupted. That's enough of that one.

Tell me about Frank's arrival.

William got a call to preach, so we moved to Richland Center, Wisconsin. There my prince was born on June 8, 1867. Some people claimed Frank looked like his father, but he resembles the Lloyd family. I wanted to name him Frank Lloyd Wright but William insisted on Frank Lincoln.

After two years, we moved to Iowa for William's work, and I had Mary Jane, named after my sisters and called Jennie.

By then, my relationship with William had deteriorated. I felt such resentment over his children, our finances brought great disappointment, and fatigue enveloped me. When we left Iowa, my family in the Valley took us in and my stability returned.

That didn't last. William moved us to Rhode Island, to the first and third floors of a house. I hated hiking up and down, and what a burden to be so destitute that we had to accept that situation. We lived on community contributions from William's preaching. At one donation party, his parish gave us twenty-nine pumpkin pies. Imagine, what could we do with that?

Give them back?

Pumpkin pies and meager rations and William's horrid child Lizzie.

How did she feel at that point?

I imagine if you'd ask her, she'd say I seemed out of control. I say, both Lizzie and William had evil intent. Neither acknowledged my physical and emotional exhaustion. When Parmelia's mother asked Lizzie to live with her, I felt such a relief.

After she left, I insisted William have little contact with her, so he tried to hide her letters, but I read them. We fought about that and about William's distain for paying trades-men's bills. Once again we had to beg for a roof over our heads, so we moved to Connecticut to live with William's father, Reverend David. Before Frank turned eleven, we lived in six towns in four states. I wanted a stable home of my own.

Our next move to a prosperous suburb of Boston provided some pleasure. William ministered at a prosperous church, and Frank attended their private school without paying the fee. I enjoyed concerts and lectures in Boston and bought the latest books. There I had Margaret Ellen. We called her Maggie Nell, which turned into Maginel. What a fragile baby. At night I put her on a pillow in front of me and sat with my arms around Jennie and Frank. We sang and had story hour, and I told fairy tales. I spoke of sacred places in Wales and supernatural events. Over and over I told the story of Taliesin, a poet, savior, magician, and seer.

Your children didn't find magical stories and the supernatural frightening?

No, it kindled their imaginations and took them away from the reality of poverty. Over and over, that irresponsible William resigned or got fired and we had to move.

Was there anything William contributed?

Only one thing: music. He taught Frank to play viola in our family orchestra. He used Bach and Beethoven to show structural comparisons between music and buildings, which later helped Frank apply musical form and composition to his architecture. Are you aware that education is the direct manifestation of God?

It sounds plausible. So William did a good job with education?

There's always a flip side with William. I called his educational method detached disciplinarian, since he rapped Frank's knuckles with a pencil if his hand position faltered on piano. When Frank was only seven, he made him pump the organ bellows while William practiced singing. He exhausted Frank, and I hated him for it. He was moody and withdrawn, and when Mam died, he didn't even help me. I pulled through because I needed to teach Frank to be self-reliant.

Sometimes Frank's nature fought against my dream for him. He was small and solitary and spent too much time in his imagination. He wanted to read and play viola and piano, and he didn't like to play with other boys. Instead, he drew and painted and worked on his printing press or made things up in his mind. His visual memory was excellent, but at school he wasn't properly taught. When he failed algebra, I attributed it to poor schooling. The same was true of rhetoric, botany, and physics, where he had poor to average grades.

Why did you keep him in school?

Education provides an awareness of natural law, so I made sure he stayed in school and I helped him learn. I told Frank there was nothing as sacred as an architect—a "builder contractor," they called it then. When he was a baby, I hung beautiful wood carvings in his crib and played the best music. When he was nine, I introduced him to Froebel's games and exercises. I knew about them from teaching and from my sisters, but I learned more when I visited the Philadelphia Centennial Exposition in the summer of 1876. The exposition taught me the new ideas of the Aesthetic Movement, and modern refinement in the home became important to me. To cultivate Frank's mind, I read Whittier and Lowell and quoted Emerson in the evenings. A special favorite of Frank's came from Shakespeare.

And this our life, exempt from public haunt
Finds tongues in trees, books in the running brooks
Sermons in stones, and good in everything.

My sisters and I gave him books, and Ruskin became an early favorite of his. Did you know that Ruskin worshiped the natural landscape?

I did not.

He appreciated life as art. Frank and the girls had oil painting lessons, and I taught them how to arrange flowers, branches, and leaves to make the room come alive. Curtains, floors, light, beauty, culture; I nurtured their minds. For physical health, I made sure they ate good meats, fruits, and vegetables and very little of cakes and pies.

You sound like you were more settled at that point.

I was, for two reasons. William left the Baptists and became a Unitarian, and we moved to Madison to a house by Lake Mendota. William had a stable job so at last I had modern refinement, with maple floors, sheer white curtains, and Indian and Oriental rugs. In that house, I planned Frank's future.

What changes did you make?

I wanted Frank to spend summers with one of my brothers, either Thomas, the builder, James, the farmer, or John, the miller and postmaster. Frank preferred James. I cut off his curls, packed his things, and wept. I calmed myself and remembered family bonfires and skating parties, Halloween fun, and molasses taffy pulls. James was a stern taskmaster, but he had a kind and generous nature.

Did Frank like the farm?

That first summer he found it ugly. He hated the animals' sick smell and the sight of a rooster's head chopped off. His body ached from work, and he despised dark morning rises. Each time Frank ran away, a family member found him and took him back. I knew nature would eventually pull at him in a positive way.

Did it?

Over five summers, I watched him change. He came to love the hills and the color contrasts of light and earth, and the landscape later affected his art. My brother Thomas and the stonemason David Timothy gave him a good foundation in building, and John showed Frank how to make his famous seed wheat cereal. My freethinking relatives provided camaraderie and love.

I was a fearful child, but I felt more comfortable with my cousins. Did Frank become more social because of those summers?

Yes. He felt shy around girls, but he became popular. During the school year, he had invitations to parties and after-dinner singing sessions, and he and a friend published a one-sheet neighborhood newspaper.

Frank became a man. Of course, with almost no help from William. That worm acted cold towards Frank, and Frank didn't love him either. The opposite was true with that nasty Lizzie, who adored her father.

Did she ever marry?

Yes, at our house. William presided over her marriage to John Heller. The entire day, William fawned over her. He spoke too often that Father David was no longer with us and couldn't be there, and he praised his monetary gift that paid off the debt on our house. Of course, not one word was said about my family's contributions. With William, everyone else came before Frank and my girls and me. Our fights increased during Lizzie's visit, and after she left, nothing changed. I had such contempt for him that I refused to have closeness of any sort with him. I wouldn't occupy the same room, and I didn't make his bed or do his mending. I changed Frank's middle name from Lincoln to Lloyd, since Frank belongs to me. Finally William took his clothes, his violins, and his old mahogany secretary and deserted us. When the neighbors questioned William's whereabouts, Frank asked me how to reply.

"Say he's dead."

We divorced and I gained custody of my three children. Frank never saw his father again. When William died, none of us went to the funeral.

Did your children want to attend?

Why should they have?

How did you make your way with William gone?

My brothers supported us. The girls and I moved in with James and kept house since his wife was on an extended vacation to visit her family. Frank boarded with neighbors nearby. High school was hard for him. No one understood his high intelligence and extraordinary visual memory. He read constantly but received low grades, so he dropped out of high school. Because of his natural intellect, the University of Wisconsin in Madison allowed him to take part-time classes as a special student. At that time, the school had no course in architecture, so he studied as a civil engineer. The classes gave him emotional distress and a sickening sense of fear, since he preferred things his way. I stood by him through his difficulties. I knew he had charm and energy and needed an individual path along the sacred road to architecture.

Did he work in that field while he studied?

As a favor to my family, Allan Conover, a professor of engineering at the university, hired Frank part time. At first Allan gave him menial tasks, but soon he taught Frank the fundamentals of draftsmanship and civil engineering. A problem developed between them, and after two semesters of classes, Frank decided to move to Chicago.

How did you react?

I thought Frank was far too young and innocent. I wrote to Jenkin for advice, since he was an important congregational leader in Chicago, and Jenkin told Frank not to come. He said Frank would waste himself on fine clothes and girls. I agreed. Frank didn't smoke or drink, and I didn't want bad influences in his life.

What did he do?

He was furious with us. He sold his father's old books, pawned my Swiss gold watch, sold the mink cape collar I'd sewn onto his coat, and left for Chicago without a word.

Did you feel betrayed?

Another mother might have felt that way, but I knew he had to find his own path.

What kind of work did he find in Chicago?

He got a job with the architect J.S. Silsbee on the construction of a new church for Jenkin's congregation. Frank learned all he could and then got another job as a draftsman with Adler & Sullivan. Sullivan had studied at the Massachusetts Institute of Technology, which had the first school of architecture in the United States. Frank did a lot of drawing, and he and Sullivan discussed architecture and design for hours.

Frank seemed content, but I fretted over his roving eye for women. I wrote weekly letters, told him to emulate Lincoln and Christ, and stressed the importance of proper diet, correct friends, warm underwear, and of course, goodness and truth. I reminded him that if I'd been born with his advantages, there would be nothing I couldn't do. When I worried about the debts he left behind, I begged him to change his spending habits. Since the girls and I had no income, I persuaded him to invite us to move to Chicago. He found a little house for all four of us in Oak Park, where our life revolved around Jenkin's church.

A church can be a wonderful place for young and old to socialize.

One day, at a church costume party and dance social, Frank met blue-eyed Catherine Tobin, a girl from a prosperous Unitarian family. Frank liked Kitty's curly red hair, and he called her gay spirited. I found her sensible, but she never stopped talking. Her parents and I didn't approve of the match because she was only seventeen and still in school. I sought out Frank's friends to try to talk him out of it. I convinced Mrs. Tobin to send Kitty away to a relative on Mackinac Island for three months, but it didn't change a thing.

When Kitty turned eighteen, Frank went ahead without our approval. I fainted from the shock of it, and Kitty's father burst into tears. Their June wedding day was one of the worst days of my life. Jenkin officiated at the ceremony and it rained all day. They honeymooned at the family farm in The Valley.

That must have pleased you.

It did, especially when my clever sisters stepped in and gave Kitty advice about how to care for Frank. I suddenly realized a wife meant no hungry women to distract him from his purpose.

Kitty and Frank returned to Chicago?

Yes, Frank signed a five-year contract with Adler and Sullivan and bought land to build a house. I gave him the money left over from the sale of my lake house, and he borrowed the rest from Sullivan. Their association seemed complicated to me, with Sullivan's unusual interest in Frank. Frank didn't feel the same way towards Sullivan, and he told me their relationship involved only work, nothing strongly personal.

Frank built his house and remodeled a small, Gothic-style frame house on the property for the girls and me. After they moved into the beautiful main house, Frank added leaded glass windows. Kitty hid in the closet to escape or sat around pregnant and miserable.

So Frank became a father.

Kitty had six children, and she raised them. Frank didn't have much interest in the father role, and he hated the sound of "Papa." With the boys, he acted like a playful uncle. They boxed and pulled practical jokes. But he made sure all his children studied music. His oldest son, Lloyd—born Frank Lloyd Wright Jr.—played the cello, John the violin, David the flute, Frances the piano, Catherine sang, and Llewellyn played guitar and mandolin. With Kitty on piano, they had a family orchestra. Most evenings, the family played music or read. Frank kept to his true vision and planned additions and changes to expand his house.

All those children made too much noise, so Frank's work suffered. Kitty didn't understand his vision and complained he had more interest in the house than in her. The woman couldn't remember the names of his clients, and she needed her mother and grandmother close. I argued with all three of those women when they complained about the money Frank spent, and his reluctance to pay his bills. Frank ignored their meddling and forged on. Then came a change. Remember I spoke of Mam's intuitive sense?

I believe it's inherited. Do you?

Yes. I possess the gift; so does Frank. He has an excellent sense of people's true nature. With that intuitive ability, Frank saw Sullivan's true self, and they had a falling out. Frank received other offers but chose to work on his own and make all the decisions.

One thrilling project for me was a windmill Frank designed for my sisters, Nell and Jane. They founded and ran the Hillside Home School in Spring Grove, Wisconsin. When they needed to pump water out of their well into a reservoir, they asked Frank to build a pretty windmill. After Frank sent his design, my brothers studied it with skepticism and a local builder mocked his design, and yet my sisters stood firm. You should see it, what a beautiful octagonal tower. Frank calls it "Romeo and Juliet."

I would love to see it. Your son does beautiful work.

I'm proud of him. Kitty never felt the same way, though she had no trouble with fine clothes, handmade automobiles, or performances of the Chicago Orchestra. When she boasted about Frank's thoroughbred horses or her grand piano, she never acknowledged he made it all possible. Instead of appreciation, she spewed critical words and found fault in everything Frank did. He finally had enough of her emotional pressure and left.

The papers were full of his life in Europe with his com-

panion.

Mamah Cheney. He called her his soul mate. They went to Berlin and then Italy.

How did Kitty and his children react?

They were devastated, but Kitty and Mamah's husband should have seen it coming. Frank had built a house for Mamah and her husband, so he spent vast amounts of time with Mamah. All their children knew the importance of their relationship. Frank admired her intellect—she had a master's degree in teaching—and her hearty laugh and open spirit charmed him. Frank asked Kitty for a divorce, and she agreed, if he waited one year.

At the end of that year, reporters ferociously questioned Kitty about Frank. She spoke of his goodness and honesty and called Mamah a vampire. After the interview, Kitty seemed upset, but I couldn't get involved. I keep the thoughts Frank confided to me to myself. I will reveal one thing Frank wrote to me when he lived in Europe.

"I am a wild bird and must stay free."

So you understood his feelings?

I did, though I missed him terribly during that long year. When he returned, I bought a few hundred acres of land from John, right next to Nell and Jane's school. My sisters worried their school's reputation would suffer because of all the negative things about Frank in the newspapers. To appease them, Frank published an affidavit that he had no connection with their school. On that land, Frank built Taliesin, named after the legendary Welsh bard from the stories I told him. Taliesin means "shining brow," and it became a divine work of art.

Frank and Mamah took up residence, and to satisfy the

press, Frank made a statement that he'd married too young. He said he and Kitty had a difference in interests that made it impossible for him to work as an artist while living with his family. Nothing stood in Frank's way, not even a car accident that left him unable to use his injured arm and hand for months.

I'm glad he recovered. When he was injured, what did he work on?

He lectured and wrote articles, and in 1913 he traveled to Japan to meet with representatives from the Emperor, since the Court wanted to replace the dowdy Imperial Hotel. At last everything seemed on an even keel, with my daughters, Jennie and Maginel, married and Maginel's successful career as an artist. By then, my sister Nannie's death had fallen out of my mind. I forgot that heartache lies in wait.

Tell me about the heartache.

It happened the summer of 1914. Frank had work in Chicago on the Midway Gardens, so Mamah and her children John and Martha stayed behind in Wisconsin. With no warning, a madman servant set the Taliesin house in flames and used an ax to attack and kill Mamah and the children. Four other people perished. Frank returned immediately, grief stricken.

"Days strangely without light would follow black nights," he said.

How horrible. With all that sorrow, could Frank continue with his work?

His work became automatic, and I felt helpless. Only time would heal him. I stood by him as he built Taliesin II, with a wing for me and my sisters. During his absences, I took charge of the project, and when he returned, I nurtured him.

In the midst of his vulnerable state, Frank received a condolence letter from a mysterious spiritual woman named Miriam Noel, who originated from a wealthy family and claimed to be an artist. Certainly her turban and ropes of beads made her look like one, but I saw a Christian Scientist adventuress who smoked cigarettes. Frank couldn't see her true nature. Instead he saw beauty, brilliance, and clairvoyance.

Did you really think he would live alone for long?

I knew Frank would find another woman, so when Miriam moved into Taliesin II, I tried to accept her outspoken nature. Here is one example. She stated in a newspaper interview that by living together, she and Frank were superior to ordinary mortals. In public, Frank praised her, but in private, her wild swings of mood caused quarrels.

In December of 1916, they sailed to Tokyo, where Frank designed and supervised the construction of the Imperial Hotel. When I received word that he'd fallen ill with dysentery, I crossed the Pacific to nurse him.

Did that sea voyage remind you of your childhood?

I thought about Nannie and what type of woman she would've become. Mostly I worried about Frank. When I landed, Miriam had choice words for me.

"I can nurse Frank on my own," she said.

Frank didn't welcome my presence, but he needed someone to truly care for him. He spent several weeks in bed and blamed his illness on the humid climate. I too suffered with dysentery, so we ate nothing but flavorless boiled rice. My recovery was more rapid than Frank's, so I took in the sights, mostly to get away from Miriam, who considered my presence unendurable. I ignored her and found comfort in my son. He adored Japan and its architecture.

Suddenly I feel exhausted.

I'll leave now. Thank you for your time and your attention to detail.

I'm glad I had strength today. Too often I'm frail with fainting spells and disorientation. I don't mention it to Frank since he's upset that I can't get along with Miriam. I am not fond of her cruel and tyrannical ways. But Frank, Frank is my golden light, my playful and creative protector. A commissioned portrait of me hangs in his studio. That proves love.

INTERVIEW WITH FRANK LLOYD WRIGHT ON THE DEATH OF HIS MOTHER

Mother died in February of 1923. She was eighty-four. At times she had a pious and irritating manner, but I found her sassy and heroic in her aspirations for me. I couldn't attend her funeral due to preplanned business appointments.

11

Interview with Ann Geilus Astaire

MOTHER OF FRED ASTAIRE,
DANCER, BORN MAY 10, 1899

———— ⟨⟨⟩⟩ ————

*The hardest job kids face today is learning
good manners without seeing any.*
—Fred Astaire

JAN HELEN MCGEE

I know music but so little about dance. You move so elegantly as you walk. Did you dance too?

ANN ASTAIRE

No. I wanted to, but my family believed it was sinful.

JAN HELEN MCGEE

So your dreams took shape through Fred?

ANN ASTAIRE

My husband Frederick and I both had unfulfilled dreams. That disappointment led us to mold Fred—we call him Sonny—and our daughter, Dellie, into entertainers.

Did you ever have any doubts about the path you chose

for your children?

I had a slew of mixed feelings. They missed some childhood pleasures and stage life took us away from Frederick, who worked in Omaha to support us. For twenty years I managed their dance career and felt the sting of criticism that people fling at stage mothers. No matter how hard I worked, people judged me unfairly. I knew the stage destroyed some lives, but anyone who watched our children dance could see they thrived. All four of us sacrificed, and it hit Frederick the hardest and then Dellie. Mothers have regrets. I certainly have them.

I never realized that your daughter was such a large part of Sonny's dance career. How did that begin?

Dellie's gifts became evident as soon as she could stand. She was born first, on September 10, 1897, and we named her Adele. Sonny was born two years later on May 10, 1899. He is Frederick Jr. My husband noticed Dellie's talent as he played piano, when suddenly our living room became a stage for Dellie to strut and play-act. He had a better eye than I did for talent since he grew up with concerts and operettas in Vienna.

When Dellie turned four, she had dance lessons and she performed at churches and school affairs. During her lessons, I left with the other mothers and then returned early since Sonny and I loved to watch. At first he had no interest in lessons.

How did you know anything about the stage?

I educated myself through Frederick's subscription to the theatrical trade paper *New York Clipper*. I followed brother-and-sister acts like Vilma and Buddy Ebsen and read everything I could find about the Cansinos, a famous family of entertainers. One of the brothers, Eduardo Cansino, had a daughter who performed. After she grew up, she took the stage name Rita Hayworth.

I know of her! She's clever. When I was eight I took dance, but I had no talent. I could never remember whether to move left or right, and my feet had trouble with the beat. As an adult, I still can't master simple steps. I like show business though.

How marvelous for you to even try.

Please tell me how you and Sonny are alike.

Fragility and steel, both of us. I'm delicate in my choices but present myself in such a way that people assume I'm detached. I'm not. The truth is, if I don't like someone I remove myself from the situation to evade any messiness. I'm a perfectionist, and I think life should be a certain way, with proper manners at the fore of every situation. You understand, since you arrived promptly. And while I have veered off the subject, I must tell you I admire the cut of your dress. Such lovely fabric.

Thank you. I'm not one for fashion, so a friend helps me. You look wonderful.

I'm fascinated with style, and I like things clean and neat. I know life can't stay perfect, so when something goes wrong I steel myself and don't get angry. The opposite side of that coin is when I decide to enchant. Then I can charm a snake. Sonny's the same.

Tell me about your husband's background and how music became a part of his life.

Frederick was born in Vienna, Austria, and his last name

was Austerlitz. He worked in the beer trade, and then he had some trouble with his older brother, so in 1895 he left for America.

What did he do when he got to Ellis Island?

He headed west to Omaha, Nebraska, to a leather trade job that a friend arranged. He hated leather, so he found work as a salesman for a brewing company. That suited him. Everyone enjoyed his sense of humor.

"There are only two kinds of Austrians: rascals and musicians. And I play the piano," he told customers who wanted to talk about life in Vienna. He had a repertoire of little stories from his past, but mostly he chose to live in the present.

My family originally came from Alsace, France. Frederick and I met in Omaha right after I graduated from Catholic high school. He was ten years older and gallant.

What did he like about you?

My eyes, my lean figure, my fashion sense. I told him how my parents said entertainers were sinful, and my childhood dream had been to escape Omaha and enter show business. We shared so many dreams, and I began to think another life was possible. We married within a few months.

How did you transition from Omaha to show business?

It was 1904, and I felt as if I were in the middle of a bad dream. Dellie was about six, so Sonny was four. The state of Nebraska enforced a ban on alcoholic beverages, and Frederick lost his job at the brewery. Late into the night, we had long talks about our children. Friends and relatives warned against the perils of a stage career for Dellie, but we knew she had talent. As for Sonny, he claimed he wanted to be a baseball player, but what four-year-old knows his future? We decided the children and I would go to New York City to get better training for Dellie and Frederick would stay in Omaha to earn a living.

That train ride took almost three days. We checked into a hotel, and I enrolled Dellie in Alvienne's Dancing School, where they taught both dance and dramatic reading and emphasized the importance of proper speech. Since we spent a lot of time waiting for Dellie to finish her classes, Sonny was bored, so he did imitations with his little steps. Some of the other mothers marveled at his ability to move. I discussed that turn of events with Frederick and enrolled Sonny in classes.

We all worked hard. In between her classes, I taught Dellie arithmetic, grammar, and other subjects, since I had some training as a teacher. At first Sonny listened as Dellie studied, but after he learned to read on his own, I included him in our lessons. As both children became proficient in dance, I noticed that Dellie had great talent and Sonny had durability, so I decided to find an agent. That was difficult. Every day while the children danced, I made calls in the city. I visited seedy offices full of men who assumed I was the typical stage mother who would do anything for her child. What distaste, to be lumped into that category.

It sounds like hard work. What did you do for enjoyment?

Our biggest pleasure came from Broadway shows. We knew if the children were going to be stars they had to study musical comedy, drama, and dance. Over and over we saw Ethel Barrymore in *The Soul Kiss*. Most of the performances met with my approval, but when they shocked me, I talked to the children about what we saw. I explained the difference between proper behavior for children and adults.

I loved those days with Dellie and Sonny, but sometimes I felt a weakness raising them alone. Frederick wanted to be supportive, but those early years were difficult, especially that first year of preparation. I remember one tiff with Frederick when I used our savings to buy props and costumes. We had so little money, but I appealed to his intellect and smoothed it over with him. One time, and the thought of it makes me laugh because of their later success, we had exactly one egg left for supper. I scrambled it and divided it between the two children and chose not to eat. Those days brought the three of us closer.

We missed Frederick, but he cheered us on with support and ideas. He was the first to recognize Dellie and Sonny's distinct styles. Dellie had a feminine and carefree manner while our shy Sonny worked hard and pushed himself with study and practice.

Did you ever want to throw in the towel?

We never gave up hope. Our perseverance paid off with a lucky break in 1907 when Dellie and Sonny debuted at a tryout theatre in New Jersey. Before the show I got everything ready. I assembled the wedding cakes we used as props during the show and cued the electrician on the split-second timing of the lights. Dellie and Sonny wowed the audience and got glowing write-ups in the newspaper.

THE GREATEST CHILD ACT IN VAUDEVILLE! one article claimed. For that engagement, they earned fifty dollars a week.

Vaudeville seems really foreign to me. Tell me more

about it.

Vaudeville presented situations that other children would never encounter. Instead of school days and children their own age, Dellie and Sonny's peers were acrobats, comics, clowns and animal trainers. But life does not fit into a box. Children learn from various sources, and luckily for me, Frederick agreed. His support continued with the money he sent us and his good ideas. One idea was to change our last name, Austerlitz.

"Too hard to spell, too hard to remember, and not American enough," he said. He suggested changing the children's name to Astaire, from my uncle L'Astaire. Later I too changed my name.

When Frederick could manage it, he hopped a train to join us for a few weeks at a time. His male presence worked well for making calls. He charmed agents and producers, booked our first tour at one hundred fifty dollars a week, and off we went. After each show, Sonny begged to stay at the theatre to further his "ham" education. He called it learning a lot of things and not getting any smarter. His freedom didn't worry me, but I got anxious for Dellie's safety since girls are more at risk. I insisted she return with me to whatever fleabag hotel functioned as our current home. There I read and she played with her paper dolls.

You mentioned that you tutored both children?

During the tour in the mornings, I taught them mathematics, history, and geography, and they studied in boarding houses and Pullman cars. Our one obstruction had nothing to do with education. The Gerry Society, headed by Elbridge Gerry, claimed the stage too sinful for children under sixteen. He and his self-appointed group of people decided they were in charge of public morals and the intellectual rights of children. I told Frederick I didn't feel our lives were Mr. Gerry's business, but in public I acted accommodating since he was a powerful man who had a way with lawmakers. I used cunning to obtain a waiver that explained my proper supervision and tutor work with my children. Anyone who met us knew I was adamant about school subjects. Outside of that, show time became a lesson in itself. We stood quietly in the wings and observed other performers and then shared what we learned and decided what to include in our own act.

After that twenty-two week tour, we signed on for another. By then, Sonny had mastered tap dancing and developed his own choreography ideas. He learned to play the piano, accordion, a little bit of clarinet, and he took singing lessons. Dellie sang and played piano. In their act they played the role of a couple, so they had to move as a team and look the part.

Was that a problem for either of them?

I don't believe so. They understood the difference between reality and make-believe. When Dellie hit her teens and grew four inches taller than Sonny, we had to temporarily retire to wait for him to reach her height, so we rented a house across the river from Manhattan. The respite from touring gave them a chance to do normal things, and Sonny's intellect meant he skipped fourth grade and enrolled in fifth. Outside of school, both of them took dance and I gave them French lessons.

French lessons? How wonderful. How did you reenter show business?

In two years Sonny's height caught up to Dellie's. We

moved to a boardinghouse in the city, and I enrolled them in Ned Wayburn's Dancing School for a combination of tap, step, and ballroom dancing. I respected Mr. Wayburn and paid him one thousand dollars to create a sophisticated act, although money was tight. Frederick had little outside work and our bookings were infrequent. In retrospect, I see it wasn't all bad, because Dellie and Sonny's performances in small-town houses improved their new act.

Travel life seemed hard, but I did what I could to keep Sonny's spirits positive. With Dellie I had no problems. With her bubbly personality, she saw traveling as a lark, but Sonny missed baseball and playing pool. I tried to emphasize his gains and highlight how much he loved to watch the ballroom dancing of Vernon and Irene Castle, even though their dancing didn't fit his style. He analyzed the beat of every type of music and reminisced about the days when his old dance professor, Alvienne, pounded out rhythms with a wooden stick against the back of a chair. As Sonny searched for a style to call his own, he studied the Negro tap dancers and their reactions to jazz and ragtime.

With our more relaxed work schedule in 1914, we had time for a wonderful summer vacation at the Delaware Water Gap in Pennsylvania. Dellie loved to boat and dance with the socialites, and Sonny rode horses and played golf. I liked carefree days and quiet evenings.

As a young man, did Sonny's interests expand?

After that vacation, Sonny visited the sheet music companies and searched for hits in Tin Pan Alley, on West 28th St. between 5th and 6th Avenue in New York City. At Remick's he made friends with George Gershwin, who worked as a song plugger.

Gershwin is a fabulous musician. Tell me about their commonalities.

The two of them felt a strong bond with their connection to music. George liked Sonny's new ideas and his left-hand-ed, hard-thumping way on the piano. They shared their dreams for the future. George told Sonny he planned to be a songwriter and Sonny confessed he wanted to be a Broad-way star, so they dreamed of doing a show together. Years later, George played rehearsal piano for a show where Sonny danced, and eventually they did work together on Broadway. Did you know that George Gershwin wrote over six hundred songs?

No, I didn't. That's a prolific amount.

It's an incredible outlay, and how sad about his passing. He was so young.

It was a terrible loss to music lovers. I admire all of his songs. Can you think of anything else about Sonny and Dellie's early career?

They did a tour in New England that we called "New Songs and Smart Dances." Those Yale boys loved Dellie, and the tour brought success, which meant Frederick could buy a back page ad in *Variety* for the critics' positive reviews. Next came Broadway, with Dellie and Sonny's first show, *Over the Top*, in 1917.

With Frederick so far away, how did you cope?

Sometimes I found it difficult. I was married, but my hus-band lived in Omaha, and I worked in a world of men. I think some people might have wondered if I liked women in a certain way because I definitely stayed away from other men. As far as Frederick, he lived his separate life in Omaha and I didn't pry. I knew when I met him that he was a salesman in the beer trade, and I accepted that it meant alcohol mixed with some unusual behavior.

Frederick had a need to feel strong and successful, which meant that even when he had financial difficulties, his pride prevented him from living off the earnings of his children. I guess at some point I could have joined him in Omaha. When Sonny and Dellie found work in Broadway shows, they no longer had to tour. I didn't join him though. I remained with Dellie and Sonny in their suite overlooking Central Park West.

What changes happened when Dellie and Sonny became adults?

I had time to relax and Sonny took over the business affairs. He dressed in smart, stylish clothes like George Cohen and visited potential backers. Sometimes in social situations he had a problem with stammering, but not when he played pool and craps with his friends. Sonny liked a grounded life.

Dellie was the opposite. She was happy anywhere. By then, each of them found their place in the team. Sonny created new ideas and took care of the day-to-day logistics, and Dellie was funny and beautiful with an airy, nutty, but tasteful style. She loved the attentions of the young men who showered her with flowers and presents.

Outside of work, Dellie took a jog in the morning and played table games like Scrabble and canasta later in the day. In private, Sonny called her "funny face." She had a short temper and spoke with swear words. She loved to make trouble, but Sonny never let her outrageous comments bother him. He had a set response to anyone's questions.

"That's my sister," he said.

Sonny was quiet and reserved, a caretaker who avoided trouble. His serious nature had a positive influence on Dellie. Even when he was a boy, he coaxed her to practice the routines over and over with him. She called him "Moaning Minnie."

"Nothing ever pleases you," she said.

It was sometimes true. Sonny could be a perfectionist, with a tendency to be grumpy when provoked. Early in their career, when Dellie was the brilliant one and the critics wrote about her performances, Sonny played supporter in the background. Dellie captivated audiences while Sonny provided discipline. They were good for each other.

I wish I could feel close to my own brother. Did Frederick ever join the family permanently?

Eventually he did come to live with us and we all had to adjust. We had enough money by then, but Frederick still had that Old World belief that a man should support his family. He engaged in several business ventures, and when all of them lacked success, his cheer turned to depression. I had hopes that would change when Dellie and Sonny got an offer to do a show in Europe. I pleaded with him to join us for a vacation. His failing health worried me and I thought it would be good for him to get away. He insisted we go without him and promised to join us when he felt better.

I never should have left, but I did what he suggested and took my first Atlantic crossing to England on the *Aquitania*, which they called the "Ship Beautiful." On the trip, the crew talked Sonny and Dellie into being part of a charity show, which turned out differently than they planned. What happened was this: a storm made the sea so choppy that it affected their movements and made their dance routine hilarious. The audience loved it. Sonny always remembered things like that and used the idea for future shows. But a black cloud hung over us.

Did something happen in Europe?

Not right away. After we arrived in London and got settled, Sonny and Dellie appeared in the stage show *Stop Flirting*. As it toured other cities, they moved with the show, and during that run we received the horrifying news. Frederick was gravely ill. I returned immediately to the United States and took Frederick to Wernersville State Hospital in Pennsylvania to help him recuperate from serious complications of his illness.

On the day I had to send the telegram to Sonny and Dellie that Frederick had died, I didn't know what to say. I cried the whole time I dictated it. Their producer offered to close the show and give them time off, but they chose to keep working. In the midst of tragedy, Dellie and Sonny wanted to be strong. We were separated for so long, and now when we looked forward to being together, it had disappeared in an instant. I wrote letters to both of them about our grieving emotions. In between sentences of sadness, I encouraged them to live their lives.

When did you feel some relief from the pain?

It took a while, but one bit of news helped. After a show one night, Sonny and Dellie met Prince George of Wales and little baby Elizabeth. Prince George became Sonny's friend, and from then on Sonny and Dellie were crazy for the English and their way of life. Sonny claimed the English were mad, all mad. In London he developed a passion for horseracing, which at that time was sporty and not as commercial as it is now. He loved the track, the jockeys, and his trainer friends. I think the horses' graceful movements appealed to him. He bet for fun after he studied the forms, and he made his own betting systems. Sonny and Dellie were both sad when they had to leave England and return home.

I love England. The people are so different from Americans. What was their next show?

They got busy with a performance in the Broadway show *Lady, Be Good.* George Gershwin wrote the musical score, and his brother Ira penned exquisite lyrics. At last, Sonny and George could work together and combine their talents. One critic wrote that he didn't know if George was born to write rhythms for Sonny's feet, or whether Sonny was born to show how Gershwin music should really be danced. I adored the song "Fascinating Rhythm," and I loved to watch my children dance to it. After the show, the accolades continued. Fans surrounded Dellie and Sonny.

Dellie gradually realized she was losing interest in professional dancing and the stage, so Sonny had to plan his own future. When he got a call to help rehearse the leads for *Girl Crazy,* he began to imagine other partners. The female lead they chose was a young, Midwestern girl, Ginger Rogers, who sang two songs: "But Not For Me" and "Embraceable You." With all the rehearsal space in use, Ginger and Sonny had to practice her dance routine in the foyer of the theatre. Can you picture them dancing on the rug out there?

I would have liked to be the manager of that theatre so I

could watch.

In *Girl Crazy*, Sonny's romantic appeal and Ginger's magic mesmerized the audience. I liked the show when it came out. Ethel Merman made a hit out of the Gershwin's song "I Got Rhythm."

Everyone likes that song. I love the line, "Who could ask for anything more?" Were you surprised at Dellie's loss of interest in dancing?

She had danced for twenty-four years, so after she turned thirty, I noticed she wanted her days to be her own. I can't say I was surprised. In retrospect, I wonder if I influenced her exit from the stage. It upsets me to think that way, and I hope I didn't play a part.

What do you mean?

I wonder now if I might have been too tightfisted. I lived with them, supervised the apartment staff, and attended to a lot of business matters. They made four thousand dollars a week, but I only allowed Dellie one hundred dollars a week. She might have resented my interference in her life.

I remember one troubling time that had nothing to do with money, an awful scare when Dellie had an accident. A boat engine blew up and burned her face, neck, and shoulders. I spent weeks in the hospital with her. Luckily, she recovered with no scars and went on to perform with Sonny on their third London hit, *Funny Face*.

The close of that show brought the biggest change to her life. Prince Aly Khan brought a friend to her dressing room, Lord Charles Cavendish. He was the Duke of Devonshire's younger brother, an English lord and a member of an ancient noble family. She adored him instantly and became intrigued with the thought of becoming an English lady. So at age thirty-three, Dellie retired from show business to marry Charlie. I adored Charlie. He called me "Mother Ann," and I called him my naughty son. He and Dellie moved to Ireland and Lismore Castle, which was given to them by Charlie's father as a wedding present.

Were you still able to see her?

I divided my time between their household and Sonny's and helped out wherever I could. When I lived with Dellie and Charlie at Lismore during the second war, I mended every single one of the shredded tapestries that hung in the library. Dellie did marvelous needlework, and we both worked to keep the estate going. When Sonny visited, we had such fun. He wanted no one to recognize him on his daily walks to the betting shop in the village, so he wore dark spectacles. It didn't work. He was so dapper no one could mistake him for someone else.

Was there any friction after Dellie left the team?

Oh no, they loved each other. When Sonny had to leave after his visits, his emotional support continued. Poor Dellie had such trials; my heart went out to her. All three of her children, a daughter and twin sons, died a few hours after birth. I could do so little to ease her pain. Her worst physical problem came after her daughter's death, but the psychological toll seemed even worse. It was not a good time for her.

In time she embraced a positive outlook. She loved to hear of her brother's success and she never seemed to regret her retirement, even when she read the news articles about Sonny dancing with Ginger Rogers. She knew they had wonderful chemistry and vitality. Part of their appeal came from the creative moves they learned from Hermes Pan, the brilliant choreographer. That man insisted on perfection. He worked wonders for Sonny's career and so did Ginger. As a new and unrelated partner, she helped Sonny overcome his shyness, which might have helped in his relationship with Phyllis Baker.

Let me put a sweater over my shoulders, and we can walk a bit while we talk. As I get older I cannot seem to regulate heat and cold.

Can I help in any way?

Don't worry about me. We can walk to the hedge and back. My strength is not what it once was.

I'll distract you with romance. How did Sonny meet Phyllis?

The two of them were first introduced at a golf and luncheon party at the Vanderbilt's. They sat together and shared their life stories. When Sonny met Phyllis, she was married and in the midst of both a divorce and a custody battle for her son, Peter.

Sonny liked Phyllis from the start. She was tiny and attractive with a willowy figure and an adorable little lisp to her R's, so she called Sonny "Fwed." She could be both proper and relaxed, and in fashion she liked clean lines, nothing splashy. Sonny was lovestruck.

"He wanted me desperately and felt determined to have me," Phyllis said. Sonny even stopped working for a time to pursue her.

Dellie and I were thrilled. We got along well with Phyllis, especially me since we were a lot alike, strong-willed and interested in fashion. Two days after Phyllis got custody of

Peter, they married. Phyllis was twenty-five and Sonny thirty-three. They moved to California and Sonny entered the world of moving pictures.

Did they have more children?

Three years after their marriage, Fred Jr. was born, and later, little Ava. Fatherhood suited Sonny. He had a special way with children and loved to watch them develop into adults. I admired that Sonny accepted Peter as his own child and that he respected Fred Jr.'s decision not to dance. The boy had absolutely no interest. By then, Sonny and his family enjoyed a quiet life. Phyllis ran the house and their ranch and did the tax returns. She acted a bit possessive and kept Sonny on a tight rein, but he didn't seem to mind. He played golf with friends, but when Phyllis wanted to play, they golfed together.

Did anything change with Dellie in Europe after the advent of the war?

I worried about her, because after the war broke out she refused to leave Ireland and return to the United States. She wanted to help the war effort. Poor Charlie fell ill from alcohol when Dellie was off working with the Red Cross. Because of the raging war, she couldn't get a permit to cross the Irish Sea, so Charlie's mother had to nurse him. Dellie was devastated when Charlie died at age thirty-nine. I miss him. We all do.

Did she return to the United States after he died?

Not right away. At first, I joined Dellie in Ireland and helped her run Lismore Castle. She felt lonely without Charlie even though she had support from friends and her seventy workers.

What did all those people do?

They raised crops and cattle, cut timber, fished the river for salmon, and took care of the house and grounds. For quite a while, Dellie mourned Charlie, but she had a good attitude and chose to stay lively. Everyone commented on how marvelous it was to talk with her. She was popular and a bit of a clown. As her grief eased, she didn't lack suitors.

After about three years, Dellie married Kingman Douglass, an investment banker. They have homes in New York and Jamaica, but Dellie never acts spoiled. And neither does Sonny. By the time he became a huge success, he was in his midthirties and old enough to have a level attitude towards fame. He dislikes pretentious people and avoids them. Anything ostentatious has no interest for him.

Sonny is such a talented man. Is he vain about anything? His hair?

I imagine you are referring to the hairpiece he wears. I won't speak any more of it. I can tell you, Sonny loves the simple things in life: food, television, and friends. His eating habits aren't fancy, and he loves homemade soup and meat loaf. His favorite soap opera is *The Guiding Light*. Dellie and Sonny and I spend hours on the phone discussing various episodes and characters. Sonny prefers television to reading, but most of all he prefers the company of men. He and a friend rent a boat and fish near Catalina Island. Off they go in their gray flannels.

This might interest you. Sonny doesn't tell jokes as many men do, just amusing stories of his everyday life. Let me give you an example. Every Sunday morning Sonny went with me to church. Once in a while George Roosevelt, who is somehow related to Franklin, helped with the collection. One day Sonny attached a piece of string to the dollar bill he donated, and pulled it off just as George stepped away. Sonny can be such a tease. After church he played gin rummy with his best friend Bill.

What do Sonny and Dellie do when they're together now, and what are some other pastimes of his?

They don't attend the ballet or the opera as some might think, because Sonny dislikes both. They play backgammon, which they learned from a stagehand when they were younger. When Sonny is alone, he plays the drums, and he even has an entire percussion set in his dressing room. His excellent rhythm and timing lends itself to dance.

Besides hard work, what is it that makes him such a talented dancer?

Whenever Sonny dances he has an uncanny ability to focus, like Japanese theatre. One of his signature moves involves a sudden movement from a big outburst of tap dancing to a sublime swish. I'm sure you've seen it in his shows.

I have, and it's delightful to watch. Tell me more about the women he has worked with.

He met Audrey Hepburn at Paramount on a big stage with just a piano and Sonny's choreographer Hermes Pan. They practiced for hours and hours. Sonny's nonchalance and perfectionist nature influenced Audrey, and Audrey in turn influenced Sonny. All his dancing partners did. He likes feminine, strong women and feels protective of them. As far as dancing partners, he liked Cyd Charisse and, of course, Ginger. Hermes Pan claimed that Sonny even taught the Prince of Wales to dance.

Who was his biggest influence?

George Gershwin. Sonny's grief overcame him when George's illness struck so suddenly and viciously. I have to say again, what a cruel thing to happen to such a talented man. At the end, George could barely talk. His brother Ira told Sonny that the last word he spoke was "Fred."

Tragedies might not define us, but they shape us.

Every family has them. We certainly had ours. In 1954, our dear Phyllis died of lung cancer. She smoked. After her death Sonny just cried and cried, even at rehearsals. He suffered so much pain it nearly killed him. They had been married twenty-one years. Ava was only twelve when she lost her mother, so she and Sonny found solace in each other, and from then on Ava was a companion and hostess to him. They would come to New York and spend Christmas with me, and then I went to live with them in California. Ava was a plump child but she grew into a beauty. How wonderful she is, bright and warm.

Any romance for Sonny now?

Sonny met Robyn Smith, a jockey, in 1973. She raced horses for Alfred Vanderbilt and he introduced them. Even though she's forty-five years younger than Sonny, they have an excellent friendship. Sonny contemplates leaving professional dancing. He feels tired.

Do you have any closing thoughts?

Sonny is never too tired to care for me, and I appreciate it. He treats me like a queen, with a chauffeured car. I put on my little black coat, and off I go. Sometimes I feel like he's the father I wish I had. Before he goes out with friends, he comes to my room to kiss me goodnight.

Both Sonny and Dellie brought me joy. For those people who accuse me of pushing them through dance school, into vaudeville, and then the Broadway stage, I say absolutely not. My children have strong wills, and if they had been unhappy they would have protested. I encouraged them, believed in them, and worked hard to make them smart and accomplished. Whatever choices a mother makes for her children, there are positives and negatives. I can close with a statement that rings true. "No mother can do everything right."

Now let me walk you to the door.

Thank you. I loved learning about dance.

And I enjoyed this visit with the past.

INTERVIEW WITH FRED ASTAIRE
ON THE DEATH OF HIS MOTHER

My mother had a stroke and died this year. She was ninety-six. I loved her deeply and I credit her for my career as a dancer. She told me when I started in vaudeville that all I needed was experience. She proved to be correct.

12

Interview with Sophia Liston, a Friend
Mother Mary Carver

GEORGE WASHINGTON CARVER,
TEACHER AND SCIENTIST, BORN JULY 14, 1864

Education is the key to unlock the golden door of freedom.
—George Washington Carver

JAN HELEN MCGEE

You admire George, but the two of you aren't related, correct?

SOPHIA LISTON

I'm George's friend, but I tease him and call myself his sixth mother. I could go on and on about that boy and his skills and the good in him.

JAN HELEN MCGEE

How did you meet?

SOPHIA LISTON

Through my friend Miss Etta Budd, the art director at Simpson Methodist College here in Iowa. When George started at Simpson, he spent a lot of time under the skylight in the art room. He felt safe there since the rest of the college was problematic for him. Before I met George, I had pockets of ignorance I didn't even know about. See, the college had three hundred white students, and George had trouble finding friends.

When he first arrived, he wanted to take in other students' laundry to make money, but he was timid and had trouble socially, so no students brought him any. His color and his living in an abandoned shack made it worse. Then George decided to take art, which was unheard-of. No Negro studied art. With an inner strength I try to emulate, he made a plea directly to Miss Etta. Not only did she work at the college, but she graduated from there.

"Why ever would you want to take an art course?" she asked George.

"I love art and I want to paint plants," George told her.

He showed her his painting of a prairie rose, and that impressed her since it didn't look like any rose she had ever seen. She felt a kinship with him like all his extra mothers do, and she wanted to help him. She had been my teacher; that's how we knew each other. She's perceptive, so she knew George and I would get along. She walked down North Howard Street and stopped at number 805. That's my house. I opened the door and invited her in.

"I have a talented Negro boy who wants to study painting. He will saw my stove wood for his tuition, but he needs a room. He's a promising young man, and we must help him," she said.

It didn't take much to convince me. I trust her, so I put on my hat and set off for George's tumbledown home, where I rapped on the door.

What was your first impression of him?

He opened the door and stood quite still. I scarcely knew how to speak to him. Something in his manner made it difficult for me to state my real errand. I guess he saw a white lady who couldn't get a word out. Then I had a thought. I'd ask for aid instead of offering it.

"Can you do some sketching for me?" I asked. "I want to paint my flower garden, but my drawing is not good enough. Will you help me with it?" George agreed. We talked and I snuck a look at his living area.

What was it like? Was he messy or neat?

It was tidy in there, but I could see he had no money. He had a battered black pan half filled with cornmeal and water, and a discarded old stove with an empty, gaping boiler waiting for wash. As we talked, I felt such trust for George. I told him a room nearer the campus would be more suitable for his laundry business, and that a friend of mine would rent him one at the corner of Detroit Avenue and Buxton, just opposite the canning factory. I never knew anyone like George, and anyone who gave him a half a chance would be intrigued. We parted on good terms.

After I left, I got busy telling all the students I knew about George's laundry business. In no time at all, he had all he could manage. But what a pack of sour pickles to keep clothes clean for a bunch of roughneck college boys.

I love laundry.

How's that?

The organization of it all. I like to fold. I relish dirty to clean. Then what happened?

The next day I took him plenty of boxes from the bookstore my husband, Arthur, and I operate. George made his furniture from them.

He turned boxes into furniture?

I never knew a young man so resourceful and industrious.

Did he eventually meet your husband?

He did, and they became friends. Arthur liked George's company. I can't count how many hours George spent studying in the bay window of our home. I love him dearly. Even after he moved away, when I write him letters, I never use my given name. "Your mother" is how I sign them.

You said you're his sixth mother. Can you tell me about his first mother?

I should have told you about his mother right off. Her name was Mary, and she was a slave. If you want to know about his grandmother, well, poor Mary never got the chance to know her own mother. The two had been separated early on, like too many slaves. When Mary was about thirteen, her owners, the Grants, sold her to Moses Carver for seven hundred dollars.

Did the Carvers have a lot of slaves?

Moses and his wife, Miss Susan, were dead set against slavery, so I should give you some background in order to understand why Moses went against his beliefs. The two of them lived in a remote area of Missouri called Diamond Grove in a cabin set out of sight of the road. They had over two hundred acres where Moses worked long hours cultivating hay and oats and vegetables and fruit and honey. That meant Miss Susan spent a lot of time alone. When she lost her only baby girl, a terrible loneliness set in. I know that feeling myself. So many of us lose babies.

It happens so often. I lost a child before it was born, just barely formed.

It's a loss that's hard to accept. With Miss Susan, she was getting up in years and must have felt worse thinking no more babies would come. She did some mothering after Moses's brother died, when she raised his three, but they eventually grew up and left. After that, her aloneness pulled on her and she needed an extra pair of hands. Moses started a search for a young woman who would work hard. The Groves had Mary for sale, so Moses put aside his opposition and purchased her. Mary was a companion for Miss Susan, and they became like sisters.

On the farm, Moses let the womenfolk go about their business and kept to himself. He thrived with animals, which he loved maybe more than people. A good adjective to describe Moses would be eccentric. He walked around all day with a pet rooster perched on his shoulder while all sorts of other critters followed behind. Because of that uncanny rapport, he had success training racehorses. As for people, he liked children and visitors. When neighbors came by in the evening, he took out his fiddle and played while the others sang and danced. On Sundays, he didn't attend church. He belonged to the Masonic Order, so that's how he practiced his faith.

What kind of woman was Miss Susan?

She believed in the Bible and had good steady words for George to live by. As far as whether she liked visitors, I only know she had a quiet way about her, did things a little old-fashioned, and kept to herself. George told me she loved having Mary for a friend. That ended too soon.

What happened? You seem upset.

I am, but I'll tell you. I hope I don't have the facts all crooked. With slaves, family lines become impossible to track. I'm so sorry for those slaves torn from their loved ones. They lived with no continuity and no way to write things down. A reliance on word of mouth had to cover everything. I thank the good Lord that slavery is gone.

Mary had five children. Her oldest was Melissa, who must have been sold away. What a fate for a loving mother. Next, Mary had twin daughters who died early on. James, who they called Jim, came four months after Mary joined the Carvers. Then a year or so later, Mary gave birth to George. I don't know about the first three children's backgrounds, but Jim's census records list him as mulatto, so his daddy could have been a white man. Maybe a neighboring slaveholder. Whoever knows, since those poor women had no men to protect them?

Do you know anything about the rumor that Moses was George's father?

No, I don't believe Moses fathered Mary's children. Back then, some owners did father children, but from how George describes Moses, he was true to Miss Susan. I guess no one will ever know who fathered Mary's babies. Those secrets go to the grave. George doesn't know his exact birth date, but he marks it as July 14, 1864. The census listed him as colored. Might be, George's daddy was Giles, a slave from over on the Grant place. After Mary moved to the Carver's, Giles used to come over and sit with Mary on the doorstep outside her shanty.

Does George know what happened to Giles?

That's another sad tale. Giles was hauling wood when somehow the ox that pulled the load got scared and bolted. The jolt caused Giles to lose his balance and fall off the wagon, and a heavy log landed on him and killed him. He could have been George's father, though Mary never confided to Miss Susan one way or the other. Or if she did, Miss Susan never told George. Neither George nor Jim had a father in their lives, but they had Moses to look up to. He did something right, since George turned out to be a fine young man.

How long was Mary with George?

Not long enough. He only knew her as a baby. Before I tell you the details of the next tragedy, I should mention that Jim grew up big and healthy, but George was a sickly baby. I think he came too soon, since his lungs gave him problems. Most nights George coughed and choked so much that Mary had to pour honey doctored with tansy into his mouth. Then that poor baby got the whooping cough, but Mary and Miss Susan pulled him through.

What happened to Mary?

This is the worst part; George lost his mother to kidnappers. It's tragic to never know your mama, and George doesn't recall anything about her. Let me tell how it happened. Back then in Missouri, even though it was a Union State, jungle law prevailed. Vigilantes and Confederate irregulars raided homes to steal money and slave women and their children. Some outlaws took slaves to sell in Arkansas because the price paid for them increased fivefold from the beginning of

the war. Other outlaws turned slaves in to the Union authorities for a bounty.

Moses Carver had his home raided three times. One time,
the outlaws strung him up by his thumbs to a branch of a
walnut tree, put burning coals on his feet and demanded
money. Moses had buried his gold and despite the torture,
he wouldn't tell, so they gave up and left. The third time the
outlaws came, Moses spotted them.

"Run Sue, run Mary," he cried as he scooped up Jim and
ran into the woods to hide behind a brush pile.

Mary and baby George couldn't get away fast enough.
The outlaws stormed in, grabbed them, threw them on their
horses and took off. Moses stood in the dirt and raged, and
Miss Susan cried.

They desperately wanted Mary and George back, so Moses
hired Bentley, a Union army scout, who understood outlaws
in the area. Moses didn't like Bentley much, but he knew his
value, so he gave him one of his racehorses and the search
party took off. Winter weather made tracking easy, and they
did find evidence, but they never caught those outlaws. The
search party had just about given up when they saw an abandoned cabin and found George in there, alone and crying.
The outlaws left him behind. It seems George's sickly constitution saved his life. There was no sign of Mary, so Bentley
returned to Diamond Grove and gave George to the Carvers.
He figured the outlaws took Mary downriver and left her for
dead.

At that point, Moses and Bentley needed to settle their
business. Moses originally promised forty acres and the
racehorse for the safe return of Mary and George, but since

Bentley rescued only George, he took only the black mare.

What a sad situation. Does George talk about her?

He thinks of his mother every day and wonders what advice she would have given him. I know she'd be proud of him since he's a talented, hardworking man. Not only that, but he appreciates how much all his mothers have taught him. And George returns the favor with his kindness.

After his mother was gone, who took over his care?

Moses and Miss Susan moved George and Jim out of the slave cabin and into their main house. Then Miss Susan set about nursing George's terrible cough. The force of it tore his vocal cords, and that's why his voice is soft, weak, and high pitched, a bit like birds chirping. His early trauma left its mark in other ways I'm sure, and one example is his stammer. It barely affects him now, but he claims he had a terrible time up until college. I guess with age, we conquer our demons. On the other hand, maybe that stammer did him some good, since it might have thrust him into his world of plants. Nature helps a quiet man bloom, and in the home of George and Miss Susan, those boys did bloom. My husband says it right.

"I take off my hat to Moses and Miss Susan for the love they gave those boys."

Both Moses and Miss Susan made a Herculean effort. They raised the boys like blood kin and insisted on being called Uncle and Aunt. But George longed to know more of his origins and pestered Miss Susan for information about his mother. When she cried with grief over the loss of her friend, he had to stop.

Did he learn any more about her?

She told him a few similarities between his mother and himself. Both had honesty in their speech and acted upright. Both had good coordination between hand and eye, and both had a quick mind. Mary couldn't read or know one letter from another, but she knew how to find any page in the almanac.

When Susan talked about Mary, George stood by her spinning wheel and longed for the day she'd return. Miss Susan knew that would never happen, so she diverted George's sadness with work. His cough meant no heavy chores, so he watered the stock, weeded, and did the housework, and Miss Susan taught him to cook, iron tablecloths, knit with four needles, and crochet. Maybe the loss of her little girl gave her the impetus to teach George things other Negro boys didn't know. Those skills set him apart and paid his way when it came time to go to school.

I can bake, but I'm not much of a cook, and I can't knit or crochet. I like the satisfaction of pressing but not in the heat of summer. Did George prefer indoor work?

He did a good job indoors, but he preferred outdoors. He cultivated a flower garden in the bushes, away from the house and out of sight of the neighbors, since they said flowers were a foolish waste of time. He took long walks in the woods and searched for plants and wildflowers to bring back home and transplant in his garden. He cried if they broke apart on the way back; that's how sensitive George is to nature. As he worked, he sang "Jimmy Crack Corn" and "Old Dan Tucker." When he sang, he had no stammer at all. George's interest in nature led to drawing the flowers and plants he collected. To this day, he loves to draw and paint.

"To those who have as yet not learned the secret of true happiness, begin now to study the little things in your own yard," he often said.

I love my pink rose bush more than any stick of my furniture. Did George ever enlighten the neighbors with his knowledge of plants?

That garden in his backyard was a secret, but in a small town, secrets rarely stay hidden. Soon the neighbors noticed his success and sought his opinion on how to cure sick plants and tend vegetables, and when to plant. They called him the plant doctor. Besides plants, George collected insects and reptiles and even snuck frogs into Miss Susan's kitchen to examine. In that way, he acted like his brother and the other boys, but most of the time he was the opposite of strong Jim. George didn't like athletic contests or boy shenanigans and no rough-and-tumble, noisy activities for him. One thing the two brothers did share was a love of clowning, mimicry, and comic recitations. Every day they tried to outdo each other. I think that led George to his interest in theatre performances.

Quiet activities came easy to George because he used to worry about his physical health. Due to his lung problems, the doctor told Miss Susan that he wouldn't live past twenty-one. He proved that doctor wrong, and later he grew strong enough to work in the fields with Moses and Jim. He walked down the rows real fast alongside Moses's niece, and he dropped the corn kernels from his little bucket. They did it in perfect rhythm: a step, drop some grain, and then over again. George liked the symmetry of it since he had a good ear for rhythm and music, which I attribute to Moses' fiddle playing and singing. In addition to the gift of music, Moses taught him not to fear being different—an important lesson to learn.

Another thing Moses and Miss Susan did for George was provide him with free time for long walks to study nature. When he took his walks, George found ways to help animals. In the forest he peeled the bark from the north side of a tree, boiled it, and sweetened it with honey and made a drench for horses that had bots, which is an intestinal or stomach problem they get. Another thing he did was collect sassafras bark and spice bushes to make the lard smell good.

Did George ever cause mischief?

All around, he was a good boy. I remember only a few stories he told me that point otherwise. One time Aunt Sue discovered Jim and George doing some nighttime wandering and she wanted to give them a switching, but Moses intervened. Another time, Moses gave both boys a thrashing for riding some sheep after they'd been warned not to do so. But that's boys' mischief, not malicious action.

George is a good person with an open heart. You would think with losing his mother so young and being raised by white people, he would turn out some kind of different. Not George. He felt at home with whites, since his aunt and uncle and most of his playmates were white. It could be that religion played a part in it. At the little Locust Grove Church, both George and Jim listened to circuit preachers, which led George to a deep belief in divine revelation and prophesy. As a child, he had a dream about a pocketknife that he deeply craved, and in the morning he found it stuck in a watermelon, just like in his dream.

"It's easy for me to foresee things," he said.

I think I have the gift of prophesy. My cousin says my great-great-grandmother had it too. People react in all kinds of ways when I tell them. How did you react when George told you?

At first I was taken aback and a little surprised. I never knew anyone who knew prophesy. I quizzed him on how he felt about it, but he didn't consider his abilities odd, only a part of him. Is that how you feel?

Yes, it's just a part of me, like my long fingers and freckles.

George was so accepting, and people noticed the goodness in his heart and his strong desire to learn. When it came time for him to read, Miss Susan used a Webster's blue-backed speller. When George's knowledge surpassed hers, she told him his next step was the Locust Grove School, located in the meetinghouse, same as the church. Sad to say, the town white folks barred George from the school, but they welcomed him for comedy productions and church on Wednesday nights and Sundays. On those days, George walked the mile to church alone, since the Carvers didn't attend. He liked the Sunday school teacher, and she took an interest in him and gave him a good foundation. She introduced him to Christianity, taught him Bible verses to recite, and gave him little Scripture cards. George showed me some of those cards he kept. They had a tiny picture of a flower or bird in the corner.

I had some myself when I was a child, though I haven't kept them. For me, the best part of church was singing.

I like to sing too. In Sunday school, the teacher sang duets with her son, so George sang with them. Soon he learned to pick out songs on the piano. That boy has talent.

How did George learn, if the townspeople didn't allow him into the school?

A smart young Negro man came to town, and Moses hired him to tutor George. When George's questions surpassed his tutor's knowledge, the man suggested a school in Neosho that accepted Negroes. George knew all about Neosho, since every year Moses allowed George and Jim to walk the nine miles over there. They had to go one at a time so they wouldn't get into mischief. Those trips opened George's eyes when he visited stores and saw new people, had adventures and spent his little bit of money. One time George brought home a steel-and-bone hook for crocheting.

Now I ought to explain why that school in Neosho existed. Back then, the law stipulated that if a county had thirty Negro children interested, there had to be a school for them. Moses suggested that George attend school during the week and come home on weekends to help out. George wanted Jim to join him, but he seemed content just to know how to read. Jim liked the farm, and by then, the Carvers paid him as their hired hand. So George packed his few things, said his goodbyes, and walked to his new life in Neosho.

Let me guess, he met his third mother there.

He did. First Mary, then Miss Susan, then Mariah Watkins, his second Negro mother. She lived with her husband, Andy, right next door to the Lincoln School for Colored Children; that's what they called it. George arrived on a Saturday, two days early, and slept his first night on the steps outside the school. The next morning, Mariah leaned over the fence to speak with George. As they talked, she took pleasure in his good manners and invited him into her home. George told me Mariah was a small, wiry woman with dancing eyes, a snippy tone, and a welcoming heart. That first morning she fed George breakfast. As soon as he started to eat, she began a lecture.

"You told me your name is Carver's George. Slavery is over. You are not Carver's George, but George Carver," she said. George sat up tall and felt proud to meet a woman of his color with a strong mind.

Later that day, Andy came home, met George, and noted his respect. Mariah and Andy laid out a plan. In return for help with the chores, George could eat and live with them in their three-room house. Those two kind people became Aunt Mariah and Uncle Andy. It was a good fit for George since Mariah was well respected in the white community and worked hard as a laundress and seamstress. Her third job as a midwife sometimes took her one hundred miles for a lying-in. When she left for birthing, George kept house for Andy, a short, strong man who did odd jobs, a man George called a smart, jack-of-all-trades fixer. The two of them relaxed only until Mariah returned. She ran a tight ship.

"Time should not be wasted," she told George, so during school recess, George hopped the fence and scrubbed laundry.

Did they work him too hard do you think?

Don't get me wrong; his life was not all work. Mariah shared her knowledge of medicinal herbs with him, and he learned a lot from her. On the Sundays he stayed in Neosho rather than return to the Carvers, Mariah took him to her church. There her personality changed. At home she liked quiet, but at church she shouted. Her yelling never rubbed off on George. I never heard him shout, but he does carry religion in his heart, and Mariah helped him in that way. She gave him a leather Bible one Christmas, and I've seen him mark his readings with a bookmark he embroidered. The two of them formed a close bond. George spoke of Mariah's acts of goodness, and she called him "my George." She taught him fine ironing and small stitches, how to plait rag rugs, and how to look at a garment and figure out how to duplicate it.

"You have a special gift from God," Mariah said

"I want to know," he told her as he watched her work. "I can do that."

What else do you know about Mariah?

She had been a slave on a huge plantation. Out of all the Negroes on that plantation, only one could read, which meant that girl had to teach everyone else. Since their owner forbade any learning, they did it at night by firelight. When George heard those stories, I think he pretended his mother was doing the telling. I don't really know for sure since we never spoke of it. What I do know is that George learned a lot from both Mariah and that Negro school. In his free time, he drew pictures on his school slate and studied, and sure enough, his knowledge surpassed that of his instructors. Those teachers did what they could, but there weren't enough of them to fill the demand for all the free schools for Negroes. George's one-room classroom had seventy-five students.

George needed to search for more education, which made sense since he was almost grown. He gave a lot of thought to the people he'd leave behind: Moses and Miss Susan, Mariah and Andy, and Jim, who had no interest in moving on, since his new trade as a plaster interested him far more than book learning. That relieved George, because if Mary came back, she'd find Jim. George had one last visit with Mariah and Andy. Mariah reminded him to read his Bible, and Andy said his will left everything to George. Jim walked with George from Diamond Grove back to Neosho, where they sat for a portrait.

He had to say goodbye to all the people he knew. That's wrenching and brave. How did he afford the move?

Things fell into place. The people down the street were packed to move to Fort Scott, Kansas. In case you're not aware, Kansas has always been a Free State, not Confederate. George thought Kansas seemed like a good place to live, so he hitched a ride in the back of their wagon. They took turns walking and riding the seventy-five miles. In Fort Scott, George heard of a household looking for help. He decided he'd use the skills Miss Susan and Mariah taught him.

"I found work as a girl," George said.

He moved into a fine house with a white family. The man was a blacksmith, so George swept the stable and delivered horses that'd been shod. Indoors he cooked, cleaned, and did laundry, and he even won a bread-and-biscuit-making contest at the church. When he saved enough money, he moved into a decrepit cabin by the stagecoach depot that cost him a dollar a week. He worked at the grocery store across the street and did laundry for guests of a fine hotel. That way he saved money to attend another school. It fit the pattern where he studied until he ran out of money and then took girl-work in different houses or chopped wood or helped in gardens. Everywhere he went, he read what he could find, usually old newspapers and pamphlets.

What prompted his next move?

A frightening thing happened. George witnessed some terrible white men hang and set fire to a Negro man, which upset him so much he left Fort Scott and became a wanderer. Along the way he bought an accordion for seven dollars and taught himself to play. That noisy instrument gave him a lot of satisfaction as he traveled. He made his own clothes and ate wild plants and mushrooms, and he'd stop here and there to attend school. In one town he worked in a greenhouse. By then he'd grown into a man, six feet tall. His quest for education continued.

I see that twinkle in your eye. Into his life came another mother?

You see a pattern here, don't you? After he traveled, he ended up in Olathe, Kansas, where he met his fourth mother, an elderly Negro woman named Lucy Seymour. She'd been looking for a hired girl but agreed on George. Her husband, Ben, farmed long hours, and Lucy ran a laundry business. George claims she was an even better laundress than Mariah, and she taught him how to iron fine undergarments and party dresses.

According to George, Lucy was a lovely, religious woman. Her only downfall seemed to be her superior attitude towards other Negroes, due to the fact that she had belonged to a nice Virginia family. But she was warm and loving to her nieces and nephews and they visited often, and George played checkers, tiddlywinks, and dominoes with them. Lucy and her husband Ben had no children, so in time, George became like a son to them.

On weekdays he attended school with Lucy's nieces. Imagine, a grown, six-foot-tall sixth grader. On Friday nights he played his accordion, and on Sundays he attended both morning and evening Methodist services with Lucy. George thought all denominations were alike, so Methodist seemed fine for him. He taught a class on Sundays, which piqued his interest in teaching. During the year that George spent in Olathe, the town experienced rapid growth from a new train line, so Lucy and Ben decided to move to Minneapolis, Kansas. Not long after they left, George joined them there.

In Minneapolis, Lucy did nursing for a doctor, and after George arrived, the doctor used him for odd jobs and lent him books to read. George did fancywork for the women of the town and hauled goods, while Ben farmed and Lucy started a laundry business.

What did he like about that area?

The wildflowers and grasses. After he and I met, he'd talk on and on about the beauty of nature and his observations. When he talks about plants, George uses a language all his own. If he could have lived only in that world, he might have found more contentment. Life can be so tough for a Negro man, and it bothered George a whole lot when he heard someone call Lucy a "darkie." Those were hard lessons to learn about survival in a hostile world. I tried to help George understand ignorance.

Life wasn't all negative, and he paid attention to the good. He attended high school, entered spelling bees, and sang in the church choir. On holidays, he loved to march in parades. In a long-tailed coat from the reverend, he arched his back and strutted like a majorette. That persona must have been like acting in plays. On stage, when he became someone else, George's stammer disappeared.

One time, the young people from his group put on a small play and gave George the female lead. He played the character as a flighty woman with a squeaky voice, which made the audience laugh. He became her so completely that even his large hands and feet didn't give him away. The audience enjoyed that play so much that the troupe performed in a nearby town, where George had his picture taken in a bustle, wig, and leg-o'-mutton sleeves. George tells that story so funny. The lady photographer chattered away and thought her subject was a girl. George liked to play his little games because he wanted people to be happy. He enjoyed some public venues, but most of the time he had a solitary nature with only a few close friends.

Then he received the sad news that his brother had died of smallpox. He did some grieving, and with no living relatives, took a hard look at his life. He'd done a lifetime of study in his twenty-five years, so he decided to apply for college. He wrote to Highland University and received a letter saying they'd be happy to have him.

Wasn't that surprising at the time, for a Negro man to be admitted to a college?

George didn't question it. He said his goodbyes to Lucy and Ben, then returned to Neosho and sat awhile at Jim's grave. Next he visited Miss Susan and Moses, who marveled at his new typewriter, the first in Diamond Grove. On that trip, he thought a lot about Mary, so he slept in her cabin and tried to feel close to a mother he couldn't remember. For many years after that visit, George returned to the Carver home, even after Miss Susan's death. On one of his last trips, Moses gave George his mother's spinning wheel and bill of sale, which he cherishes to this day.

During that visit after his brother's death, George told the Carvers of his college plans and once again said his goodbyes. He traveled to the university, where he found the admittance office and knocked on the door.

"We don't take coloreds here," the university man said.

Oh no!

That hurt George. On top of disappointment, his money was mostly gone from traveling. He had no choice but to stay and find an inexpensive room. In Highland, he attended church services and socials and met a lot of new people. When he shared the story of his rejection from the college, news spread among the churchwomen, who became indignant. They helped George find odd jobs and a place to live, but soon he took to the road again.

George wandered for quite some time and then stopped to find work in Winterset, Iowa near Des Moines. He got a job as a cook at a hotel and found a Methodist church to attend, where he met his fifth mama, a white woman named Helen Milholland.

What was she like?

She led the choir at church, and she loved his tenor voice. After she found out where he lived, she sent her husband, Dr. John Milholland out to get him. Right off, Helen took to George. She had an enormous enthusiasm for gardening and even had her own greenhouse. After they talked and shared their plant knowledge, they made their way inside her home, where George admired her paintings. Then Helen sat down to play her piano and George sang. A love of music and gardening sealed their friendship. Helen helped him with singing and George kept her painting area neat.

Did George live with the Milhollands?

No, he found a tiny cottage on the edge of town, with a kitchen shed and a parlor so he could open a small hand laundry. He found equipment that cost about fifty dollars. He used the little bit of cash he had, and the rest he secured with credit vouched for by the doctor. George had never bought on credit so it threw him into spasms. Since debt troubled him, he took on extra jobs to pay it off quickly.

By Christmas, George was just like a member of the Millholland family. The Dr. and Mrs. fell right in with George's unusual sense of fun, like when George dressed up and made everyone laugh as he distributed gifts. He gave the Milhollands some ornaments he made from chicken feathers and seed and some colored peanut necklaces. He spent wonderful evenings with that family. All day he worked hard, and after he finished, Helen wanted a detailed report about what he accomplished. She called her two children in to listen and used George as an object lesson. Her response would be the same every time.

"Who ever heard of anyone doing half that," she said. She loved George's work ethic and his dependability. "Just get George to make a promise and you can rest easy."

When George had free time, he carved corner pieces of picture frames to give away as souvenirs. When people raved about them, he had a set response.

"It cost ten cents, my Buckhorn handy Barlow blade, best old knife that ever was made," he rhymed.

Work, music, plants, carving, and learning filled George's days. He conducted his own private school for one, with a self-made schedule he rigidly enforced. His dream was to start a school in the South where he could teach. At that point, George had just about given up on college. The Dr. and Mrs. thought otherwise.

"You have to go back to school. You ought to be in school," they told him.

All summer they insisted. George knew he couldn't afford it, and he got so troubled at the thought that he stopped going to their house. Finally Helen sent her children to find out what was the matter, since their friendship had become that important. The Milhollands are fine people. After that, Dr. Milholland opened some doors and got George into the Simpson Methodist College, which had been started by a friend of President Lincoln who believed in the equality of all men. To pay his tuition, George sold his belongings and then gave his paintings on tin to Helen. He said his goodbyes and walked twenty-five miles to the college.

Oh, wonderful. Now you enter the picture?

Yes, as I said, we met through my friend Miss Etta.

What drew him to you?

George seemed so familiar to me. We had common outlooks, and a mystical religious orientation that later led me to the Christian Science faith. We helped each other spiritually in so many ways, and George brought beauty into my life. He rejuvenated my flower beds and brightened a corner with amaryllis bulbs, and he painted a picture of my garden in first bloom, which floods my senses to this day. When he gave it to me, I cried, and then he thanked me for what I had done when he first arrived.

He never found out all I had done for him. You see, Helen Milholland and I had corresponded. She told me George had written to her and mentioned how kind the people were to him, how they gave him a whole set of furniture to use instead of the boxes. I secretly had a hand in organizing that, but so many of us got George what he needed. Students and teachers would slip tickets for lectures under his door, or leave a fifty-cent piece when they were sure they wouldn't be caught. A dining hall cook gave him banquet leftovers and student saved their pencil stubs for him.

With all that support, George blossomed at Simpson. He played on the baseball team and took vocal and instrumental lessons. His vocal tones improved and strengthened until he could hit a high D and three octaves below.

I can only sing two octaves and a few notes, so that impresses me. How wonderful that you and Mrs. Milholland became friends. Did George return to visit her?

One time he took a vacation to see her and her husband. Through her letters, she kept such good contact with him, and they shared a love of words. George felt so good after he read them. "Your humble servant in God," is how he signed his own.

Is there anything else to add about Miss Etta?

At Simpson, George and Miss Etta became close. Painting lived in their hearts. Miss Etta allowed George to study art at Simpson, but she stressed the lack of opportunities for Negro men in that field. After much thought, George decided to study agricultural science instead of painting and music. Miss Etta wrote letters of introduction and enlisted the aid of her father, Dr. Budd, who worked as a professor of horticulture at Iowa State Agricultural College at Ames. They helped George get admitted there.

How did you cope with his leaving?

I hated to see him go, and I knew I'd miss him, but I believed someone in Ames would notice his greatness and help him on his path. George packed his things and said his sad good-byes.

The man does not give up, does he? What obstacles did he face at his next college?

When George got to Iowa College, he saw he was the only Negro student. On the first day, some young men yelled hateful words, and the college told George he couldn't eat with the other students. Instead, he had to eat with the field hands in the basement. George wrote to me and complained about that treatment and asked what he should do.

When I got that letter, my blood boiled. As soon as I could, I put on my best dress and hat and took the train for Ames. Every time that whistle blew, I used it as a signal to calm my anger. By the time I arrived, I had a resolve like none other. George met me at the train station. We strolled all over campus and admired the buildings and equipment, and when it came time to eat, I dined in the basement with him and the field hands. That turned some heads.

That's funny. What a great idea. What was George's reaction?

A few days later I got a letter from him. "The next day everything was different," he wrote. "The ice was broken and from then on, things went very much easier."

I was so happy to help a young man who preferred thinking to fighting, as we all should. Miss Etta helped some more too. She asked a professor of botany to find work for George. He gave him a job as North Hall's new janitor, and they became good friends.

Tell me about his everyday routines and personal customs.

We all love George, but I must say, we took note of his unusual habits. He played accordion and did crochet. Instead of a four-in-hand, he wore a cornhusk necktie or a flowing scarf. Every morning before breakfast, with a flower stuck in his buttonhole, he wandered through the woods to explore. Later in the day, he took another walk. If he came upon a friend, he spoke politely in that high-pitched voice of his. With his voice the way it was, public speaking posed a real challenge, with that breaking falsetto that he couldn't control. One teacher went so far as to tell him his voice was the most ridiculous that she had ever heard, with none quite so bad. Now how can a teacher speak so rudely? That comment hurt George's feelings, but he had a thick skin in public. His outside persona served him well.

George not only worked as a janitor but also supervised the college's greenhouse. Eventually he became respected enough to teach undergraduates. As far as other interests, George loved military science, and on campus he rose to the rank of captain. He joined the German club, the art club, and the debating society, and he was an outstanding botany student. He trained the athletic teams and helped start student prayer meetings and the campus agriculture society. Due to his plant knowledge, the other students called him "Doctor." He had an interesting saying for the uses for plants.

"They are waiting for the kindly hand of man to wave his magic wand over them that they may show forth their long hidden usefulness," he said.

His interest in plants was as great as his interest in painting. My favorite painting is his *Yucca and Cactus*, which he entered in a statewide art contest and won first prize. Later they exhibited it with honorable mention at the 1893 Chicago World's Fair. But George never thought his work was good enough, so during the winter break at Iowa, he came back to Simpson to take an art course as a special student. I was so glad to see him.

The winter after that, I hoped to see him again, so I was disappointed when he couldn't come, yet I understood. He had anemia and his nerves were in shocking condition. The doctor said he couldn't touch his brushes or paints for at least a year. I wrote encouraging letters and told him to try to take life easier.

Your reassurance must have helped him.

I hope it did. He improved.

Was he able to graduate?

In 1894, with a Bachelor of Agriculture degree, he was the first Negro to graduate from Iowa Agricultural College. He invited me to the ceremony, so I boarded the train with dozens of red carnations from members of his Simpson art class. Red carnations are their class flower. George loved it, such a triumph. He wore a beautiful gray suit and a flower in his buttonhole. After graduation, he took me to dinner in the student dining hall and we sat at the professors' table.

When it came time to leave, I held back my tears. I miss that young man every day. He does so much for his people.

I know I'm going on and on, but I love to brag on George. After he got a Master of Agriculture degree, Booker T. Washington wrote to him to come to Alabama's Tuskegee Institute, the school for Negro teachers, so he went down there to head the agriculture department. And he continued to be resourceful. He built a laboratory from things he collected at the rubbish dump.

What about romance for George?

I understand it's in a woman's nature to wonder, so I'll tell you what I know. George had very few social relationships with women and little interest in parties. Friends tried matchmaking, but despite their efforts he stayed single. Only one time did George think about marriage. He wrote and asked me for advice. He had a lady friend, Sarah Hunt, a teacher in the home economics department and sister-in-law of the Institute's treasurer. The two of them walked around campus and dined together. He admired her vivacity, and she admired his dedication. At first I felt hopeful, but I heard nothing from George that hinted romance, only friendship, so this was my advice.

"Your mind might be in it, but your heart doesn't seem to be. With your teaching, your time in the woods, and your travel, any wife of yours would be a widow no matter how long you live," I told him. He agreed that he and Sarah didn't share the same goals, and they broke it off.

How did that lack of romance affect him?

The extra time gave George the energy to do important work. On the third Tuesday of every month, he invited the Negro farmers for hymns and a meeting. He talked about planting crops and letting the ground rest to conserve the soil and suggested they eat vegetables instead of meat, meal, and molasses all the time.

Once a month on the weekend he drove off in a mule-driven wagon to educate other Negro farmers. He suggested natural fertilizer and asked them to plant peanuts and beans rather than corn, which stripped the soil of its nutrients. He taught them how tomatoes and peanuts could be used in nutritional ways to improve their diets. At that time, many Negroes thought tomatoes poisonous. Can you imagine their surprise? Those farmers learned a lot from George, not only plant information, but things like not hating.

"It destroys the hater," George said. "Good thoughts bring happiness, success, and peace."

George called his farmer's wagon a moveable school. He considers that school his most important work, even more than the hundreds of products he made for peanuts, such as cereal and soap, rubber, and medicine. I like his peanut butter the best. I guess other people feel the same, because his nickname changed from the Plant Doctor to the Peanut Man. And he found over a hundred ways to use the sweet potato. When the white people wanted to know his methods, he had to be tricky. Alabama had a law against them studying with the Negroes, so George had informal instruction in the summers.

He certainly made a difference in many people's lives. Do you have any last philosophical thoughts?

I feel so lucky to have mothered George. At his best, he is a chemist, a naturalist, and, since I do love my food, a wonderful cook. At his worst, well, with George there is no worst. It's a shame he lost his real mama so young. I think plants took her place. Yes, it could be those plants were George's true mama. That's a good way to end it. Maybe that's the key to George.

INTERVIEW WITH GEORGE WASHINGTON CARVER ON THE DEATH OF HIS MOTHER

I wish I could remember my mother, Mary. After I accepted that she was gone, I found contentment knowing that other grown women could teach me the right way to live. I took their lessons into my heart. I like to think that all my mothers look on me kindly.

I am indebted to the following authors and their works:

Walt Disney, Creator of Mickey Mouse, Michael D. Cole. *Walt Disney, Hollywood's Dark Prince*, Marc Eliot. *Walt Disney, The Triumph of the American Imagination*, Neal Gabler. *The Man Behind the Magic*, Katherine & Richard Greene. *The Story of Walt Disney*, Diane Disney Miller. *Disney's World*, Leonard Mosley. *The Disney Version*, Richard Schickel. *Building a Company*, Bob Thomas.

Einstein, Jeremy Bernstein. *Einstein*, Denis Brian. *Einstein, the Life and Times*, Ronald W. Clark. *Albert Einstein: Theoretical Physicist*, Aylesa Forsee. *Albert Einstein, Creator and Rebel*, Banesh Hoffman. *The Einstein File*, Fred Jerome. *Einstein in Berlin*, Thomas Levenson. *Einstein, A Life in Science*, Michael White & John Gribbin.

The Most Dangerous Man in America, Catherine Bowen. *The First American: The Life and Times of Benjamin Franklin*, H.W. Brands. *Benjamin Franklin*, Ronald W. Clark. *Code Number 72, Ben Franklin: Patriot or Spy?*, Cecil B. Curry. *John Adams, Party of One*, James Grant. *The Wit and Wisdom of Benjamin Franklin*, James C. Humes. *Benjamin Franklin: An American Life*, Walter Isaacson. *Benjamin Franklin*, Clara Judson. *Ben Franklin, An Affectionate Portrait*, Nelson Beecher Keys. *Book of Ages*, Jill Lepore. *The Private Franklin*, Claude-Anne Lopez & Eugenia W. Herbert. *Benjamin Franklin*, Milton Meltzer. *Benjamin Franklin*, Clifford Smyth. *The Importance of Benjamin Franklin*, Gail B. Stewart. *Benjamin Franklin, An Autobiographical Portrait* edited by Alfred Tamarin. *Benjamin Franklin*, Arthur Bernon Tourtellot. *Benjamin Franklin*, Carl Van Doren. *Franklin on Franklin*, Paul M. Zall.

George Gershwin, David Ewen. *George Gershwin, A Study in American Music*, Isaac Goldberg. *Gershwin*, Edward Jablonski. *The Gershwin*, Robert Kimball & Alfred Simon. *The Memory of All That*, Joan Peyser. *Gershwin, His Life and Music*, Charles Schwartz.

Howard Hughes, Peter Brown & Pat Broeske. *Hughes*, Richard Hack.

Norman Rockwell, a Life, Laura Claridge. *Norman Rockwell, America's Best-Loved Illustrator*, Joel H. Cohen. *Norman Rockwell, Storyteller with a Brush*, Beverly Gherman. *Norman Rockwell*, Elizabeth Montgomery. *Norman Rockwell, My Adventures as An Illustrator*, Norman Rockwell. *A Rockwell Portrait*, Donald Walton.

Roy Rogers, Georgia Morris & Mark Pollard. *Growing Up with Roy & Dale*, Roy Rogers Jr. *The Roy Rogers Book*, David Rothel. *Happy Trails: Our Life Story*, Jane & Michael Stern.

Theodore Roosevelt, Louis Auchincloss. *The Roosevelts, An American Saga*, Peter Collier. *Theodore Roosevelt*, Paul Russell Cutright. *Theodore R oosevelt*, Ann Gaines. *A merican First Ladies, Th eir Lives and Their Legacy*, Lewis L. Gould. *Mornings on Horseback*, David McCullough. *The Roosevelt Chronicles*, Nathan Miller. *Theodore Roosevelt, A Life*, Nathan Miller. *The Rise of Theodore Roosevelt*, Edmund Morris. *The Lion's Pride*, Edward J. Renehan Jr. *My Brother Theodore Roosevelt*, Corinne Roosevelt Robinson. *Grandmere: A Personal History of Eleanor Roosevelt*, David Roosevelt. *Theodore Roosevelt, The Man As I Knew Him*, Nicholas Roosevelt. *The Autobiography of Theodore Roosevelt*, Theodore Roosevelt.

The Solitary Singer, Gay Allen. *The Evolution of Walt Whitman*, Roger Asselineau. *Whitman's Journeys into Chaos: A Psychoanalytic Study of the Poetic Process*, Stephen A. Black. *Whitman, A Study*, John Burroughs. *From Noon to Starry Night, A Life of Walt Whitman*, Philip Callow. *Walt Whitman, An American*, Henry Canby. *My Soul and I*, David Cavitch. *Walt Whitman Reconsidered*, Richard Chase. *Whitman's Young Fellow Named DaPonte, Walt Whitman Review*, Durant DaPonte. *Studies in the Psychology of Sex*, Havelock Ellis. *Free and Lonesome Heart: The Secret of Walt Whitman*, Emory Holloway. *Walt Whitman: A Life*, Justin

Kaplan. *Gay American History: Lesbians and Gay Men the U.S.A.*, Jonathan Katz. *Whitman and Homosexual Tradition in American Poetry*, Myrth Jimmie Killingsworth. *A Whitman Chronology*, Joann P. Krieg. *Walt Whitman: Lover & Comrade*, American Image, Paul Lauter. *Walt Whitman, the Song of Himself*, Jerome Loving. *O Wondrous Singer!*, Barbara Marinacci. *Whitman*, Edgar Lee Masters. *Walt Whitman: The Correspondence*, Edwin Haviland Miller. *Walt Whitman*, James A. Miller. *Walt Whitman*, Bliss Perry. *Whitman and Tradition*, Kenneth M. Price. *Walt Whitman*, Catherine Reef. *Walt Whitman's America*, David S. Reynolds. *The Historic Whitman*, Joseph J. Rubin. *Walt Whitman, A Gay Life*, Gary Schmidgall. *Walt Whitman*, Frederik Schyberg. *Calamus Lovers, Walt Whitman's Working Class Comrades*, Charley Shively. *Drum Beats, Walt Whitman's Civil War Boy Lovers*, Charley Shively. *Walt Whitman*, Paul Zweig.

Many Masks: A Life of Frank Lloyd Wright, Brendan Gill. *Frank Lloyd Wright*, Ada Louise Huxtable. *Frank Lloyd Wright*, Meryle Secrest. *Frank Lloyd Wright: His Life and His Architecture*, Robert C. Twombly. *A Testament*, Frank Lloyd Wright. *Frank Lloyd Wright*, Olgivanna Lloyd Wright.

Fred Astaire, A Wonderful Life, Bill Adler. *Fred Astaire, His Friends Talk*, Sarah Giles. *Starring Fred Astaire*, Stanley Green & Burt Goldblatt. *Astaire*, Bob Thomas.

100 Greatest African Americans, Molefi Kete Asante. *George Washington Carver, the Man Who Overcame*, Lawrence Elliott. *George Washington Carver*, Rackham Holt. *George Washington Carver*, Linda O. McMurry. *Unshakable Faith*, John Perry. *George Washington Carver*, Sam Wellman.

Discussion Questions for Carriers of Genius

1. What similarities existed in the ways these mothers treated their sons?

2. Which mother do you think influenced her son the most?

3. What chapter did you find especially surprising or intriguing?

4. Which specific passages left an impression? Were they interesting, disturbing or illuminating?

5. What effect did wealth or poverty have on these mothers and sons?

6. Which mother shocked you the most?

7. What motivated these women to raise their sons in the way they chose?

8. What did you find surprising about these women's stories and why?

9. Do any of the women remind you of your mother? How?

10. Which mothers tended to live through their sons?

11. What preconceived notions did you have about these men that were changed by the book?

12. Which women did you admire or dislike?

13. What new biographical or philosophical facts did you learn?

14. Do you see time travel as a viable way to visit the past?

15. Which chapter made you want to read more about that person?

16. Did you notice family traditions similar or different from your own?

17. What similarities did you see in the spiritual mothers?

18. What was the purpose of this book, to entertain or to teach? Or both?

19. Is there a lesson you learned that can be applied to your own life? What was it and how was it important?